"Absolutely perfect! There are so many levels to this book, plots, subplots, shades of gray; it was brilliantly constructed and written. . . . Not only is the story magnificent, but it is truly one of the hottest books I've read this year."   —Rage, Sex and Teddy Bears

"A gripping, touching, and scintillating page-turner. [Day] skillfully blends a timeless tale of love lost and found. [This is] a perfect romance with excellent world-building that's rich with angels, lycans, and vampires."
                              —*Romantic Times* (4½ stars)

Praise for *A Hunger So Wild*

"Ms. Day has set this world up brilliantly. There are so many mysteries unfolding at a rapid pace the reader can't help but become enthralled with *A Hunger So Wild* and the Renegade Angels series."
                              —Joyfully Reviewed

"Day is an expert at mixing the right amount of excitement and intrigue with a sexy couple on the cusp of danger."   —*Romantic Times* (4 stars)

"Man, is it ever hot! I didn't want it to end! . . . I truly loved the first book in this trilogy . . . but this second installment takes it to a whole other level! I am seriously looking forward to the finale and I have a feeling [it] will blow me away."   —Guilty Pleasures

"Elijah Reynolds is one sexy as hell lycan (wish I could take him home) . . . This has been an amazing year for Sylvia Day's books for me and this one was no exception. Action packed, story driven, sensual and raw. An un-put-downable story!"   —Under the Covers

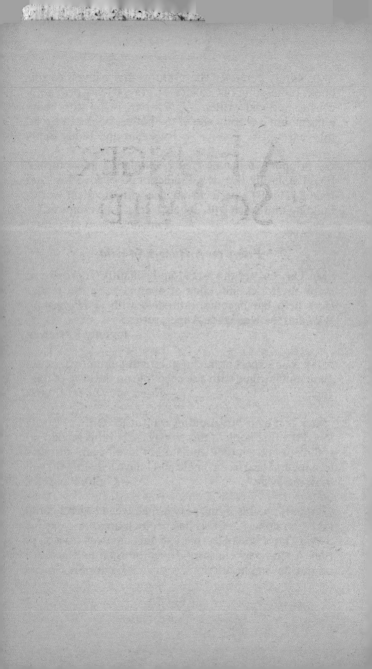

10/01

Praise for *Reflected in You*

"The steamy sex scenes and intriguing plot twists will have readers clamoring for more." —*Library Journal*

"Talk about an emotional book. Gideon and Eva have now solidified their place in my list of favorite couples." —Fiction Vixen

"This book is intense . . . crazy good sex." —Smexy Books

"Emotionally exhausting, sensually enthralling, and sexually riveting, *Reflected in You* shatters your heart and keeps you coming back for more!" —Darkest Addictions

"I am not ready to leave Gideon and Eva. I just can't get enough of them . . . smokin'-hot, dirty, sexy, panty-melting, drool-worthy, sigh-inducing sex." —Avon Romance

"Continues to grab you by the throat and does not let you go." —HeroesandHeartbreakers.com

Praise for *Bared to You*

"Full of emotional angst, scorching love scenes, and a compelling story line." —Dear Author

"Richer and more real to me than many of the contemporary books I've read in a while." —Romance Junkies

"This is one of those books that I'm glad I read and I can't wait to see what happens next to Gideon and Eva." —The Book Reading Gals

continued . . .

"A fantastic read . . . From chapter one I was ensnared in this tale of passion and intense vulnerability that Ms. Day so expertly weaved. Oh and did I mention the sex is hot? Page meltingly hot."   —Darhk Portal

"I love the writing, the sexual tension, and the intricate dance the characters do as they get together."
        —Carly Phillips, *New York Times* bestselling author

Praise for *A Touch of Crimson*

"Will rock readers with a stunning new world, a hot-blooded hero, and a strong, kick-ass heroine."
        —Larissa Ione, *New York Times* bestselling author

"Angels and demons, vampires and lycans, all set against an inventive, intriguing story world that hooked me from the first page. Balancing action and romance, humor and hot sensuality, Sylvia Day's storytelling dazzles. I can't wait to read more about this league of sexy, dangerous guardian angels and the fascinating world they inhabit . . . a paranormal romance lover's feast!"
        —Lara Adrian, *New York Times* bestselling author

"Explodes with passion and heat. A hot, sexy angel to die for and a gutsy heroine make for one exciting read."
—Cheyenne McCray, *New York Times* bestselling author

"Sylvia Day spins a gorgeous adventure in *A Touch of Crimson* that combines gritty, exciting storytelling with soaring lyricism. Adrian is my favorite kind of hero—an alpha-male angel determined to win the heart of his heroine. . . . Definitely a book for your keeper shelf."
        —Angela Knight, *New York Times* bestselling author

A HUNGER
SO WILD

A RENEGADE ANGELS NOVEL

SYLVIA DAY

A SIGNET ECLIPSE BOOK

SIGNET ECLIPSE
Published by New American Library, a division of
Penguin Group (USA) Inc., 375 Hudson Street,
New York, New York 10014, USA
Penguin Group (Canada), 90 Eglinton Avenue East, Suite 700, Toronto,
Ontario M4P 2Y3, Canada (a division of Pearson Penguin Canada Inc.)
Penguin Books Ltd., 80 Strand, London WC2R 0RL, England
Penguin Ireland, 25 St. Stephen's Green, Dublin 2,
Ireland (a division of Penguin Books Ltd.)
Penguin Group (Australia), 250 Camberwell Road, Camberwell, Victoria 3124,
Australia (a division of Pearson Australia Group Pty. Ltd.)
Penguin Books India Pvt. Ltd., 11 Community Centre, Panchsheel Park,
New Delhi - 110 017, India
Penguin Group (NZ), 67 Apollo Drive, Rosedale, Auckland 0632,
New Zealand (a division of Pearson New Zealand Ltd.)
Penguin Books (South Africa) (Pty.) Ltd., 24 Sturdee Avenue,
Rosebank, Johannesburg 2196, South Africa

Penguin Books Ltd., Registered Offices:
80 Strand, London WC2R 0RL, England

First published by Signet Eclipse, an imprint of New American Library,
a division of Penguin Group (USA) Inc.

First Printing, July 2012
10   9   8   7

This one is for all the readers who have so generously embraced the Renegade Angels. Your support and enthusiasm mean the world to me. Thank you!

ACKNOWLEDGMENTS

I remain deeply grateful to Danielle Perez, Claire Zion, Kara Welsh, Leslie Gelbman, and everyone at NAL for being so wonderful with this series and with me.

Thank you to Robin Rue and Beth Miller for handling the pesky details.

Thanks to the art department for granting my wish to have Tony Mauro design my cover . . . again. I'm thrilled.

My love to Tony Mauro for another striking cover. I'm such a fan. It makes me giddy to have his artwork on my books.

Himeko, I told you I'd make you a lycan. I did.

And thank you to all the readers, reviewers, bloggers, booksellers, and librarians who've talked up the Renegade Angels series and shared it with your friends, customers, patrons, and visitors. I very much appreciate each and every one of you!

Go tell the Watchers of heaven, who have deserted the lofty sky, and their holy everlasting station, who have been polluted with women, and have done as the sons of men do, by taking to themselves wives, and who have been greatly corrupted on the earth; that on the earth they shall never obtain peace and remission of sin. For they shall not rejoice in their offspring; they shall behold the slaughter of their beloved; shall lament for the destruction of their sons; and shall petition for ever; but shall not obtain mercy and peace.

The Book of Enoch 12:5–7

GLOSSARY

CHANGE—the process a mortal undergoes to become a vampire.

FALLEN—the *Watchers* after the fall from grace. They have been stripped of their wings and their souls, leaving them as immortal blood drinkers who cannot procreate.

LYCANS—a subgroup of the *Fallen* who were spared vampirism by agreeing to serve the *Sentinels*. They were transfused with demon blood, which restored their souls but made them mortal. They can shape-shift and procreate.

MINION—a mortal who has been *Changed* into a *vampire* by one of the *Fallen*. Most mortals do not adjust well and become rabid. Unlike the *Fallen*, they cannot tolerate sunlight.

NAPHIL—singular of *nephalim*.

NEPHALIM—the children of mortal and *Watcher* parents. Their blood drinking contributed to and inspired the vampiric punishment of the *Fallen*.

("they turned themselves against men, in order to devour them"—Enoch 7:13)

("No food shall they eat; and they shall be thirsty"—
Enoch 15:10)

SENTINELS—an elite special ops unit of the *seraphim*,
tasked with enforcing the punishment of the *Watchers*.

SERAPH—singular of *seraphim*.

SERAPHIM—the highest rank of angel in the angelic
hierarchy.

VAMPIRES—a term that encompasses both the *Fallen*
and their *minions*.

WATCHERS—two hundred *seraphim* angels sent to
earth at the beginning of time to observe mortals. They
violated the laws by taking mortals as mates and were
punished with an eternity on earth as *vampires* with no
possibility of forgiveness.

WRAITH VIRUS—the street name for a new disease
sweeping through the *vampire* ranks. Symptoms include
mindless hunger, foaming at the mouth, and graying of
the skin, hair, and irises.

WRAITHS—*minions* infected with the *Wraith Virus*.

PROLOGUE

It was fingertips following the curve of her spine that woke Vashti from slumber. She arched into the familiar touch with a purr of delight, a smile curving her lips as she floated up to total awareness.

"*Neshama*," her mate murmured.

My soul. Just as he was hers.

With her eyes still closed, she rolled to her back and stretched, pushing her naked breasts up to Charron in deliberate provocation.

The velvet lash of his tongue across her nipple startled her, eliciting a gasp that dropped her back onto the mattress. Her eyes opened in time to see his beautifully etched lips surround the hardened point and his cheeks hollow on a deep, long suckle. She groaned, her body eagerly responding to the attentions of the man for whom she drew every breath.

She moved to clutch his golden head to her breast, but he straightened, making her aware that he stood beside the bed rather than lay upon it. The sight of his fully dressed body told her why he'd woken her.

Towering over her sprawled, bared body, he stared down at her with heated eyes. The fangs peeping through his wicked smile betrayed that he, too, had become aroused by the way he'd woken her.

Her heart raced at that smile. Her chest ached from the surfeit of emotion he inspired in her. She'd lost everything; at times she still felt phantom twinges from the wings that had been severed from her back, but Char had filled the subsequent hole inside her. Now he was everything to her, the reason she rose every day.

"Save that thought," he said in his richly resonant voice. "I'll sate your hunger when I return."

Vash pushed up onto her elbows. "Where are you going?"

He finished strapping on the twin katana scabbards that crisscrossed his back. "We have a patrol that didn't check in."

"Ice's?"

"Don't start."

She sighed, knowing how much time Char had invested in training the fledgling, but the kid couldn't seem to follow orders.

Char glanced at her before securing a gun holster to his thigh. "I know you think he hasn't demonstrated sufficient accountability."

Swinging her legs off the side of the mattress, she said, "I don't just think it. He's *proven* it. Over and over again."

"He wants to please you, Vashti. He's ambitious. Ice

doesn't leave his posts to play. He leaves because he thinks he can be more valuable elsewhere. If an opportunity to impress you presents itself, he'll make the attempt. He's probably tracking a rogue now or trying to eavesdrop on lycans."

"I'd be impressed if he followed commands without insubordination." Standing, Vash stretched, then sighed as her mate came to her and stroked his elegant hands down the sides of her torso. "And he's pulling you out of our bed. Again."

"*Neshama*, someone has to pull me from it. Otherwise, I would never leave it."

She wrapped her arms around him and pressed her face into the leather vest that hugged his lean chest. Breathing him in, she thought again that he was worth falling for. If she could relive making the choice between her wings and her love for Charron, she would have no doubts or hesitation about repeating her "mistake." The curse of vampirism was a small price to pay to have him. "I'm coming with you."

Tilting his head, he pressed his cheek to her crown. "Torque says no."

"Not his call to make." She pulled back, her eyes narrowed. Torque was Syre's son, but she was the Fallen leader's lieutenant. When it came to the Fallen and their minions—collectively, vampires—only Syre could gainsay her. Even Char had to take orders from her, which he did gracefully for a man who commanded others by nature.

"He has a demon problem."

"Damn it. He should be able to take care of it." Yes,

hunting the demons who preyed on vampires was her job. No one was better at it than she was, but she couldn't be everywhere all the time.

"She's another one of Asmodeus's."

"Of course she is. Damn it. Three times in two weeks? He's fucking with us." That changed things up. Taking down a demon in the direct line of a king of hell was a bit more politically involved. Vash had a reputation for being a wild card; she'd take the heat without casting as much of a shadow on Syre as his offspring would. And now she was pissed off enough to want to deal with it herself. They may have fallen, but they weren't easy targets.

Char pressed a kiss to her forehead, then released her. "I'll be back before dark."

"Before dark . . . ?" A quick glance at the bedroom window and she understood. "It's dawn."

"Yeah." His face was as grim as she knew hers must be.

Ice wasn't one of the Fallen, as she and Charron were. He was a mortal who'd been Changed, which meant he was photosensitive. Regardless of his overeager nature, he should've checked in before sunrise. Now he'd have to hunker down somewhere until dusk came or Char found him, whichever came first. A few sips of Char's potent Fallen blood would afford a temporary immunity that would get the errant minion home.

"Have you considered," she began, pulling back, "that it might be wise to let him stew it out? How will he learn, if he never faces the consequences?"

"Ice isn't a child."

Vash shot him a look that challenged that pronouncement. Ice might be nearly as broad and tall as her mate, but he lacked Char's steely control, leaving him as impulsive as a kid. "I think you're projecting traits onto him that he doesn't have."

"And I think it's about time you trusted my judgment." His returning gaze dared her to keep pushing.

It was a look no one else would even consider giving her, and not just because of her rank. While it goaded her obstinacy, she appreciated her mate's willingness to confront her when he felt strongly about something. It was his ability to separate how he treated her as a superior officer and how he treated her as a woman that first stirred deeper feelings in her, during a time when the humanity she'd been sent to observe had begun to spread like a stain inside her.

She couldn't pinpoint when her feelings for him had deepened. One day, Charron had been just another Watcher angel like her, one of the seraphim sent to earth to report on man's progress to the Creator. The next, his smile had taken her breath away, and the sight of his powerfully graceful body had caused places low in her belly to clench. His gilded beauty—his gold-and-cream-colored wings, his tawny skin and hair, and his piercing, flame blue eyes—had morphed from being a mere testament to the skill of the Creator to being an irresistible lure to her newly awakened feminine hunger.

Hiding her new awareness of him had been torturous, but she'd done it for a time, embarrassed by her mortal weakness and unwilling to taint him with it.

When he'd succeeded in cornering her, then seducing her, he'd taken her with white-hot determination, and she had fallen from grace into his arms with full awareness of the consequences. She hadn't shed a tear or made a sound when the avenging Sentinel angels had severed the wings from her back, turning her into the Fallen bloodsucker she was today. She had, however, begged and pleaded for mercy for Charron, and she'd cried the sobs of the heartbroken when they'd stripped him of his gorgeous wings, too.

His touch on her face brought her out of her memories, returning her to the present and the man whose eyes were now the gleaming amber of a soulless vampire. "Where do you go," he asked softly, "when you drift away from me like that?"

Her mouth curved on one side. "I was telling myself how stupid it is to be irritated by your compassion and desire to mentor when I fell in love with you for those very traits. Among many others."

Char fisted his hand in her long hair, bringing the crimson strands to his lips. "I remember you in flight, Vashti. When I close my eyes, I can still see you with the sun at your back, its light shining off your emerald feathers. You were a jewel to me, with your ruby hair and sapphire eyes. I ached whenever I saw you. The need to touch you, taste you, push inside you was a physical pain."

"Poetry, my love?" she teased, although the levity in her tone was marred by the huskiness of deep emotion. He knew her so well. Read her thoughts so easily. He was her other half, the best part of her. While she was temperamental and capricious, he was levelheaded and constant. When she was impatient and easily frustrated, he was reassuring and forward thinking.

"You are far more valuable and desirable to me now than you were then." His forehead dropped lightly to hers. "Because now you're mine. Totally and completely. As I am yours. With all my faults and traits that annoy you."

Catching him with a hand at his nape, she took his mouth in a deep, lush kiss that curled her toes and quickened her breathing.

"I love you." The words were spoken against his lips, her hands clutching him with the strength of all the joy inside her. It was too much sometimes, overflowing and clogging her throat with tears of gratitude. She was embarrassed by the strength of her feelings for her mate. He was in her thoughts at nearly every waking moment and many of her sleeping ones as well.

"I love you, my dearest Vashti." He crushed her naked body to him. "I know you've given me considerable leeway with Ice, against your better judgment. I think it's time I repaid you by listening to your counsel and reining him back."

She adored that about him, too, his sense of fairness and ability to bend when appropriate. "You deal with him, I'll deal with Torque's problem, and tonight we'll drop off the map for a couple days. We've both been working hard lately. We've earned a break."

Wrapping his hand gently around her throat, he

smiled. Eyes bright with sensual promise and affection, he murmured, "With an incentive like that, I'll make damn sure I'm home early."

"We'll see how cooperative Ice is with that. He might have his ass hidden in the most out-of-the-fucking-way place imaginable."

He arched a chastising brow for her ribbing, but vowed, "Nothing could keep me away."

"Better not." She turned away and wiggled her ass at him. "Neither of you wants me hunting you down . . ."

By noon, Vashti was sashaying into Syre's office with a memento from her latest hunt in hand. The vampire leader wasn't alone, but she felt no hesitation in interrupting. The woman with him was one of countless human females who'd caught Syre's eye and lost it just as quickly. It didn't matter if they were forewarned or not; they never believed he was completely unattainable until they experienced his dismissal firsthand. He was a passionate man, but physical enthusiasm was no sign of deeper interest. Syre had lost his wings for love, then he'd lost the woman he had given them up for.

"Syre."

He glanced at her with the heavy-lidded gaze that drove women crazy. He stood with arms crossed and his hip canted into the short built-in bookcase behind his desk. Dressed in black tailored slacks and black silk tie paired with a crisp white dress shirt, he was both elegant and devastatingly attractive. His inky dark hair and warm, caramel-hued skin made him exotic in a way that was impossible to classify. Eastern European, some guessed. Syre had been favored once, much loved by the Creator. It was why, she believed, their fall had been punished so harshly—he'd had a very lofty perch to tumble from.

"Vashti," he greeted, his voice as throaty and warm as whiskey. "Things go well?"

"Of course."

The blonde who'd been overstaying her welcome shot daggers at Vash, as most of his lovers did. They mistook the connection between her and her superior officer as something far more than it was. Their relationship was personal and priceless, but it wasn't intimate or romantic. Vash would give her life for Syre's in an instant, but the love she bore him sprang only from respect, loyalty, and the knowledge that he would die as readily for her.

She gave the woman a sympathetic smile, but spoke bluntly, as was her way. "Don't call him; he'll call you."

"Vashti," Syre admonished in a warning tone. He was too much of a gentleman to make the clean breaks that would spare him a lot of messy confrontations.

She didn't have such qualms. "He wanted you, he had you, and you had a good time. There's nothing else beyond that."

"What are you?" the lovely blonde shot back. "His pimp?"

"No. That would make you a whore."

"Enough, Vashti." Syre's voice cracked like a whip.

"You're so jealous," the blonde hissed, her perfect features contorting from her frustration and hurt. Her emotional spillage contrasted sharply with her pristine, perfect exterior. Her sleek chignon, fashionable pillbox hat, and tidy feminine suit were so cool compared to her heated response. "You can't stand that he's with me."

Sadly, the woman couldn't have been farther from the truth. Vash would give up everything but Charron to see her commander happy again. If it would have made a difference to do so, she would have pointed out what a striking couple they made—the regal blonde and the debonair dark prince. But the heart Syre's mortal wife had awakened in him had died along with her.

"I'm trying to save you from weeks of humiliating yourself," Vash said as kindly as possible.

"Fuck you."

"Diane," Syre said firmly, straightening and moving to catch her by the elbow. "I'm sorry to have to end our pleasurable association so abruptly, but I can't allow anyone to speak to Vashti in that manner."

Diane's cornflower blue eyes widened and her painted mouth formed an astonished O. She stumbled along beside him as he led her out of the room. "But you allow her to talk to me the way she did? How can you?"

When Syre returned, alone, his handsome features were grim. "You're in a mood today," he said curtly.

"I just saved you from a week or more of begging and pleading. You're welcome. And you need a mistress."

"My sexual proclivities are none of your concern."

"Your mental well-being is," she shot back. "Find someone whose company you enjoy and keep her around. Let her look after you a bit."

"I don't need the complication."

"It doesn't have to be complicated." She dropped into one of the seats in front of his desk, her hands smoothing her sleek khaki pants. "I'm talking about a business arrangement. I don't understand it myself, but there are some women who can have sex just because it's fun. Set one up in a nice place and give her an allowance."

Syre shook his head. "You *are* becoming my pimp."

"Maybe you need one."

"I'm insulted by even the concept of fucking a woman who feels obligated to comply."

Her brow arched. "There isn't a woman alive who would find it a chore." Even she, a woman who was happily mated to the love of her life, wasn't immune to Syre's sexual appeal. He was the kind of man that hit a woman right between the eyes every time she saw him. Sensuous, seductive, hypnotic.

"You will cease talking about this."

"No, I won't. You need someone to care about you, Samyaza."

The use of his angelic name thrust home her seriousness. His gaze sharpened and narrowed as he sank into his chair behind the desk. "No."

"I didn't say *love* you. *Care* about you. Someone to make you coffee in the morning, just the way you like it. Someone to watch a rerun on television with you. You know, just someone who's around who knows you and wants good things for you."

Leaning back, he set his elbows on the armrests and steepled his fingertips together. "I've been asked to explain you at times. Explain what you are to me. I haven't come up with the right answer yet. You are my second, but you're not merely a subordinate officer to me. We're more than friends, yet I don't view you as a sister. I love you, but I'm not in love with you. I am aware of your beauty as any man would be, yet I'm not interested in sleeping with you. You are the most important woman in my life and I'd be utterly lost without you, but I would never want to cohabitate with you. What are you to me, Vashti? What gives you the right to discuss such personal matters with me?"

She frowned. Categorizing what they were to each other was something she'd never done. For her, their relationship just . . . was. She was an extension of him in many ways.

"I'm your right hand," she decided, then she tossed him the object she held.

He caught it deftly, his reflexes quick and agile. "What is this?"

"Half of a charm I took off Asmodeus's lackey. I left the other half on the pile of ashes she turned into when I killed her. When it was whole, it bore Asmodeus's sigil."

"You're taunting him."

Vash shook her head. "Three in two weeks? That's not a coincidence. He's allowing, maybe even encouraging, his underlings to toy with us. We're a prize—angels who were thrown away like garbage."

"We have enough enemies as it is."

"No, we have jailers—the Sentinels and their lycan dogs. The demons are possible enemies, *if* we don't correct them. We have to take a stand."

"This isn't the way I would see things handled."

"Yes, it is. That's why you put me in charge of dealing with demon annoyances." She crossed her legs. "You can shake on a truce with your other hand. I'm the hand that flips them off."

A commotion in the hallway pushed her swiftly to her feet. Vash moved to the open doorway with preternatural speed, beating Syre by a mere millisecond.

What she saw froze her blood.

Raze and Salem carried an all-too-familiar body into the house, making a beeline for the dining room, where they laid him on the long oval table.

"What the fuck happened?" she snapped, entering the room and staring at Ice's motionless body. The minion's skin was burned black in places and blistered all over. Blood soaked his T-shirt and stained his jeans to the knees. Tears in his clothing revealed the clawing marks of lupine paws.

His hand reached out lightning quick, caging her wrist. He opened bloodshot eyes. "Char . . . help . . ."

For a moment the room spun, then everything drew inward, coalescing in frigid clarity. "Where?"

"Old mill. Lycans . . . Help him . . ."

Yanking one of Raze's blades free of the scabbard on his back, Vash spun on her heel and raced into the gloaming.

CHAPTER 1

Elijah Reynolds stood naked on a rock in the woods surrounding Navajo Lake and watched his dreams burn along with the decimated outpost below him. Acrid black smoke plumed into the air in wide, thick funnels that could be seen for miles.

The angels would know a rebellion had begun long before they reached the ruins.

Around him, lycans yipped with celebratory joy, but he felt none of it. He was cold and dead inside, his life as he'd known it scorched to embers in the smoldering devastation that had once been his home. He excelled at one thing: hunting vampires. Doing what he enjoyed came from working for the Sentinels—the most elite of all warrior angels. That indentured servitude, while chafing, was a small price to pay to do what he loved. But very few lycans felt the same, which had led to this result. Everything that mattered to him was gone, and what was left was a battle for independence his heart wasn't invested in waging.

But it was done and couldn't be undone. He'd live with it.

"Alpha."

Elijah's jaw clenched at the designation he'd never wanted. He glanced at the nude woman who approached him. "Rachel."

Her gaze lowered.

He waited for her to speak, then realized she was doing the same in reverse. "*Now* you want to follow orders?"

Her hands linked behind her back and her head dropped. Irritated by her lack of conviction, he turned away. He'd told her a revolt was suicide. The Sentinels would hunt them, exterminate them. The lycans' one purpose for existence was to serve the angels; if they no longer did that, they no longer had a place in the world. But she wouldn't listen. She and her mate, Micah—Elijah's best friend—had incited the others to this act of sheer fucking stupidity.

He sensed the approaching male lycan before he heard him. Turning his head, Elijah watched a golden wolf step into view, then shift midstride into the form of a tall, blond man.

"I've rounded up those with self-preservation instincts, Alpha," Stephan said.

Which confirmed Elijah's suspicion that some had fled the battle without considering the brutal days certain to lie ahead. Or perhaps some of the smarter ones had returned to the Sentinels. He wouldn't hold it against them.

"Montana?" Rachel asked hopefully.

He shook his head, reminding himself that he'd promised Micah on his deathbed that she'd be looked after. "We'd never make it that far. Sentinels will be breathing down our necks within hours."

One of the Sentinels had flown away during the conflict, blue wings spread wide as she raced to report the uprising. The rest had stayed and fought, but the razor-sharp tips of their wings had offered too little protection against the size of the Navajo Lake pack, which had needed thinning for months. Seriously outnumbered, the Sentinels had fought to the death, knowing that's what their captain, Adrian, would do and expect. During the weeks that Elijah had been a member of Adrian's pack, he'd seen for himself how tenacious and committed the Sentinel leader was. Only one thing could split Adrian's focus, and even she couldn't dull the angel's killer instinct.

"There's a network of caves near Bryce Canyon." Elijah turned his back to the Navajo Lake outpost for the last time. "We'll hole up there until we're organized."

"Caves?" Rachel asked, scowling.

"This was no victory, Rachel."

She flinched away from the undercurrent of anger in his tone. "We're free."

"We were hunters and now we're prey. That's not an improvement. We kicked the Sentinels when they were already down. They were outnumbered twenty-to-one, taken by surprise, and lacking Adrian, who's dealing with so much shit right now his head isn't fully in the game. This was a one-shot, one-kill deal."

Rachel's shoulders went back, thrusting her small breasts forward. Nudity was nothing to a lycan; flesh or fur, it was all the same. "And we took it."

"Yes, you did. Now trust me to handle the rest."

"This is what Micah wanted, El."

Elijah sighed, his anger swallowed by a tide of regret and grief. "I know what he wanted—a home in the suburbs, a nine-to-five job, carpools, and play dates. I would do anything to give you that dream . . . to give it to any other lycan with a wish for the same . . . but it's impossible. You've dumped a task in my lap that I failed before I began, because there's no way for me to succeed."

And they couldn't know what that failure cost him. He would never say. He could only make the best of what he had to work with and try to keep those who were now dependent on him alive.

He looked at Stephan. "I want teams of two sent to the other outposts. Preferably mated pairs."

Mates would protect each other to the death. In times like these, when they would be hunted while separated from their pack, they'd need all the support they could get.

"Notify as many lycans as possible," he went on, rolling his shoulders back to ease the tension in his neck. "Adrian will cut off outside communication to and from all the outposts—cell phones, the Internet, snail mail. So the teams will need to tackle the task directly, face-to-face."

Stephan nodded. "I'll see to it."

"Everyone needs to withdraw whatever money

they've got socked away before Adrian freezes their accounts." As "employees" of Adrian's aviation corporation, Mitchell Aeronautics, their stipends were deposited in an employee credit union that Adrian had complete access to.

"Most have already done that," Rachel said quietly.

So, she'd thought that far ahead, at least. Elijah sent her off to gather the others; then he turned to Stephan. "I need the two lycans you trust the most for a special assignment: Find Lindsay Gibson. I want her whereabouts and status."

Stephan's eyes widened with surprise at the mention of Adrian's mate.

Elijah struggled through the driving urge to find Lindsay himself, a mortal woman he considered a friend, the only one he had left now that Micah was dead. In so many ways, she was a mystery. She'd stumbled into their lives without warning, displaying skills no mere human should possess and garnering the Sentinel leader's attention in ways Elijah had never witnessed or heard of.

Unlike the Fallen, who had lost their wings because they'd fraternized with mortals, the Sentinels were angels above reproach. The sins of the flesh and the vagaries of human emotion were far beneath their lofty stations. Elijah had never seen a Sentinel show even a flicker of desire or longing . . . until Adrian took one look at Lindsay Gibson and claimed her with a fierceness that surprised everyone. The Sentinel leader protected her life with more care than he did his own, putting Elijah in charge of her safety despite knowing that he was one of the rare, anomalous Alphas that were swiftly weeded out of the lycan packs.

It was during the course of his protection of Lindsay that a friendship had developed between them. Their easy camaraderie ran deep enough that they would die for each other. *I'd take a bullet for you*, she had told him once. Not many people had friends like that and Elijah had none now but her. He may have become the lycan Alpha, but Lindsay's safety wasn't a concern he'd ever relinquish. She had gone missing under the Sentinels' watch, and he wouldn't rest easy until he knew she was okay.

"I want her found and safe," Elijah said, "by whatever means necessary."

Stephan nodded. The unchallenged acquiescence gave Elijah the first hope that they just might have a chance in hell of surviving after all.

"Fuckin' A." Vash eyed the hazmat suit she held in her hand and felt a shard of icy fear pierce her gut.

Dr. Grace Petersen rubbed at one bleary eye with a fist. "We're not entirely sure how the disease is transmitted. Better to be safe than sick—trust me. Bad piece of business."

Pulling on the suit, Vash forced her mind to clear out the rising panic. She focused on reviving the scholarly skills and mindset she'd been sent to earth with as a Watcher. It had been a long time since she'd approached anything without the warrior's mindset she'd cultivated as a vampress, but this was a battle she couldn't fight with her fangs or fists.

"You've got balls of steel, Gracie," she said through the receiver in her headpiece.

"So says the woman who takes on opponents the size of a double-decker bus."

Suited up, they entered the sealed antechamber of the quarantine room, then stepped through to the inner room once given the green light to do so. Inside, a man lay on an exam table as if sleeping, his features peaceful in repose. Only the intravenous lines in his arms and the rapid lift and fall of his chest betrayed his illness.

"What are you giving him?" Vash asked. "Is that blood?"

"We're transfusing him, yes. We're also keeping him in a medical coma." Grace looked up at Vash through her face shield, her features weary and austere. "His name is King. When he was mortal, he went by the name of William King. He was my primary assistant until this morning, when he was bitten by one of the infected vamps we caught yesterday."

"It takes hold that quickly?"

"Depends. According to preliminary reports from the field, some vamps are immune. Others take weeks to show symptoms. Still more are like King and succumb within a matter of hours."

"And what are the symptoms, exactly?"

"Mindless hunger, unreasoned aggression, and an unnaturally high tolerance for pain. We're calling them wraiths."

"Why?"

"They're shadows of their former selves. Lights on, no one home. Their minds and personalities are shot, but their bodies are still cruising right along with the party. The ones I've managed to keep alive more than a handful of days lose pigment and melanin in their hair and skin. Even their irises turn gray. And check this."

Grace brushed the bangs back from King's forehead with a gentle, slightly trembling hand. "Sorry, buddy," she whispered, before reaching for a corded, handheld device that looked like a retail checkout scanner. Holding his wrist, she aimed at his forearm and activated a pale bluish glow. Ultraviolet light.

Vash bent closer, examining the targeted skin. It rippled minutely, as if the muscle beneath it was having a spasm, but that was the only sign of irritation. "Holy shit. UV tolerance?"

"Not quite." Turning off the device, Grace set it aside. "There's no real immunity at work—the flesh is still burning; it's just healing at an accelerated rate. The damaged skin cells are regenerating as quickly as they're being destroyed. Ergo, no visible or lasting damage. I ran some tests on two of the other subjects we had in here. Same deal."

Their gazes met.

"Don't get excited," Grace muttered. "That cellular renewal is what's causing all the other symptoms. The insatiable hunger comes from the need to fuel the massive energy expenditure required for regeneration. The aggression comes from the hunger, which has to feel like starving to death—all the damn time. And the high pain tolerance comes from the fact that they can't focus on anything else but the need to feed. They can't seem to *think*, period. Have you seen a wraith in action?"

Vash shook head.

"They're like frenzied zombies. Higher brain function is subverted by pure instinct."

"So you're transfusing him because he'll die without a continuous intake of blood?"

"I learned that the hard way. I sedated two of the captures so I could study them—you can't get near them when they're fully functional—and they liquefied. Their metabolisms are so accelerated that their bodies pretty much digested themselves. Pile o' mush. Not pretty."

"Is it possible that Adrian cooked this up in a lab somewhere?" The Sentinel leader had been tasked with leading the elite unit of seraphim enforcers that had severed the wings from the Fallen. Using lycans as herding dogs, Adrian prevented the vampires from expanding into more widely populated areas. The result was both territorial and financial suppression.

"Anything is possible, but I wouldn't have made that leap." Grace gestured at King. "I can't see Adrian doing this. Not his style."

Truth be told, Vash couldn't either. Adrian was a warrior to the core. If he wanted a fight, he'd do it face-to-face and hand-to-hand. But he had a lot to gain if the vampire nation withered away to nothing. His mission would be over and he could leave the earth—and its pain, misery, and filth—behind. Assuming he'd even want to leave now that he had Lindsay, a mate who couldn't go with him.

Softening her voice, Vash conveyed her sympathy. "I'm so sorry about your friend, Gracie."

"Help me find a cure, Vash. Help me save him and the others."

That's why she'd come, the reason Syre had sent her. Reports of the illness were cropping up all over the country, the spread so swift it was quickly becoming an epidemic. "What do you need?"

"More subjects, more blood, more equipment, more staff."

"Done. Of course. Just get me a list."

"That's the easy part." Crossing her arms, Grace shot another glance at King. "I need to know where the Wraith Virus first appeared. Which part of the country, which state, which town, which house, which room in the house. Down to the minutia. Male or female. Young or old. Race and build. I need you to find the very first person who got sick. Then I need you to find number two. How did they know number one? Did they live in the same house? Share the same bed? Or was the connection more tenuous? Were they blood relations? Then, find number three and four and five. We're talking six degrees of separation gone wild. I need enough data to establish a pattern and point of origin."

Suddenly feeling suffocated by the hazmat suit, Vash strode toward the door. Grace met her there and typed in the code that released the seal to the antechamber.

"You're talking about a hell of a lot of manpower," Vash muttered, following Grace's example and standing on a painted circle on the floor. Something sprayed from the exposed piping over her head, surrounding her suit in a fine mist.

"I know."

There were tens of thousands of minions, but their inability to tolerate sunlight seriously hindered their usefulness. The original Fallen had no such restriction, but there were less than two hundred of them. Far too few to provide the blood to minions that would grant them temporary immunity. Certainly not enough to manage the pavement-pounding necessary to carry out the requested task in a timely manner.

Shrugging out of her suit, Vash rolled her shoulders back and set her mind. The initial reports of the illness had surfaced at the same time as Adrian's lost love. Nailing down a timeline would help her to decide if the Sentinel leader had culpability or not. "I'll make it happen."

"I know you will." Grace paused in the act of ruffling her choppy blond hair and her gaze moved over Vash. "You still dress in mourning."

Vash looked down at the black leather pants and vest she wore and managed a shrug. After sixty years, the pain was still there, throbbing to remind her of the vengeance due her for Charron's brutal slaying. One day she'd find a lycan who could give her the information she needed to pick up the trail of Char's killers. She could only hope that happened before the ones responsible died of old age or on a hunt. Unlike Sentinels and vamps, the lycans had mortal expiration dates.

"Let's get that list," she said crisply, ready to start on the monumental task ahead of her.

* * *

Syre watched the video to the end, then pushed to his feet in a burst of agile movement. "What are your thoughts on this?"

Vash tucked her legs up beneath her on the chair that faced his desk. "We're fucked. We don't have enough people to attack this as quickly as the virus— the Wraith Virus, she called it . . . As fast as it's spreading, we don't have the resources to tackle it."

He shoved a hand through his thick, dark hair and cursed. "We can't go down like this, Vashti. Not after all we've been through."

The Fallen leader's pain was a tangible force in the room. As he stood before the windows that overlooked Main Street in Raceport, Virginia, a town he'd built from the ground up, it appeared as if the weight of the world was on his shoulders. It wasn't just the problems they faced that pressed down on him. He was in deep mourning, grieving the loss of his daughter after centuries of praying for her return. And he was altered by that loss. No one else had noticed it yet, but Vash knew him too well. Something had changed in him, a switch had been flipped. He was harder, less flexible, and that was reflected in the decisions he was making.

"I'm going to do the best I can," she promised. "We all will. We're fighters, Syre. No one will give up."

He turned to face her, his beautiful face set in fierce lines. "I received an interesting call while you were with Grace."

"Oh?" His tone and the glitter of his gaze set her on edge. She knew that look of his, knew it meant he was resolved to his course but expected resistance.

"The lycans have revolted."

Vash's spine stiffened painfully, as it always did when discussing the Sentinels' dogs. "How? When?"

"Within the last week. I assume Adrian's distraction over my daughter was seen as a prime opportunity to break free." His arms crossed, his powerful biceps flexing with the movement. Adrian had first been attracted to Lindsay Gibson because she was the latest incarnation of Shadoe, Syre's daughter and Adrian's longtime love. In the end, it was Lindsay who'd won both Adrian's heart and the right to her own body, leaving Syre mired in grief over the loss of his child and Adrian knocked a bit off his game. "The lycans will need us if they want to stay free, and it appears we need them just as badly."

She pushed to her feet. "You can't be serious."

"I know what I'm asking of you."

"Do you? This is akin to me asking you to work with Adrian, knowing he's the reason your daughter is gone. Or me telling you to partner with the demon who killed your wife."

His chest expanded on a slow, deep inhale. "If the fate of every vampire in the world was dependent on my doing so, I'd do it."

"Fuck you and your guilt." The words slipped out before she could hold them back. Whatever else Syre was to her, he was first and foremost her commanding officer. "I'm sorry, Commander."

He dismissed her concern with an impatient flick of his wrist. "You'll pay me back by finding whoever the lycan Alpha is and offering an alliance."

"There are no lycan Alphas. The Sentinels have made sure of that."

"There has to be one or the revolt would never have happened."

She began to pace, her heeled boots rapping out a quick staccato on the hardwood floor. "Send Raze or Salem," she suggested, offering up her two best captains. "Or both of them."

"It has to be you."

"Why?"

"Because you hate lycans and your reluctance will hide our desperation." He rounded the desk, then half sat on the front edge, his long legs crossing at the ankles. "We can't give them an advantage. They have to believe they need us more than we need them. And you're my second. Sending you delivers a powerful message as to how seriously I would take the proposed alliance."

The thought of working with lycans stirred a rage inside her that fogged her vision. What if she inadvertently worked alongside one of the lycans who'd ripped Charron to ribbons? What if she saved one of their lives, thinking they were an ally? It was so perverted it made her stomach roil. "Give me some time to try to handle this on our own. If I don't make sufficient progress within a couple weeks, we can revisit."

"Adrian could exterminate the lycans by then. The timing has to be now, while they're still on uneven footing. Think about how quickly we could search with thousands of lycans at our disposal."

She continued to traverse the length of the room at a

pace that would make mortals dizzy to follow. "Tell me your request has nothing to do with your hatred for Adrian."

Syre's mouth curved on one side. "You know I can't. I want to kick Adrian while he's down. Of course I do. But that wouldn't be enough to ask you to do this, knowing what it's going to cost you. You mean far more to me than that."

Coming to an abrupt halt, Vash approached him. "I'll do this because you're ordering me to, but I won't set aside the retribution I'm owed. I'll use this opportunity to find those responsible for Charron's death. When I act on that information, I won't be held liable for the consequences. If that's not acceptable to you, I'll present your offer of an alliance, then I'll go my own way."

"You will not." Syre's low tone held a wealth of warning. "I'll support you, Vashti. You know that. But at this moment, the exigency of the vampire nation must come first."

"Fair enough."

He nodded. "The revolt began at the Navajo Lake outpost. Start in Utah. They can't have gone far."

Chapter 2

"We need to find out whether or not there are other Alphas." Elijah glanced at the lycan who walked beside him, wondering at how easily Stephan had stepped into the role of his Beta.

Instinct weighed heavily on everything they did as a fledgling pack, a truth that unsettled Elijah more than it soothed. He would prefer that their destinies be shaped by their own hands and not by the demon blood that flowed through their veins.

But as he traversed the long stone hallway, the number of verdant gazes staring back at him was irrefutable proof of how dominant a lycan's baser nature was. Every one of them had the luminous green irises of a mixed-bloodline creature. They lined the walls by the hundreds, staring as he passed them, forming a gauntlet through the red rock caves in southern Utah that he'd selected as his headquarters. They thought he was a damn messiah, the one lycan who could lead them into a new age of independence. They didn't realize that their expectations and hopes for freedom imprisoned him.

"I've made it a top priority," Stephan assured. "But half the lycans we send out don't return."

"Perhaps they're returning to the Sentinel fold. As far as quality of life goes, we had it better working for the angels."

"Is any price too high to pay for liberty?" Stephan asked. "We all know the Sentinels don't stand a chance if we take the offensive. There are less than two hundred of them in existence. Our numbers are in the thousands."

The gentle prodding for Elijah to be proactive instead of reactive wasn't lost on him. He could feel it in the air around him, the crackling energy of lycans ready and willing to hunt. "Not yet," he said. "It's not time."

An arm shot out and grabbed him. "What the fuck are you waiting for?"

Elijah paused and turned, facing the brawny male whose eyes glowed in the shadows of the cave. The lycan was bristling and half shifted, his arms and neck covered in a grayish pelt.

The beast in Elijah growled a warning, but he held it in check, a control that made him Alpha.

"Are you challenging me, Nicodemus?" he asked with dangerous softness. He'd been waiting for this, had known it was coming. It would be only the first of many challenges until he established his dominance through physical prowess in addition to a lycan's instinctive need to follow a leader.

The lycan's nostrils flared, his chest heaving as he fought against his beast. Lacking Elijah's control, Nic would lose.

Prying the man's grip from his arm, Elijah said, "You know where to find me."

Then he turned his back to the challenge and walked away, deliberately baiting Nic's beast. The sooner they got this over with the better.

Nic had asked him what he was waiting for. He was waiting for cohesion, trust, loyalty—the cementing framework that would hold all the packs together. Greater numbers or not, there was no way they'd win against a tightly commanded elite military unit like the Sentinels if they didn't work together.

A female approached him at a near run, agitation radiating from her tense frame. "Alpha," she greeted him, quickly introducing herself as Sarah. "You have a visitor. A vampire."

His brows rose. "*A* vampire? As in one?"

"Yes. She asked for the Alpha."

Elijah's curiosity was more than piqued. The lycans had been created by the Sentinels for the sole purpose of hunting and containing the vampires. The fact that the lycans had revolted from Sentinel control didn't mean they'd forgotten their ingrained hatred of blood-suckers. For a vamp to walk into a den alone was suicidal.

"Show her to the great room," he said.

Sarah turned and ran back the way she'd come, with Elijah and Stephan following at a more sedate pace.

Stephan shook his head. "What the fuck?"

"The vamp's desperate, for some reason."

"Why is that our problem?"

Shrugging, Elijah said, "Could be our gain."

"Do we really want to become a safe house for bloodsucking losers?"

"Let me get this straight: we rebel and we're better off, but a vampire bolts and they're a loser?"

Stephan scowled. "You know as well as I do that the pack won't take in vamps."

"Times have changed. In case you hadn't noticed, we're pretty damned desperate, too."

Elijah was stepping over the threshold into the great room when he heard the growl behind him. Lunging forward, he shifted into his lupine form before his paws hit the rock floor. He whirled around at the same moment he was charged by Nicodemus, taking a full-on ramming in the side that knocked the wind from him. Rolling over, he regained his feet, righting himself in time to catch his challenger by the throat mid-leap. With a toss of his head, Elijah threw the other lycan across the room. Then he howled his fury, the sound reverberating through the massive room.

Nic skidded sideways on his paws, then found traction and attacked again. Elijah rushed forward to intercept him.

They collided with brutal force, their jaws snapping for purchase. Nic caught him by the foreleg and bit hard. Elijah went for the flank, his teeth digging in deep, his beast growling at the heady taste of hot, rich blood.

Kicking off his attacker, Elijah turned, ripping a chunk of flesh away. Nic yelped and came back around, limping. Elijah crouched, prepared to leap, when the lush scent of ripe cherries slid across his senses in teasing tendrils. The fragrance swept through him, burning through his blood and sending aggression pumping through his veins.

He was abruptly sick of playing with Nicodemus. Elijah vaulted ahead, twisting midair to avoid Nic's snarling maw and coming down on the lycan's back. Catching him by the throat, Elijah pinned him to the floor, his jaws clenched tight enough to wound and warn but not enough to kill. Yet. Just the slightest increase in pressure would cut off Nic's air.

Nic writhed for a few moments, his limbs flailing in an effort to shake off his opponent. Then blood loss and exhaustion stole his strength. He whimpered for his release and Elijah let him go.

Elijah's low growl rumbled through the room. He turned, his gaze meeting those of every lycan in the cave. They stood around the perimeter, their gazes lowering quickly as he dared all comers.

Satisfied that he'd made his point for the moment, he shifted and faced the arched entry to the great room, his attention riveted to that ripe, sweet scent that was making his dick hard.

"Get me a change of clothes," he said to the cave at large, not caring who did it, just that it got done. "And a damp towel."

He'd barely finished speaking when she appeared, looking just as he remembered her—black high-heeled boots, black Lycra bodysuit that clung to every curve, scarlet red hair that fell to her waist, and pearly white fangs. She looked like something out of a BDSM-laced wet dream and he wanted to fuck her nearly as badly as he wanted to kill her. The lust was instinctual and unwelcome; the fury was laced with grief and pain. She'd killed his best friend in a slow, agonizing death while trying to get to him, mistakenly believing he'd murdered her friend Nikki, a vampress who'd also been Syre's daughter-in-law.

Be careful what you wish for, bitch.

Baring his teeth in a semblance of a smile, he said her name. "Vashti."

Her gaze narrowed as she picked up his scent. "You."

Shit.

Vash stared at the naked, blood-spattered lycan standing across the room from her and her fists clenched. The lack of the familiar weight of her sword sheaths on her back had already been driving her nuts, but now it pissed her off.

He'd killed her friend, and he was going to pay.

She stalked closer, her booted heels clicking across the uneven stone floor. They lived in a goddamn cave and fought among themselves like animals. Fucking dogs. She'd tried for days to talk Syre out of this fool's errand, but the vampire leader would not be swayed. He believed the old "the enemy of my enemy is my friend." She might've agreed with that if they were talking about anyone but lycans.

"The name is Elijah," he corrected, watching her with the focused gaze of a natural hunter zeroing in on its prey.

Another male approached him with a towel in one hand and clothes in the other. Elijah took the towel and began to wipe the blood from his mouth and jaw. His gaze never left hers as the cloth moved across his broad chest and arms.

Vash found her attention reluctantly drawn to the stroking of white terry cloth over golden skin. He was ripped with powerful muscles from head to toe, beautifully defined in a way she couldn't help but appreciate. There wasn't an ounce of extraneous flesh on him and his virility was unquestionable, even without his display of impressive cock and weighty testicles. His scent was in the air, an earthy yet exhilarating fragrance of clove and bergamot that was rich with male pheromones.

He handed the towel to the lycan standing next to him, then stroked his long, thick penis from root to tip.

"Like what you see?" he taunted in a deep, rumbling voice that affected her physically. Blood oozed from a nasty gash in his calf, the scent so delicious her mouth watered for a taste of it.

She forced her gaze to lift from his groin with insolent leisure. "Just marveling that you don't smell like wet dog."

His nostrils flared. "You smell like sacrificial lamb."

Vash laughed softly. "I'm here to help you, lycan. You're safe while you're underground. But you'll have to surface at some point, and beneath the open sky is where the angels will slaughter you all. Since you're already fighting among yourselves, you won't have a chance in hell against Adrian's Sentinels without allies."

The lycans around the room rumbled their disgust at the very idea. She raised her voice and spoke to the assembly at large. "I absolutely agree with you. I don't want to work with you either."

"Yet you came when Syre sent you," Elijah said, stepping into a loose pair of jeans. "Walked straight into a wolf's den at his order."

She faced him again, her chin lifting. "We're more civilized than you, lycan. We know the value of a hierarchy of power."

He approached her, his barefooted stride sleek and predatory. The tight roping of muscles over his abdomen flexed as he walked, riveting her gaze. A surge of heat moved through her as his scent grew stronger.

Fuck. She'd been celibate too long if a lycan could make her hot.

Her hands fisted as he stopped in front of her. Too close. Invading her personal space. Trying to intimidate her with his powerful body and sharply edged hunger. She saw his need in his eyes and smelled the enticing pheromones in the air around him. He hated her, yet he desired her.

Despite her height and heels, Vash had to tilt her head back to look up at him. "Just tell me to fuck off and I'm out of here. I only agreed to present the offer. I really don't want you to accept."

"Ah, but I have no intention of turning you down

until you go into the details." He caught a lock of her hair between his fingers and rubbed it. "And I want to see your face when you find out I didn't kill your friend."

Her breath caught. She told herself it was from surprise and not from the feel of his knuckle brushing over her breast. "My sense of smell is damn near as good as yours."

One side of his mouth lifted in a cruel smile. "Did you check my blood sample for anticoagulants?"

She stepped back in a rush. She knew the Sentinels kept samples of every lycan's blood in cryogenic storage facilities at the lycan outposts, but she hadn't considered that those samples might be vulnerable to abuse. "What the fuck?"

"I was set up. You, however, *are* guilty of killing my friend. Hopefully you remember him, since his murder signed your death warrant. The redhead you pinned to a tree and left for dead?"

He circled her. Dozens of pairs of emerald eyes watched her with open hostility. The chances of getting out of the cave alive diminished to zero.

"If you kill me now," she warned, "you'll have both the vamps and Sentinels after you."

"That's problematic," he murmured, rounding her shoulder from the back.

"But there's something I want more than my life. If you help me get it, I'll let you kill me in a way that looks like self-defense."

Elijah stopped in front of her again. "I'm listening."

"Clear the room."

With a wave of his arm, he gestured everyone out.

"Alpha . . . ?" Stephan questioned.

"Don't worry," Elijah said. "I can take her."

She snorted. "You can try, puppy. Don't forget I have a few eons on you."

In less than a minute, the room was emptied.

"I'm waiting," he said, his eyes glittering dangerously.

"One of your dogs killed my mate." Familiar rage and pain raced through her veins like acid. "If you think what I did to your friend was bad, it was nothing compared to what was done to Charron. You help me find the ones responsible and let me kill them, I'm all yours."

His gaze narrowed. "How do you plan on finding these lycans? What are you looking for?"

"I have the date, time, and place. I just need to know who was in the area then. I can narrow it down from there."

"Such bloodthirsty loyalty."

She turned her head to look at him. "I could say the same about you."

"You'd have to stay with me," he pointed out. "I expect to be present anytime you question a pack member. It could take days, maybe weeks."

The scent of his lust grew stronger by the moment and she—damn it all—wasn't immune.

"I've been searching for years. A few weeks more won't kill me."

"No, but I will. Eventually. In the meantime, I don't have to like you," he said softly, "to want to fuck you."

She swallowed hard, damning the elevated rate of her pulse, which she knew he could hear. "Of course not. You're an animal."

He circled her again, leaning in and inhaling deeply. "What's your excuse?"

She had none, which was screwing with her head. In all the years since Char had been killed, the need for sex had been less than an itch. But she wasn't about to confess that he was getting to her in a way no man had since her mate. Especially when she was certain her reaction had less to do with him than with her own anxiety at being in a den full of creatures she hated without a weapon on her back. With her fangs and claws, she could take down a half-dozen lycans; with Charron's twin katanas, she could hold her own against a legion. Only Char himself could rival her skill with the swords. "No excuses necessary. I'm a heterosexual woman and you're an exhibitionist who likes to fondle his big dick. The show had its merits."

He bared his teeth in a semblance of a smile and crossed his arms. "What does Syre want in return for protection from the Sentinels?"

Vash studied him, noting his wide-legged stance and uplifted chin. He was a solid, anchoring presence. She could almost imagine him remaining an immovable object in the midst of a tornado. Although his rage was a tangible force, battering her senses along with his desire, his beautiful emerald eyes were shadowed with pain. Whatever else he was, Elijah was loyal. If he was trustworthy as well, he could be an asset to the vampire nation. And to her.

Her arms crossed in mimicry of his pose. She watched his eyes dip to the vee of her neckline and his jaw clench. He didn't want to want her. That made her smile inwardly. She'd been using her sexuality as a weapon since Charron died; she was as deadly with it as she was with a blade.

Something Elijah was about to discover firsthand.

"You're going to kill me," Vash said softly, "in retaliation for the death of your friend, who died because I was seeking the same vengeance for Nikki. No . . . let me finish before you argue. I'm not going to renege on our agreement. When all is said and done, you'll be doing me a favor. I'll even lay my neck across a stump and make it easy for you."

The lycan's gaze sharpened. "Your point?"

"I'm not asking for your sympathy or compassion. I just want you to look for the same fidelity in me that I see in you. I'll come into this alliance with all I've got. You do the same and we'll both end up with what we want."

"Will we?" His tone was low and intimate, belying the anger that thinned his sexy mouth.

"If you keep your wants realistic," she qualified drily.

"You're dodging my question, Vashti. What does Syre expect to gain from this?"

"It's an almost even trade." Lifting her hand, she ran her fingers through her hair, noting how his eyes followed the fall of the crimson strands. She meant to tease him with what he hungered for, but instead found herself heated by the fierceness of his regard. The desire of such a gorgeous, virile beast of a man was a seduction all by itself. "We both need bodies."

"I won't lead the lycans into war with the Sentinels."

"No? Still feeling the pinch of the collar?"

"Still aware that the Sentinels serve a purpose," he shot back. "They're needed to keep the rogues in check. That's why I think Adrian hasn't fallen like you did, even though he's crossed the same line. He's the weight that balances the scale, which makes him too necessary to throw away."

Her jaw clenched, pushing infuriating thoughts of the Sentinel leader aside because she needed to keep her head cool. "You also need money now that you're all unemployed. The vampire nation has amassed considerable wealth."

"You want me at a disadvantage. You want me grateful." He unfolded his arms and stroked a hand down his chest, rubbing his palm over one beautifully defined pectoral. Showing off his mouthwatering body. Playing her game. His voice was gravelly. Warm crushed velvet. It brushed over her like the stroke of a tongue. "I won't subordinate the packs to anyone. We're equals or we're nothing."

Her mouth curved. "You can't afford to see this fall through."

"I know what I can afford. And what I'm willing to pay. I've got nothing left to lose, but that doesn't make me desperate. Take it or leave it."

She started to turn away, hiding a smile. "I'll grab

what I need and return tomorrow. Be ready to get down to business."

"Vashti."

Looking over her shoulder at him, she realized he could hold his own. Sandwiched between two power-houses like Adrian and Syre, she felt little doubt that he could and would take on either side in battle if necessary. The submissive qualities she was so used to seeing—and disparaging—in other lycans were notably absent in the Alpha. Yet Adrian had kept him in service, a marked deviation from his usual practice of segregating Alphas from the others. Not only that, the Sentinel leader had trusted Elijah with Lindsay's safety.

"Yes?"

"Don't play me." His voice rumbled with warning, setting off a sweep of goose bumps over her skin. "I've admitted I want you, but I won't be led around by my dick. Two can play the game. It won't leave my mind that you want me, too. I don't need to hear you say yes when I can smell it."

"I hate lycans," she said without heat. It was a simple fact, best laid out there in case he missed the memo. "The thought of fucking one makes my skin crawl."

"But the thought of fucking *me* makes you wet." His tone was as emotionless as hers had been. "Let's put that on the table from the start. I'll wring you out and you'll milk my last drop, and we can still hate each other in the morning. Nothing is going to change how this association will play out."

Genuine amusement slid through her. "Good to know."

His gaze dropped to her throat. "And whoever's been feeding off you is done. The only lips that will be touching your skin are mine. I don't share."

Her fingers lifted involuntarily to the twin fang tears that were healing with unusual slowness. Lindsay had taken the bite out of her after Syre's failed attempt to recover the soul of his daughter, Shadoe. Vash was reminded that the first time she had seen Elijah he'd been with Lindsay, protecting Adrian's mate with his own life. "Not that it's any of your business, but it won't be happening again."

She began the long walk back to the cave entrance, feeling unsettled in a way she hadn't in . . . forever. Elijah was going to help her find the lycans she sought. As adversarial as their "association" was, she trusted that he'd follow through, if only to get his revenge at the end. That should make her feel good about working with him. Instead, she felt twitchy.

She was now dependent on the trustworthiness of a creature whose breed she'd long reviled for its treachery. The lycans had once been Watchers. Instead of taking the same punishment as the rest of their brethren and becoming vampires, they'd begged the Sentinels for leniency. Adrian had given it in the form of indentured servitude as lycans. With transfused werewolf blood sliding through their veins, they'd lost their wings but retained their souls . . . and their mortality. They lived, they whelped, and they died as slaves, which is the least of what they deserved.

But now they'd betrayed the Sentinels—just as they had the Fallen—by switching allegiances again.

She'd be damned if the dogs would have the opportunity to be faithless to the Fallen a second time. Whatever she had to do, she'd make sure that if someone was going to get a knife in the back, it would be a lycan.

CHAPTER 3

"I have the right to kill her," Rachel snapped, her eyes lit with a roiling fury. "You can't take that from me."

Elijah stood with his palms flat on his desktop. He kept his gaze on the schematics in front of him, following the red lines that showed where electrical cables would transfer power from generators into various caverns. "I can delay that right and I am."

Because they weren't the only two people who had a claim to a piece of Vashti's luscious hide. Lindsay, too, had lost a loved one to the vampress.

"Micah would have avenged you, El. Don't forget he died protecting you. Vashti killed him trying to find out where you were."

To avenge Nikki's death, because his blood had been planted to frame him for the crime. It didn't matter that he was innocent of Nikki's abduction. He was nevertheless guilty of being the reason Micah died. "Micah didn't have thousands of lycans depending on him, Rach. We need this alliance to keep us all alive."

"Damn you. You want her."

He lifted his head and looked at her.

"Don't try to deny it." She held his gaze. "It's obvious."

"He's still going to kill me," Vashti interjected as she joined them.

All eyes turned toward the arched entrance and the vampress who strode through it. In direct opposition to her appearance the day before, Vash had returned armed to the teeth. Katana scabbard straps crisscrossed between her lush tits, and two knife sheaths hugged her lithe thighs. She carried a small navy duffel in her hand. Her stride was long and sure, her chin lifted high and proud. As usual, she wore black from head to toe, this time sporting skintight cotton pants topped with a leather vest that was secured with brass snaps down the front. Her hair was twisted atop her head into a bun that was secured with what he suspected were slender throwing knives.

Like the first time he'd seen her in a parking lot in Anaheim, the look of her hit Elijah like a fist to the gut. His visceral response to her was so strong he sucked in a breath to push through it, then forced himself to exhale slowly.

Rachel growled, and he glanced her way. He took her sneer as his due, knowing how he would feel if their positions were reversed.

"Vashti." He straightened. "This is Rachel, the mate of the lycan you killed. Rach, this is Vash, Syre's second."

He watched the two women carefully, painfully aware of how difficult it must be for Rachel to face her mate's killer and be forbidden to seek revenge by the very man who'd contributed to Micah's death. His hand lifted to his chest, rubbing at the ache that shortened his breathing.

Vash dropped her duffel on the floor in front of his desk. "It won't comfort you to hear that I know how you feel, Rachel, but I do. My mate was killed by lycans."

"Was he mortally wounded and left to die over the space of several days?" Rachel asked bitterly.

"No. He was disemboweled and had his vitals eaten while he was still alive."

"You lie," Rachel spat. "Lycans don't hunt that way."

"Sure. Whatever you say."

Elijah gestured at his Beta, who worked on a laptop at an adjacent desk. "That's Stephan over there."

"Hi, Beta," she greeted him. Then she smiled at his upraised brows. "Takes one to know one."

Stephan acknowledged her with a brisk nod.

Vashti kicked at a rock on the floor. "I love what you've done with the place, El. You take rustic charm to a whole 'nother level."

The look he shot her said everything he needed to say about her sarcasm.

She stepped closer, looking down at the schematics with a wry twist to her mouth. "Cute. But you can put those away. We're not staying here."

He sank into his chair and reclined, waiting for her to get to her point.

She half sat on his desk. "I'm not sticking my guys on cave-watching duty. They're not going to be happy about this alliance as it is. Besides, we need more power than generators are going to provide. No way you've got Internet or cell reception in this hole in the ground, and you'll need both to have the information and communication necessary to pull the packs together. And I need the same to keep track of my men and my agenda."

"Which is?" Elijah glanced at Rachel, and his voice softened. "Let the others know we'll be vacating shortly."

"Just like that?" she asked, wide-eyed. "She says jump and you do?"

"Look at it however you want." As much as he regretted the position he was forced to put her in, he wasn't going to argue his point with anyone. His word had to be law if they were going to survive. "You can stay here, if you prefer. Tell the others they can stay with you or come with me—their choice."

Stephan rose to his feet as Rachel stomped out. "I'll see to it, Alpha."

"I'll have you follow up. For now, I'd like your input here."

Vash shook her head. "I hope you can keep a lid on the drama. We have enough on our plates."

"Such as? The time for showing your hand is now."

She hesitated a moment, her lips pursing slightly as she considered whatever it was she had on her mind. "We have a situation."

"Tell me something I don't know. You wouldn't be here otherwise."

"I need to run some background checks, and I need

bodies pounding the pavement during daylight hours. I don't have enough of the Fallen to cover the ground necessary in the time we've got to work with." Her fingertips drummed on the desktop, betraying her restlessness. "I'll cover your ass and provide safe passage for the lycans fleeing the other outposts. In return, you put those lycans to work helping me dig for information."

Elijah waited for her to elaborate. In the interim, he took her in, noting the fine texture of her creamy skin and the darkness of her thick lashes. The amber of her eyes, a trait universal among all vampires, was striking against the brazenly bold hue of her hair. He wondered what she'd looked like with the flame-blue eyes of a seraph angel. Like a china doll, he imagined. There was an elegant fragility to her that wasn't immediately apparent and totally lost at a distance. Her penchant for black leather and Lycra distracted one from noticing how softly feminine she really was.

With a sigh, she capitulated and withdrew a flash drive from her cleavage. "This will explain everything better than I can."

Stephan retrieved his laptop from the other desk and set it up in front of Elijah, who plugged the drive in. Shortly, a video began to play. It was clearly surveillance video of a cell in which a vampire with foam at the mouth and bloodshot eyes bashed his head against a brick wall until it burst.

"I've seen an infected vamp like this before," Elijah said.

"You have?" Vash stood and faced him, her focus razor sharp. "When? Where?"

He leaned back again. "The first time was in Phoenix, about a month ago. I believe she was the friend you wanted to avenge—brunette, petite, a pilot."

"Nikki." Vash took a deep breath. "Jesus. I thought Adrian was full of shit when he said she was fucked up."

"We cleaned out a nest in Hurricane, Utah, two days later. Half the occupants were foaming at the mouth like that."

Bending down, she dug in her duffel and pulled out an iPad. She typed as she spoke. "We don't know what the hell this sickness is, how quickly it's spreading, or where it started. That's what we need to determine and what we need you for—we have to work night and day. We can work in shifts."

"Maybe this is population control."

Her head lifted. "Don't play me. I don't play nice."

"Have any of the Fallen been infected?"

"No." She set the tablet in front of him, revealing a map of North America dotted with multicolored spots. "The red spots are the first reports. You can see Nikki's appearance in Phoenix was part of the first wave. Orange is second. Yellow is the most recent."

Stephan leaned closer. "They're all over the map."

"Right. You'd expect to see an outward spread from one point, but it looks like there were four, as if they were deliberately spaced to speed the rate and area of infection. We know Sentinels raided a nest outside of Seattle, and you can see that's one of the first known cases."

Elijah shook his head, knowing where this was going. "Adrian's clean on this."

"You sure?"

"Yes. Doesn't mean a Sentinel isn't responsible, but Adrian is in the clear."

"Shit." Vash began to pace, briefly distracting him with her graceful and agile stride. "And the Sentinels won't act without his orders, so that leaves us with what? Demons? A lycan?"

"Don't rule out the Sentinels."

Stilling, she looked at him. "Why not?"

"A woman was taken from Angels' Point while under Sentinel guard."

"Then they allowed it to happen."

"Not to this woman. Adrian would kick off Armageddon first."

"Would he? Hmm . . ." She spun on her stiletto heel and left the cavern.

Elijah was right behind her, following in her cherry-scented wake. He was damn near dizzy by the time he reached the surface, his chest expanding on a deep breath that cleansed his lust-addled brain. He watched Vash pull an iPhone out from under a crimson bra strap and hit a speed-dial button. A moment later, the vampire leader appeared on her screen via a video feed.

"Vashti." Syre greeted his second-in-command with warm familiarity. "Are you well?"

Elijah interjected. "You didn't care about that when you sent her to me alone and unarmed."

"Let me see him," Syre said, prompting Vash to angle the screen in Elijah's direction. "Ah. The lycan Alpha. You're precisely what I expected."

"I expected you to be smarter." Elijah crossed his arms.

"You'd be an idiot to harm my lieutenant. I would hunt you down and spread your hide in front of my fireplace as a rug."

"My hide is worth the same as hers?" He glanced at Vash, irritated that he gave a shit about the respect—or lack of—that she was shown by her commander.

"If you'd been able to take her down, yes. She's a damned fine warrior, armed or not."

Vash flipped the phone back around to face her. "How did you get your hands on Lindsay?"

The hair on Elijah's arms and nape rose with his sudden fury. He'd pinned the vampress to a tree by the throat before she knew what'd hit her.

Vash found herself flattened into the coarse bark of a tree trunk by over six feet and two hundred twenty pounds of bristling, growling lycan. Her fury over being caught unawares was exacerbated by her prickling dislike of Elijah's proprietary feelings toward Lindsay Gibson.

"What?" she taunted, catching the wrists of his hands presently wrapped around her neck. His heavily muscled thigh was shoved between hers and his lean hips pressed against her pelvis in a way that set her heart racing. "Got a hard-on for Adrian's woman?"

"Where is she?"

Her smile was mocking. "Why do you care?"

"Lindsay saved my life."

"I knew I hated that bitch for a reason."

"She's with Adrian."

Elijah's head turned toward the iPhone on the ground and Syre's steely-eyed visage. "Is she unharmed?"

"If she's still alive, she's healthier than she's ever been."

A chill slid down Elijah's spine. He looked at Vashti, whose eyes were bright with challenge. While a mortal would have lost consciousness by now from lack of air, the vampress was merely flushed, which made her even more beautiful. "What did you do to her?"

"What she wanted done," Syre answered. "Release my second, Alpha, before I decide you're more trouble than you're worth."

"Not yet." Maybe not ever, if his growing suspicions were realized. His gut knotted as the fear deepened.

Vash smiled. "How did you get her, Syre?"

"She was brought to me by members of the Anaheim cabal."

Elijah growled. "There's a vampire nest in Southern California?"

"We prefer to call them cabals or covens," she corrected, "depending on the size." She turned her gaze to Syre. "Did they tell you how they got her out of Angels' Point?"

It was no secret that Angels' Point, Adrian's compound in Anaheim Hills, was a fortress. Set high above the city, it was guarded by Sentinels and lycans—before the revolt—as well as the finest electronic surveillance millions could buy.

"No." The turning wheels in Syre's mind were evident in his contemplative tone. "I assumed they'd acquired her somewhere between her work and the Point."

"We need to talk to them. They have a winged contact they're not sharing."

"I'll see to it. And I've sent the Alpha's blood sample from the scene of Nikki's abduction out to be analyzed for anticoagulants, as you requested. I'll let you know the results when I have them." There was a pause. "Are you all right there, Vashti?"

The circle of her fingers released Elijah's wrists, freeing her hands to slide up his arms like a lover. Teasing him. Goading him. "Of course."

"Check in regularly, so I can be certain."

"Yes, Syre."

Yes, Syre. Elijah was determined to hear her cede to him as thoroughly . . . while she was beneath him, taking hard, deep thrusts of his aching cock. That he could want her and want to kill her at the same time was fucking with his head. Rachel's pain was a vice around his chest . . . Lindsay had lost her mother to Vashti's viciousness . . . yet still he craved the vampress with a ferocity that shook him.

She squeezed his shoulders with a vampire's strength, which just happened to be the exact pressure he most enjoyed. Her hands ran down either side of his spine, kneading, before reaching his ass and palming it. Her tongue peeped out and slid over her full lower lip.

"You can't have Lindsay, you know. She's brain-dead over Adrian. Gave up her life for him."

He fought the seductive lure she was trying to wrap him with. "What—exactly—did you do to her, Vashti?"

"You've been a Sentinel dog for years. Bet you've never seen Adrian look twice at a woman. Why her? What's special about her?"

"Get to your point."

"She's—well, she *was*—Syre's daughter."

Elijah froze, his fingers going slack with shock. "Impossible."

None of the vampires could procreate—soulless creatures couldn't create a being with a soul. But . . . Lindsay had shown anomalous traits almost from the beginning.

"She was born with another soul inside her. The reincarnated soul of Syre's naphil daughter, created before he fell."

"What did you do, Vashti?" he repeated.

"What had to be done for one soul to overcome the other."

Rage burned through his blood like fire, tightening his hands around her throat. In that moment, he was a breath away from separating her head from her neck.

"Did you Change her?" he snarled, fighting off the shift rippling just beneath his skin. "Did you kill her spirit? Is Lindsay gone?"

For the first time, fear shadowed her eyes and whitened her lips. As his claws extended and pierced through her pale skin, blood slid over the upper curve of her breasts in crimson tendrils. "She's still Lindsay.

Shadoe's soul was lost when Syre finished the Change. And he wasn't lying—Lindsay wanted it."

"Bullshit. She hated vampires because of you. Because you killed her mother. She would never become one willingly."

A frown marred the space between Vash's brows. "What the fuck are you talking about?"

"Two decades back. A pretty little blond five-year-old and her mother, having a nice picnic in the park . . . until a pack of vamps decided to have a snack."

"No." The confusion cleared. Her gaze bored into his. "Not my style. And if you don't believe me, you can ask her. She must've figured it out when she gnawed these holes in my neck and dug into my blood memories. She had me down and pinned with a sharp piece of wood nearby; she could've vanquished me, but she let me go."

Needing definitive answers, he pushed away from her plush, pliant body. He derided himself for wanting to believe her. "I need to know she's okay. Make it happen."

"You've got bigger things to worry about."

He staked her to the tree with a fierce glance. "*Now*, Vashti."

Cursing under her breath, she retrieved her phone from the ground and riffled through her contacts. A moment later, ringing came over the phone, followed by the clipped greeting of a receptionist at Mitchell Aeronautics. "Adrian Mitchell, please. Tell him Vashti is calling."

Elijah's arms crossed as he waited, his mind spinning from the fact that the vampires had once had Lindsay in their clutches and had let her go back to Adrian, effectively forfeiting the Sentinel leader's only weakness. Why?

"*Vash.*" Adrian's richly sonorous voice flowed through the phone's speaker, sans video.

"How's the new love of your life, Adrian?" Vash's mouth curved bitterly. "Did she make it?"

"She's exceptionally well. How's your neck?"

"Still holding my head and body together."

"You continue to have vicious rogues in your numbers, Vashti." Despite the harshness of his words, the Sentinel leader's tone remained as even and smooth as always. "We'll be hunting them."

All of the Sentinels displayed that steely control and neutrality of emotion, but Elijah had heard Adrian speaking with Lindsay and he knew the angel's still waters ran deep.

She snorted. "Not everyone in your ranks is toeing the line either, I hear."

"You'll stay away from Lindsay. She's no longer any concern of yours or Syre's."

Vash looked at Elijah. "She's a vampire, Adrian. That makes her one of us."

"She's my mate; that makes her mine. Forgetting that will see your neck no longer serving its purpose."

"I love it when you talk dirty," she purred. "Give my regards to Lindsay." She ended the call, then redialed. The video activated and Syre's face appeared. "Lindsay's okay. And Adrian threatened me over her, so he's still protecting her. She's in loving hands, Samyaza."

Elijah stepped closer, his gaze riveted to the vampire leader's haunted eyes. A long moment later, Syre swallowed and a deep exhale escaped him. "*Todah*, Vashti."

"You're welcome." Her face and voice softened. "I should have checked sooner. I'm sorry I didn't think of it."

Silent understanding passed between the two vampires. The instinctive exchange bespoke of a long relationship and deep compassion. Elijah was contemplating his own changing perceptions about Vashti—most especially his absorption of her as a person who had a soft heart beneath the hard exterior—when she ended the call and faced him.

She arched a brow. "Feel better?"

"Enough for now." He wouldn't feel totally settled until he spoke with Lindsay himself, but at least he knew she was with Adrian, who would die for her. His friend was safe for now.

"Less inclined to kill me now?"

He bared his teeth in a smile.

She shrugged. "Worth a shot."

CHAPTER 4

As Vash opened the rear hatch of her Jeep, she felt Elijah's stare move down her back.

Something had shifted between them a moment ago. She'd felt it, even if she couldn't define it.

"What are you doing?" His rough, rumbling voice at her shoulder prompted a deep, cleansing breath, and she closed her eyes.

The hardest transition from Watcher to Fallen hadn't been the loss of her wings; it had been the surge of emotion that shattered her previously inviolate equanimity. Since Charron, the only blessing she'd received was the numbness of all-encompassing fury. That a lycan—one of the very creatures who'd made her what she was today—should be the one to break through her shell and rattle her was the most heinous irony.

"These are surveillance cameras." She pulled out one of the long rods that had a camera on top of it. "You'll want to get some of your men to place them around the perimeter in widening circles. Then station a team on the surface to monitor the feed."

Stepping back, she let him see that the rear seat had been laid flat, expanding the cargo area to hold dozens of cameras.

"Jumping in with both feet," he said, glancing at her with those brilliantly verdant eyes.

She set the tip of the camera pod on the ground and leaned her weight into it. Syre didn't want the lycans to know just how much they were needed, but there'd been too many skeletons popping out of closets already. Considering who they both were—hunters of the highest caliber for their respective factions—there would certainly be more transgressions they'd hate each other for. Neither of them could afford to hold back from this point forward, just as they couldn't delve too deeply into their pasts. Theirs was a merger of necessity. Regardless of the things they'd done previously, they needed each other now. Digging up secrets would only make the going more difficult; it couldn't change the route.

Vash met his gaze. "What choice do we have?"

"Right." But the line of his mouth softened.

"These are just a temporary precaution. We'll start moving your people out of here in the morning. I know you'll want to be near rural areas, but we need a command center with easy transportation access. I've got specs on some properties that meld the two needs. Money isn't a concern."

He shifted his stance, and his irises took on a preternatural glow. Her hackles rose. She spun around before she heard the rustle behind her, kicking herself inwardly for being caught unawares, another sign that Elijah had knocked her off her game.

A slender woman stepped into the clearing. Dressed in a simple sleeveless floral dress with buttons down the front, she looked fresh and innocent except for her eyes, which were narrowed and hot with hatred.

Rachel. The mate of the lycan Vash had tortured in an effort to find Elijah, whose blood had been left at the scene of Nikki's abduction.

"Back off, Rachel," Elijah warned.

"She's mine, El."

Vash moved subtly, firming her stance and preparing to unsheathe the blades on her back. She commiserated with Rachel's loss and she didn't disagree with the lycan's right to challenge her—after all, revenge for a murdered mate was a goal they shared—but damned if she'd go down for anyone without fight.

"No, Rachel," he growled softly. "She's *mine*."

"You owe me this. He died protecting you."

"He didn't give me up. I won't deny that." He moved closer, stepping in front of Vash, acting as a shield. "But Micah set me up in the first place. He planted my blood, and that lured Vash to hunt me."

Rachel's mouth curved, but the smile didn't reach her eyes. "How would he do that? Only Sentinels have access to the cryogenic storage facilities."

"The same Sentinel or Sentinels who took Lindsay from Angels' Point?"

If Vash hadn't been watching so closely, she might've missed the shiver of fear that raised the hairs on Rachel's arms. As it was, Vash felt a grudging admiration for the Alpha, who was so swiftly piecing together a picture of double-crosses and fractured loyalties.

Rachel ripped open the front of her dress and shifted, and Vash whipped out her blades. Elijah darted forward in human form, catching the snarling she-wolf in the air and deflecting her.

If Vash had harbored any doubts that he was an Alpha, they would have been completely dispelled. She'd never heard of a lycan able to resist a shift while under attack. Never thought she'd see it.

"Stop it," Elijah barked, his words cracking like a whip.

But Rachel was beyond caring. She hunkered low and came at Vash again. Vash leaped to the roof of the Jeep to gain the high ground and prepared to slice back, but Elijah pivoted with a roar, grabbing Rachel and crushing her spine to his chest. Standing on her hind legs in lupine form, the female was bigger than he was. She clawed at the air with her forepaws, her jaws snapping over her shoulder.

"Cut it out." His bare feet skidded on the ground as he wrestled her writhing body. "Don't make me hurt you, Rach. Don't— Damn it."

Rachel's back paw scraped his calf, eliciting a bellow of pain and fresh gushing of blood as his injury from the day before rent anew. The potent scent of his blood filled Vash's nostrils. Her fangs descended; her body tightened with hunger. She crouched, her gaze shooting to the mouth of the cave. A witness would be helpful, but she saw none forthcoming.

Elijah hurled the wolf aside again and tore open his button fly. In a split second, he'd shifted into a pony-sized wolf with rich chocolate fur and a lupine face as majestic as his human one was gorgeous. He howled, the sound echoing off the red rock and rolling like thunder through the canyon.

Rachel slinked across the dusty ground, her lips pulled back in a snarling display of wickedly sharp teeth. Elijah stalked her, growling low and deep with unmistakable menace. Vash's breathing quickened. She smelled the third lycan before she saw him.

In human form, Stephan leaped onto the rooftop beside her and landed nimbly on his feet. "Jesus," the Beta hissed. "This is the last thing we need."

"You're my witness," she said, before diving off the SUV with her blades leading the charge, her body stretched to its full length.

The she-wolf pounced with a bark, meeting her halfway. Her katanas were a mere inch from fur-covered flesh and muscle when Elijah tackled Rachel from the side, slamming her out of the way. Vash's blades sank into the ground where the she-wolf had been a mere second before. Using the anchored swords as leverage, she held the hilts and flipped, her legs arcing over her head and landing on the other side. She hit the ground in a crouch, her boots pounding into the dirt. The sickening crunch of broken bone sounded behind her.

"Fuckin' A," she cursed, knowing death when she heard it.

*   *   *

Elijah shifted forms, the power of his lycan sight diminishing into that of a human's, then blurring with tears. He stared down at the lycan lying at his feet, watching fur melt into flesh as life flowed out of Rachel's body from the punctures in her broken neck. Dropping heavily to his knees, he threw his head back and howled his grief.

"Damn it," Vash snapped at his back. "You should've let me do it. It would have been self-defense. The others would've accepted that easier than they will you killing a lycan while protecting a vamp."

A growl at his back alerted him to Stephan's presence behind him. Bracing for the agony of a bite he wouldn't defend himself against, he was startled when the expected attack didn't come and Vashti spoke instead.

"I'm not going to hit him while he's down, Beta," she said drily. "You don't have to protect him from me, even if he does need a smack upside the head for jumping in when I can protect myself."

"I didn't do it for you." Gathering himself, Elijah stood and collected his jeans, yanking them on. "I can't afford disobedience now. Letting you two get to each other after I ordered Rachel away would only prove that my word isn't law, and it needs to be."

His chest heaving, he swiped his tears away and fought down the rising bile in his throat. An icy lump had settled in his gut, guilt eating through him like acid. He'd killed the woman he had promised to protect from harm, the widow of his closest friend. While her death had been certain from the moment Micah died—lycans couldn't live long after the loss of their mate—he'd never imagined the nightmare of being the hand that dealt the fatal blow.

Stephan shifted, but kept a defensive position between Elijah and Vash.

"Alpha." His voice was calm and controlled. "How do you want to handle this?"

Elijah faced him. "I'll inform the others. Take whoever you need and see Rachel buried as well as possible. Then take these cameras and set them around the perimeter in ever-widening circles. If you need help setting up the feed, Vashti will assist you."

"I'll take care of it."

Stephan's immediate compliance might've soothed him, if that had been even remotely possible. Before his Beta walked away, he stopped him. "Stephan . . . thank you. For everything."

Giving a brief nod of acknowledgment, Stephan gathered his clothes from the ground and moved away.

Elijah set off toward the caves. Remorse weighted his shoulders and stung his eyes. He'd never wanted this, never wanted the responsibility of making such brutal decisions or having the power to see them enforced.

"Hold up, Alpha." Vash drew abreast of him, swords still in hand. "I'm coming with you."

The way she strode by his side, armed, offered her support without words. They were a united front. Allies. He almost laughed at the terrible absurdity.

"You have to put it away, Alpha."

He came to an abrupt halt, his hands fisting at his sides.

"Wanna take it out on someone?" she asked softly, facing him and sliding one blade into its scabbard. "I'm your girl. I'm always up for a heated sparring match. But you'll regret carrying that baggage in front of the others. Trust me. I know."

"Do you?" he challenged. "Have you killed someone you promised to protect with your life?"

Amazingly, her beautiful amber eyes softened with something like sympathy. "I've done some horrible things, things I'm not proud of and have a hard time living with. It's part of the job of being a leader. I'm not saying you should suck it up and get over it, because you're not going to get over it. That's also part of the job—if you stop caring, you're worthless. I'm just saying you can't stand in front of your troops seething with guilt, because that implies culpability and this was an assisted suicide. Rachel had to know she couldn't possibly win against you or me. She was ready to go, and this was how she chose to do it."

"Is that supposed to make me feel better?" His friendships were precious to him. As frustrated as he was with Rachel, she was still a friend and a pack member and he ached from her loss.

Vash shrugged. "Nothing will. But you didn't do anything wrong. It was a shitty thing to do, yeah, but it had to be done. For her sake, my sake, your sake, and the sake of this alliance that we both really fucking need. As I said, if you wanna knock it out, I'm here. Just don't take it in there."

"There will be more," he muttered, respecting her counsel and appreciating—however reluctantly—that she'd offered it. "The others didn't know what they were getting into when they orchestrated this revolt, and many of them aren't going to be happy with the decisions I'm making."

"Fuck 'em. Until they've been in command, they can't know what it's like."

He snorted. *She* knew what it was like, which created an unexpected affinity between them.

She smacked him on the shoulder. "Ready, puppy?"

Fuck. She was hot as hell but totally crazy. Irreverent and unpredictable, too. Yet when he'd researched her, he'd heard the stories of her hunts—she was like a lycan on the scent when she pursued, dogged and unwavering, dependable for those who hunted with her. And now it seemed there was a method to her madness.

He growled. It'd been better when the only thing he admired about her was her tits. "Stick close to me."

"I've got your back."

"Fine. Make it easy for me to have yours."

She glanced at him as they entered the main cavern. Blood still stained the ground from his earlier fight and he was trudging in more, his wounded leg leaving a crimson trail in his wake.

Throwing his head back, he howled, a purely inhuman sound. Within moments, the space began to fill. Vash appeared startled by the number of lycans who poured in. "Jeez. Who knew so many furries could fit in one cave?"

Elijah waited until the room was so full that a mere five feet of clearance surrounded them. He relayed the recent events without inflection—starting with Vashti's arrival and ending with his reason for taking the life of a packmate. His remorse and frustration roiled, twisting around his vitals, but he contained them, even as he expressed sincere regret that they'd lost one of their own.

As some of the lycans in the room shifted into their lupine forms, Vash lifted her blade and set the flat of it against her shoulder. While her pose was casual, it conveyed her battle readiness. The beasts paced and she tracked them with her gaze.

"I'm asking you to trust the orders I give and the actions I take," he finished, "whether you understand and agree with them or not. If you can't, I won't stop you from leaving and I won't think less of you. If you stay, some of you will be on the move tomorrow and working with vampires. In either case, try to get some rest tonight. Things will be stressful for all of us for the next while."

He started forward, heading for the cavern he was using as sleeping quarters. The female who'd announced Vash's arrival the day before stepped into his path. Sarah was a young Omega—he guessed mid-twenties—and exceptionally pretty, with long straight black hair and tip-tilted eyes.

"Alpha." She met his gaze shyly. "Allow me to tend your wounds."

He almost brushed her off, his emotions too volatile to welcome company. But her earnestness touched him. While there were many who would challenge him, there were others who needed a different sort of guidance—

a soft touch and gentle words to go along with a firm hand. It was the sort of leadership he longed to provide and hoped he could eventually achieve once their situation became less precarious. "I'd be grateful if you would, Sarah."

Battery-operated lights lined the passageway. Gesturing at his office, he spoke over his shoulder to Vashti. "Grab your bag."

She muttered something under her breath, but complied. She joined him a few minutes later in his room, entering at the moment he had his hands on his fly. He shed his ruined pants and sat on the military locker placed at the foot of his air mattress. Sarah sank to her knees between his spread legs and opened the first-aid kit.

"I'm not interrupting anything, am I?" Vash queried tightly.

Elijah looked up at her, noting the rigidness of her jaw and her narrowed gaze. Nudity was nothing to a lycan, but perhaps it meant something to Vashti. Wondering if the vampress could possibly be feeling as proprietary about him as he felt about her, he reached out and tucked Sarah's hair behind one ear. Vash stepped closer, the hand not holding her duffel wrapping tightly around the hilt of a blade strapped to her thigh.

"Where's my room?" she demanded. "I'll give you some privacy."

"You're standing in it."

Her gaze lifted from his cock to his eyes. "What?"

"You're rooming with me."

"Like hell."

Canting his arms back, he gripped the rear edge of the trunk and stretched his wounded leg out. "It's the one place I can trust you'll be safe."

"I can damn well take care of myself."

He took a deep breath, released it. "No argument, but the odds are against you."

"If I can't fight off a pack of puppies, I deserve to bite it."

"And Syre would come down on me in a swarm of vamps. How much shit am I expected to have shoveled on me?"

That knocked her back a bit. She looked at the queen-sized air mattress, clearly debating the risks and benefits of sharing it with him.

"We're both adults," he pointed out. Then he groaned softly as Sarah smoothed ointment over his torn skin. He'd be healing faster if he was eating properly, but he was quickly becoming undernourished on the sparse amount of food to be found while roughing it. "Nothing will happen that you don't want."

"I don't want anything besides you keeping your end of our agreement."

"Then you've got no worries. Why don't you show me those property specs you mentioned?"

Vash stared at him for a long moment, then muttered something beneath her breath and dug in her bag. She set it down on the ground a moment later, her hand emerging from the depths with a folder clutched in her grip. She looked at Sarah, who was tying off a bandage. "Are you done yet?"

Sarah's gaze searched Elijah's face for instruction.

He dismissed her with an easy, "Thank you, Sarah."

The lycan closed the first-aid kit and said, "I'll get you some dinner, Alpha. Esther made an awesome venison stew."

"I appreciate that." Ideally, they'd each be eating their own deer, but they weren't in a position to dine well under the circumstances. Instead they were divvying up what they caught among everyone, which kept them alive. Barely.

"Also . . ." She offered a timid smile. "I'd like to stay with you when you make the arrangements to send some of us out with the vampires."

"Aw," Vash crooned with syrupy sweetness. "Puppy love. How touching."

Sarah rose to her feet with graceful dignity, but the look she shot Vashti was poisonous, a rare display of hatred from an Omega.

"I'll work something out," Elijah answered, his decision taking into account her innate Omega gift for soothing and comforting others. She'd be best utilized in a support position, rather than on a hunt.

"Thank you, Alpha." She left the room in a calm, graceful glide.

Pushing to his feet, he rolled his shoulders back, feeling better already. He felt Vash's gaze slide over him and he glanced at her with an arched brow.

"Will you put some damn clothes on?" she snapped.

"Why don't you take yours off?"

She bared her fangs. "In your wet dreams, lycan."

He shrugged. "Worth a shot."

CHAPTER 5

They were on the road before dawn and across the Utah/Nevada border before midmorning.

Vash gripped the steering wheel and tried not to think about the restless night behind her. Elijah, damn him, had slept like a log, which said more clearly than anything that he didn't consider her a threat at all.

She'd tried to work. There was so much to be done. But she'd been distracted by the way he had stretched out next to her with one arm tossed carelessly over his head, showing off beautifully defined biceps. And the way the sheet had clung tantalizingly low on his hips . . . A tiny tug would have revealed all of his impressive assets.

Vash loved a healthy man's body as much as the next woman, but Elijah's was a work of art, his powerful frame covered in mouthwatering ridges of muscle she wanted to trace with her tongue and hands and—

"These are all warehouses," Elijah muttered, looking over the property listings she'd printed out.

"Warehouses with plenty of parking, room for a helipad, top-of-the-line electrical systems, and air-conditioning." She glanced at him. "I know how touchy you lycans get when you're overheated."

"It's not easy being furry."

It took a moment for the levity of his dry statement to sink in. Looking out the windshield, she felt her lips curve. He was feeling more himself, it seemed, and she was relieved. His pain yesterday had moved her, made her see him in a far more personal way than she would've wished. His sincere grief proved his strength of character in many ways—he'd taken an action he knew would cost him personally to benefit the many. She respected both that toughness and his willingness to shed tears without shame.

"These properties are expensive," he said bluntly. "Syre's making a hell of an investment in an alliance that hasn't been tested."

"I'll kill you if you double-cross me. Stake your head on a pike for other lycans to see."

"You're expecting me to screw you over."

"Your breed's track record isn't so hot. Your ancestors ditched us for Adrian to save their hides and you just ditched Adrian, once again to save your ass."

His gaze seared her profile. "You're skipping over millennia and multiple generations. With the average lycan lifespan being two hundred and thirty years, there's not a single lycan in existence who's been touched by what happened to the Watchers. Most of them couldn't even tell you which angel they're descended from."

Yet the memory of her fall was as fresh to her as if it had occurred mere weeks ago instead of lifetimes. "So if you forget an obligation, it doesn't count?"

"Not what I meant. It's just a tough sell enforcing promises made on behalf of someone who's centuries away from being born."

"Your great-great-grandwolfies made that decision for you. A shame you can't ask them about it." Familiar bitterness coated her tongue. "I expected fidelity from the angels who served beside me. We made our beds— it's not a tough sell thinking they'd be honorable for lying in them."

"I was told the Fallen who became lycans hadn't broken the laws the rest of you did," Elijah said.

Vash shot him a scathing glance and became even more irritated by how delicious he looked. She would've thought that after seeing how impressive he was naked, seeing him dressed would be no big deal. But he managed to make the casual attire of wide-legged jeans and plain black T-shirt look stunning. He was a big, brawny hunk of a male, capable of taking on a woman of her strength and force of will in a way very few men could. That got to her. Made her hot and hungry for the greedy touch of a passionate man's hands. *His* hands. The hands she'd watched stroke over his bare skin in deliberate provocation.

Of course, she wasn't even sure she remembered *how* to have sex anymore . . .

She looked away. "That's a cop-out. We all lost our way in some manner or another. We were tasked with observing and reporting. Any sort of contact with mortals was outside our scope as Watchers—seeing, talking, hearing, touching, teaching. But we were scholars. We thirsted for knowledge, the giving and receiving of it. We couldn't resist the desire to interact."

He tucked the property spec sheets back in the file. "But you didn't. Not like the others did."

"I took a mate."

"Charron. Another Watcher like you. Not a mortal."

"I know what they say about me, that I martyred myself out of a twisted sense of loyalty to the others, that I wasn't as guilty because I mated with another angel. But I fraternized in nonsexual ways. I taught what I knew, gave man knowledge they weren't ready for yet. So when I walked up to a Sentinel with my head held high and accepted my punishment without a fight, it's because I deserved it. I also thought His fury was just a test of our resolve. The Creator had never allowed the shedding of an angel's blood before. I thought if we showed our remorse and repentance that we'd be forgiven our trespasses." She blew out her breath in a rush. "And then the Sentinels were created."

Her eyes lost their focus on the road, her mind rewinding to that bleak, heartrending time of her life. She would never forget looking down from her hidden vantage, seeing Adrian and Syre battling in the field below while Sentinels rimmed one side and the soon-to-be-Fallen Watchers the other. The deadly dance had been terrifyingly beautiful. Adrian with his alabaster wings and Syre with wings of iridescent blue. Both men tall and dark. Works of art lovingly crafted by the

Creator. The best and most favored of their respective castes.

Their fists had pummeled each other viciously; tenderizing flesh and rippling muscle. Twisting and lunging, their wings had swirled fluidly around them like massive capes.

But Syre had been no match for the honed instrument of punishment that was Adrian. Syre was a scholar; Adrian a warrior. Syre had been softened by the humanity that seeped into him via his love for his mortal mate. Adrian was too new to the earth; his control and purpose had yet to be eroded by emotion of any kind. And his entire body was lethal. Unlike the Watchers, the Sentinels were weaponized from head to toe. The tips of their feathers sliced like knives, and their hands and feet clawed with talons that shredded through skin and bone.

Syre had been vulnerable; Adrian inviolate.

In the moment after the Sentinel leader had severed the wings from Syre's back, his head had lifted and his flame-blue gaze had locked with hers. There had been nothing in the cerulean depths but angelfire, the scorching vengeance of the Creator from which he'd been forged. Over time Vashti would watch those eyes change, as the Sentinel leader settled into his life on earth and fell prey to Shadoe's erotic hunger.

"Hey." Elijah's voice broke into her reverie. "Where'd you go?"

"Adrian's getting a taste of his own medicine now," she said hoarsely, thinking of the Sentinel's beautiful crimson-tipped wings. Those ruby bands of honor were the bloodstains that marked him as the first being ever to draw the blood of an angel. "I hope it goes down like acid."

He withdrew the aviator shades he had slung over his collar and put them on. "There are very few people I admire more than Adrian."

"He's a hypocritical asshat. A total douche for breaking the very rules he busted our asses over."

"Wasn't his decision to punish you, and it isn't his decision to not be punished himself. That order has to come from the Creator, right? If you break a law in front of a cop and the cop doesn't arrest you, whose fault is it that you don't get punished?"

"So? He could at least show a little remorse. A little guilt. *Something.* He's completely unrepentant."

"Something I admire him for."

"You would."

"To me an asshat is a guy who'd fuck around, angst about it, then fuck around again as if angsting about it absolved him in some twisted way. Adrian owns his mistakes and he owns his feelings for Lindsay, which is just what you did when you gave up your wings without a fight. I think he'd do the same thing, if the punishment comes his way. He certainly wouldn't make excuses, because he's not making any now."

Frowning, Vash stared across the hood at the expanse of flat nothingness that hugged the stretch of Nevada highway they traveled on. Resenting Adrian was one of her tenets. She wasn't prepared to lose it alongside losing her hatred of every single lycan in existence. One truce was enough for now. "Shut up."

She didn't look at him, but she suspected he was smiling. Smug bastard.

"Our exit," he said, and she pulled off.

"This works."

Vash looked at him. "Just like that? First place we see and you're done."

He glanced around the vast open space again and shrugged. It had been the distribution center for a small import company that hadn't survived the economic downturn. The exterior was marked by loading bay doors and the interior by soaring ceilings that suspended moving cranes on elaborate tracks. Skylights flooded the space with illumination, dissipating any possibility of feeling closed in. "It has everything you say it needs. No point in wasting the day looking at more of the same. Besides, you liked this one best, and it's your dime we're dropping."

It didn't bother him to take the handout and it didn't shake his confidence, which she grudgingly admired. "I didn't say I liked this one best."

He shot her a look.

"Okay, then." She pulled out her iPhone and called Syre's assistant, Raven, to complete the sale. Then she speed dialed Raze. "Hey," she said when he answered. "You win. And . . . I didn't cheat."

"Ha! Be there in ten."

She ended the call and met Elijah's gaze, explaining, "He was sure you'd go with my choice."

Amusement warmed his eyes. There'd be no repudiations from him, no defensiveness, even though it could be easy for her to say he was so used to following commands that he was easily led. His poise and self-possession stirred her admiration. And her desire. There was nothing so attractive as a powerful, handsome, and self-assured man.

God. What the hell was the matter with her?

She needed to eat. That was it. She hadn't fed in days, and hunger was making her vulnerable to Elijah's appeal and making it too easy to forget what he was.

Trying to get her mind off it, she texted Salem to make sure he was en route with the busload of lycans Stephan had been tasked with rounding up. Assured that everything was on track, she took a moment to make sure the Alpha was on track, too.

"Are you all right?" she asked him. "About yesterday."

"No." His face shuttered. "But I'll survive."

"You handled the announcement well last night. I meant to tell you that." But she had been distracted by aggravation with the fawning lycan who'd patched him up. Not that she'd ever admit it.

He stared at her a minute. "Thanks. And thanks for the pep talk."

"No problem." Suddenly feeling awkward, she gestured toward her Jeep. "Help me unload before Raze arrives."

They were just finishing up when the sound of a helicopter approaching signaled Raze's arrival. He landed smoothly in the empty parking lot and cut the engine. The remote location of the property spoke to the ambition of the previous owners—they could've expanded indefinitely as business grew. Instead, the rising cost of fuel and weak retail traffic in stores had led to a short sale. Their loss was now her gain.

The heavily muscled vampire, one of the Fallen like her, climbed out of the aircraft with a grin, his eyes hidden behind wraparound sunglasses, his shaved head shining under the desert sun. He sized up Elijah with a long, sweeping glance. Then he looked at Vash. "I'll have to make another trip, at least. Maybe two more."

She nodded. "Let's get you unloaded, then."

It took all day to move the necessary supplies into the building, even with the help of the four dozen lycans they'd brought in via bus. In addition to the electronic equipment, which took priority, they set up rows of bunk beds that drew groans from the lycans, because they were identical to the ones they'd been provided while indentured to Adrian. Cameras were set up on the roof, since any angelic incursion would come from the air, and the windows were covered with UV-blocking film, to create a safe haven for the minions that would join them in a few hours under cover of darkness.

The most important thing for Vash, however, was the van-sized map that showed the pattern of contagion around the country. She stood in front of it with her hands on her hips, knowing the radiuses had extended in the last few days she'd spent setting up the lycan/vampire alliance.

Turning her head, she watched as the lycans worked alongside her most trusted captains, Raze and Salem.

Lycans and vampires working together. It was insane, really, considering the seething hostility that weighted the air, like flammable gas awaiting the strike of a match. She was restless in anticipation of a sparking event, knowing it wouldn't take much to set off an explosion that could devolve into a bloodbath.

It didn't escape her attention that Elijah was the force keeping it all together. As the temperature rose, he took most of the outside shifts, hefting the heavy equipment and carrying it into the loading bays without a word of complaint. She knew how lycans hated the heat; she'd exploited how testy they became when uncomfortable countless times on hunts. But Elijah was such a powerful example of grace under pressure that the others were shamed into good behavior—lycan and vampire alike.

Although sweat poured down the lycans' laboring bodies and their chests heaved, they worked quickly and efficiently. And the vampires gave the Alpha only a token amount of flak when he directed their efforts with firm, unwavering command. They didn't trust him, but they couldn't fault his leadership style. It was impossible to do so. There was something inherently majestic about Elijah, a core strength of will that was unshakable. And he was compassionate. He took the time to speak to each lycan individually, putting a hand on their shoulders and gifting personal words of thanks and praise.

More than once she found herself staring at and admiring him. *We're equals or we're nothing*, he'd said, referring to vampires and lycans as a whole. But it was true for them as individuals, too.

No, she corrected herself. *He outranks me.* His equals were Syre and Adrian. For the first time, she was confronted with an attraction to a man who wasn't beneath her in rank. She was startled at how much that changed the dynamic.

"If this alliance sticks," Elijah said at the end of the day, "it'll take me years to get used to."

"How many of these lycans can you trust to have your back?"

One slashing brow rose. His hair was damp from a recent shower, inciting a mental picture him of standing beneath a spray of water, naked and wet and irresistibly sexy . . .

"Hell if I know," he said without heat.

Honest to a fault. She liked that about him, among too many other things. He was a goddamned lycan, a race of beings that couldn't be trusted—

His other brow rose to match the first. "Problem?"

"No problem." She brushed past him on her way out, her nostrils filled with the wildly clean fragrance of his skin mixed with the earthy pheromones he exuded as a matter of course . . . pheromones her senses soaked up as if starved for them. "I'll see you in the morning."

She didn't hear him come up on her, but she felt him. Was overly attuned to him. Damn it all to hell. "Don't nip at my heels, puppy," she snapped.

"You're charming when sexually frustrated."

Her fists clenched. "I'm hungry for food, not you."

"I am your food. We discussed this."

"*You* discussed it." She stepped outside into the

chilly desert night and took a deep breath of air untainted by the primal scent of hardworking lycans. As she walked, her head began to clear . . . Then Elijah cut her off by stepping in front of her, fogging her mind with the exotic scent that was unique to him, a fragrance reminiscent of cinnamon and cloves. It was delicious, as everything about him was.

"You stay with me," he said. "That part of the deal was mutually agreed to."

"I'll be back. I need to take care of something." She needed blood, and—for the first time in damn near sixty years—sex. Then she could deal with him without tripping over how scorchingly beautiful he was.

Sidestepping him, she reached into her cleavage for her Jeep key.

He caught her wrist before she passed him. "How much shit have you got in there? Cell phones, jump drives, keys."

Yanking her hand free, she gestured at the skintight, sleeveless black catsuit she wore. "Where the hell else am I going to carry things?"

His hand, however, didn't budge, despite the ferocity of her movement. It remained suspended by her shoulder, close enough that she tensed in expectation of his touch. Slowly, as if she might yet bolt, he adjusted his position to bring them face-to-face again and reached for the exposed zipper that was nestled between her breasts. Breasts that swelled and began to ache, growing heavy in anticipation of his touch.

She'd forgotten what it felt like to be physically aroused, forgotten how intoxicating it was, how it im-

peded the ability to think rationally and act with common sense.

"Keep your paws to yourself," she bit out, stepping back.

"What are you afraid of?"

"Not wanting to be mauled doesn't make me scared, asshole."

Emerald eyes glittering with challenge in the moonlight, he held up both hands. "I promise to keep my paws to myself. I just want to see what else you've got in there. Cash? ATM cards? Spare tire?"

"None of your business."

"I've shown you mine," he taunted softly, goading her with a lycan's overt sexuality. Vampires were sexual creatures, too, but lycans were pagans, their demontainted blood spurring wild natures. Elijah was more brutally sexual than any other lycan she'd ever met, his confidence and quiet command stemming from his comfort with himself, his luscious body, and his awareness of his virility and strength.

She couldn't get the image of him out of her head— naked, bloody, his big hand stroking his big cock, his eyes dark and hot with wanting her. The memory had haunted her all night while he slept soundly. Fucker.

Pissed at the imbalance in the attraction between them, Vash yanked her zipper to her navel and pulled the separated halves aside. Her breasts bounced free, the tips hardening as a cool breeze slid across them. She was braless due to the natural constriction of the suit, which hugged her so tightly any underwear would have marred the sleek lines. The garment was comfortable, affording her full range of movement, and it distracted her opponents—win/win all around.

He stared, unblinking, his face hardening into an austere mask of ferocious hunger. His arms fell slowly to his sides, his hands fisting.

"Jesus," he hissed.

Pure feminine power slid through her, her anger and frustration soothed by his undisguised helpless captivation. When she moved to close her top, he growled low and deep, the rumbling sound an unmistakable animal warning. She stilled instinctively, her body freezing in place as if lack of movement would make her invisible to the predator stalking her.

In her haste to retaliate, she'd awakened the beast. Now the steady, powerful drumming of his heartbeat was spurring her potent vampiric needs. The intrinsic hunger for blood and sex. *His* blood. *His* sex. That's what she craved with a force that shook her, as if the desire for a man's touch had always been inside her. Lying dormant. Waiting for the right man to jolt it to life.

That man stepped closer. Then lowered his head . . .

"Elijah." She breathed his name, her pulse pounding violently. Her body was straining toward his without her volition, every muscle taut with expectation and wanting. She should've backed away again, would have done so if she'd been capable of moving. Instead it felt like her feet had been encased in concrete, rooting her in place.

His breath gusted hot over her nipple, his lips hovering over the stiffened peak. "No paws," he whispered.

Then he stroked his rough tongue across her with a long, leisurely lick. Her gasp was a whiplash in the still of the night; her body jerked as if she'd been tasered. She felt as if she had been. Needles of sharpened awareness swept over her skin from head to toe. The roots of her hair stood on end, tingling with the need to feel his grip fisting the crimson strands.

He groaned, the sound filled with pleasure and torment. "Offer yourself to me," he ordered roughly, licking his lips.

She swallowed hard, tasting blood and realizing her fangs had descended and pierced her. Her hunger beat at her senses, rushing through her veins, mingling with her sexual desire until they were one and the same. She didn't realize she'd cupped her breast and lifted it to his mouth until she was scorched by the heat of his lips. The drenching burn was quenched by a sudden hard suck that made her moan and stumble a fraction of an inch closer. His tongue fluttered maddeningly over the elongated tip, worrying it, making her sex clench in jealous greed.

The wind blew softly, riffling through his dark hair and urging the thick silk to brush over her tender skin. He touched her nowhere else, with nothing else but his mouth, which began to tug with rhythmic pulls. The measured tempo pulsed through her, making her wet between the thighs and achy with emptiness.

He released her with a pop of breaking suction.

"I love your tits," he growled, each word said with arousing vehemence. "I'm going to squeeze them in my hands, holding them together as I slide my dick through all this lush, firm flesh until I come all over you."

No man had ever talked to her that way, so crude and raw. No man would dare.

Taming Elijah would be impossible, she realized, quivering with longing tinged by apprehension. She was a strong woman, but she couldn't imagine bending him to her will. Because he was strong, too. Maybe even stronger than she was.

Elijah looked up at her as his head turned slightly to bring his mouth over her neglected nipple. "You want that, too. I can smell how it turns you on to think about giving it up to me however I want it. Giving up all that power and command you're used to shoving everyone around with."

"Fuck you."

"Oh . . . you will, Vashti. Long and hard. It's only a matter of time."

He was suckling her before she could retort, pinning her nipple to the roof of his mouth and massaging it with his tongue. She almost came from the sweet sting of it, the delirious pleasure/pain of voracious draws so powerful they hollowed his cheeks. He was relentless in his taking, his teeth sinking into the turgid peak with just enough pressure to send a shiver of wariness through her.

"Vash."

Salem's voice behind her startled her into jerking away from the wicked ecstasy of Elijah's mouth. She cried out at the sharp scrape of teeth over tender flesh, then again with surprise at the orgasm that was *almost* triggered by the bittersweet pain.

Elijah had her zipped up and steadied with lightning-quick efficiency. If not for his labored breathing, she might've thought he was unaffected. Then he caught her hand and cupped it around his erection, grinding himself into her palm.

"We're here," he called out, pushing her hand aside and taking a step back.

They were only yards away from the door. Salem would have seen Elijah's bent head and smelled their mutual arousal.

"I need your wheels," her captain said, lingering by the warehouse instead of approaching. Agitated by the scent of desire, he shoved a meaty hand through his electric orange hair. It was a testament to how bad-ass he was that he could flaunt a hair color that was a bull's-eye on his massive cranium. "Time for a run to Shred."

Swallowing hard, she stared at Elijah but spoke to Salem. "I'll go with you."

Shred was one of Torque's most exclusive and secretive dens. Located far off the Vegas Strip, it was a way station for fledgling minions and older vamps alike, offering safety, sex, and blood.

"I'll drive," Elijah said, bending to pick up the car keys she'd unknowingly dropped from her lax hand.

Any one of the lycans in the building could have snuck up on her and she would never have noticed, her brain fried by the heat of Elijah's mouth on her breast.

It was unacceptable. She needed to get her shit together before she got herself killed. "I'm not telling you where it is, lycan."

"You don't have to." He turned toward the Jeep. "I've hunted there before."

CHAPTER 6

Pissed off and frustrated by his own weakness where Vashti was concerned, Elijah made no attempt to hide his raging lust from either Vash or Salem. Instead he obstinately pumped pheromones into the air around him, permeating the Jeep's interior until Salem cursed viciously and adjusted himself in his leather pants. Vash had chosen to take a seat in the back, a mistake that guaranteed the smell of his need whipped across her face and through her hair, carried by the wind surging through the window Salem opened.

"Cut it out, Alpha," she shouted, punching her fist into his seat back.

He met her furious gaze in the rearview mirror, his own hard and brittle. She was as angry as he was; he had made sure of it by reminding her that he'd hunted her kind, that he'd observed and studied their habits and places of congregation in minute detail so he could kill the ones who stepped out of line.

She deserved to be uncomfortable for putting him through this hunger, for making him want her more than he'd ever wanted anything. The moment he'd stroked his tongue across her skin, her taste had exploded across his senses with the force of an incendiary grenade. There was nothing reasoned or calculated in his response to her. It was pure primal recognition of a unique and potent physical attraction. Lust at first sight, exacerbated by their heightened lupine and vampire natures.

He could still taste her, damn her. Smell her. His palms burned with the need to feel her. Inside, his beast howled with rage to be freed, forcing him to struggle in a way he'd never had to before. Because he : . . liked her. Crazy as that was. Crazy as *she* was. Controlling his baser nature had always been as easy as breathing, but it was exhausting him now. Wearing him down. Clawing at him from the inside and shredding what restraint he had left after a week of painful blows and savage lows and highs. She'd witnessed those trials and, in her own way, been an asset to have around while going through them.

He growled. Vashti's returning feminine hunger was eating at him like a cancer. As tough as she was, he now knew he could make her soft and submissive, and he wanted her like that. Wanted her limp and panting beneath him, completely at his mercy. He could accept nothing less.

The nearly two-hour drive to Shred ended up feeling like two years, and not just for him. Salem unfolded from the Jeep before it drew to a complete stop and was through the thick metal entrance door in a flash. Vash was fast on his heels, fleeing Elijah as if the hounds of hell were after her. When the door slammed shut behind her, he barked out a mirthless laugh.

As if a simple door could prevent what was coming. If only it was that easy.

Needing to get himself under control before he entered a vampire den, Elijah took his time locking up the SUV and scoping out the exterior of the unobtrusive building for changes. He surveyed the immediate area, refreshing his memory of the industrial properties on the periphery that had closed long before the party got started. He took note of the armed vampires on the roof before they deliberately made their presence known. They smelled him coming, and because he was spoiling for a fight, he lifted his hand and flipped them off.

One decided to oblige him, leaping agilely from the top of the three-story building and landing in a graceful crouch. The vamp was sleek and sinewy, his world-weary eyes and economy of movement betraying significant age. They circled each other slowly, baring fangs and canines, claws extended. Neither of them looked away from the other when the door opened and a masculine voice shouted out, "Dredge! Leave him alone. He's Vashti's."

The vampress's protection so enraged Elijah that his spine rippled with a partial change. He didn't fucking need her to clear the way for him. He could damn well do it himself.

"Are you a pet, dog?" Dredge taunted, his amber eyes glowing. "Or a meal?"

Elijah's mouth curved. "Maybe she's a lycan's bitch."

Dredge lunged. Expecting the reaction, Elijah met the vamp's incoming face with his fist, hurtling him backward across the parking lot and into the side of a delivery van, creating a massive dent that mimicked the shape of his body.

Shaking the sting out of his fist, Elijah turned toward the open door, his ears trained for the sound of a retaliatory ambush from the others on the roof. But none came, proving the extent of Vash's power—her word was law for vampires. Seeing the proof of it made Elijah's dick impossibly harder, spurring his need for her, which had grown steadily over days of watching her run the show. She wielded power with the same control and skill that she used to wield her katanas, which turned him on as much as her body did.

Once inside the outer door, he encountered a second entrance. It opened as soon as the first door shut, releasing a flood of pounding techno-pop music and the rich metallic smell of freshly spilled blood. The scent of sex engulfed him in a steamy mist, spurring his ferocious mood. He wanted to fight and fuck with unmitigated ferocity, and the need to do both increased with every second that passed.

Rounding a corner, he was thrust into a massive room filled with writhing vampires. Some were dancing, grinding their undulating bodies against whoever was close enough. Others were feeding, their bloody mouths latched on to throats, wrists, and thighs. Still more were openly fucking, like Salem, who was drill-

ing a vampress from behind as she drank from the
femoral artery of a woman spread-eagled in front of
her.

The unrestrained hedonism bombarded Elijah's ravaged senses, the thick humidity in the space almost suf-
focating him. Maddened to the edge of insanity, he
searched for Vash among the crowd, his beast lunging
against the cage of his control, trying to batter its way
out at the thought that she might be spread for someone else.

Leaping onto a tallboy table, he roared, drowning
out all sound. The room froze, the music becoming
glaringly loud within the absence of sound. Then a
slender blonde mimicked his leap and gained the bar
top. She ripped her shirt apart and exposed her tits,
shaking them with wild abandon and screaming, "Fuck
yeah!"

The crowd ignited into a frenzied mass. Drunk on
endorphins, they resumed their carnal excess, the
pounding bass of the music spurring them like a war
drum.

Elijah vaulted up to the second-floor balcony, hunting his vampress.

Vash entered the third-floor VIP lounge and scanned
the room's occupants with a sweeping glance. She was
searching for something in particular and she found
him. He was long and lean. Blond. His eyes were
heavy-lidded, his lounging pose was insolence person-
ified. His chest and feet were bare; his skin was pale
and smooth. The antithesis of Elijah. But best of all

were the piercings riddling his body—his ears, brows, nose, lips, nipples, navel . . . She was certain there would be more in places she couldn't yet see. And the carvings in his skin. Intricate designs that had been sliced by a skilled blade and prevented from healing by application of silver-laced cream or shavings.

The man enjoyed pain. Sought it out deliberately and found beauty in it. And she wanted to inflict pain on someone who could take it and wanted it. Because she hurt and was infuriated by that hurt. Because she'd pushed her way through dozens of beautiful, desirable male bodies to reach the lounge, and none of them had moved her or stirred the hunger simmering in her blood. Because she was dead to every male just as she'd been ever since the day Charron died . . . every male but one.

"You." She beckoned her quarry with a crook of her finger.

He straightened with a slow, sensual smile and came to her with a leisurely, confident stride. Reaching her, he took her in from head to toe with a covetous glance, then licked his lower lip. "I was beginning to think you'd never come for me."

Bored already, she raised her brows. "Oh?"

Tilting his head, he exposed his neck . . . and the tattoo that was written there with silver-tainted ink: VASHTI, BITE HERE.

A shiver moved through her at the craziness of the act. They'd never met, yet he'd marked himself as her property.

Of all the men to meet her criteria for the night, she

had to pick a groupie, one of the far-too-many minions who were aroused by the thought of being a blood slave to one of the Fallen.

She almost waved him away—there was enough crazy in her life as it was. Then she heard Elijah's roar, felt it vibrate through walls and rattle the bloodstained glasses on the tables. The fierceness of the desire that shot through her made her sway on her feet, as if she was hardwired to answer that dominant call. She didn't have time to be discerning. She needed blood to manage her desire for Elijah and she needed it *now*.

Knowing she had maybe five minutes at most before the lycan worked his way through the crush of bodies on the stairs to get to the third floor, Vash shoved the vamp into a chair and circled him, grabbing his jaw from behind and yanking it out of the way to expose his neck. She'd prefer his wrist, to keep it impersonal, but she needed to be quick and nothing beat an arterial gush for speed.

Her fangs descended, her gaze riveted to the thick pumping vein at his throat. As her stomach gnawed in hunger and dizziness swept through her from the need to feed, the lounge door was ripped off its hinges and thrown over the balcony into the teeming mass of vampires below. Elijah filled the threshold, his body big, hard, and virile. His irises glowed in the shadows cast by the muted wall sconces.

"*Mine*." Just the one word, spoken low and terrifyingly deep, as if ripped from the beast inside him instead of from his human throat.

Something warm and slightly twisted slid sinuously

inside her, some alien feeling of . . . pleasure that such a magnificently masculine creature should be so powerfully possessive of her.

His gaze dropped to the minion seated in front of her. "Go, before I kill you."

"I need to eat, damn you!" she shouted, weary of fighting herself over him and desperately clinging to the hope that a replenishment of nutrients would free her from her inexplicable fascination.

But she knew he wouldn't let her drink from anyone else, not now. The act of feeding was too innately sexual, even when the only contact was fangs to vein and lips to skin. He was too territorial to allow that connection, however impersonal. Yet she couldn't afford to drink from him . . . *wouldn't* drink from him, because she knew, instinctively, that she would have the same reaction to the taste of him as he'd had to the taste of her—the hunger wouldn't be appeased; it would grow. She would crave more. More of his potent lycan blood. More of *him*.

She would have to restrain him long enough to get a meal in edgewise.

Taking command of the situation, Vash closed the distance between them and caught him with a fist in his shirt. "Come with me."

She pulled him, but succeeded only in ripping the shirt off his back. Elijah didn't move at all, was too powerful for even her vampire strength. Her sex clenched with greed for this male who was more than a match for her.

Flushed and breathless, she skirted him and exited

to the hall, trying to get herself under control before he realized how close to the edge she was. If she wasn't careful, he'd have her begging for his cock. The thought of that weakness terrified her as nothing else could. She had to be strong, for herself and for Char, and for all the vampires who needed her to keep them alive and thriving.

Elijah followed so closely she could feel his heavy exhalations on her nape. Stalking her again. And she couldn't deny that some recessed part of her wanted him to. Because it ratcheted up her desire, made her hot and wet.

Vash saw the small green light lit above a door and went to it quickly. There were more doors and more lights. Most were red, which signaled locked and occupied. Some were yellow, which signaled vacant but in need of housekeeping. Only a few were green and she chose the nearest one, opening the door and cursing as Elijah crowded her into the small playroom. He caught her around the waist and tossed her onto the massive bed, barely giving her the time to scoot up before he pounced.

"Elijah," she gasped, as he landed neatly on all fours, caging her to the bed with his hands pressed to the mattress at her shoulders and his knees hugging the sides of her thighs. Fear paralyzed her, not of him but of the raging desire that was quickly consuming her. The need to arch upward and offer herself to him was a driving force. It pounded her heart against her ribs and squeezed the air from her lungs.

Her eyes adjusted to the dimness of the room, the

only illumination provided by recessed lighting in the baseboards. His eyes glowed with preternatural green fire and his head lowered, his chest expanding on a deep inhale as he breathed her in.

"Should've brought us here when we arrived," he said gruffly. "You'd be coming now."

He took her mouth before she could reply, his lips sealing over hers and stealing her breath. His tongue swept inside her on a groan, his hand moving to her zipper to slide it down to where it ended at her pubic bone. She'd barely swallowed her first rich, dark taste of him when he pushed his hand beneath the edge of her suit and claimed her breast in one big, hot hand.

Her fangs sharpened in a rush of need, piercing his tongue. His blood flowed into her mouth, the flavor intoxicatingly exotic. He kneaded her breast, plumping it, then focusing his thumb and forefinger on the tip, rolling and tugging on her hardened nipple until her sex spasmed in the same rhythmic tempo.

Out of her mind for him, Vash sucked on his tongue with the same voracious pull with which he'd sucked her nipples earlier, drawing more of his blood over her taste buds. Her eyes rolled back in her head, her ability to reason lost to the addictive deliciousness. He growled into her mouth and sank between her thighs, grinding the rigid length of his cock into her aching sex. Whimpering, she gripped his hips and tugged him into her, rocking her hips upward to stroke her clit against his erection.

Elijah lifted his head and watched her as he rolled his hips, watched her head arch back as an orgasm hovered just out of reach. "Tell me you want it, Vashti. Tell me you need my cock in you like you need blood to live."

Her body quaked violently as he gave voice to her greatest apprehension.

I won't be led around by my dick, he'd said what seemed like ages ago in the Bryce Canyon caves. But she feared she wasn't as strong as he was. She'd never been so desperate for sex as she was at that moment, and he was the only man she wanted to have sex with. Her attraction to him wielded too great a power over her, and she feared giving him what he demanded of her—total surrender.

Tossing her leg over his hip, she gained the leverage to flip him to his back. Moving as fast as if her life depended on it, Vash focused on the purpose of bringing him to a playroom to begin with. In a split second, she had him restrained, his wrists and forearms banded with barbed silver-plated steel cable. He roared as the tiny rounded points pierced his flesh, scarcely enough to draw blood but enough to expose the wounded flesh to the one metal that weakened Sentinels, vampires, and lycans alike.

The bed quaked with his fury, his irises burned bright enough to light up the room. "You fucking bitch!"

But she was beyond caring now. She was slick and swollen between her legs, her breasts were tender and heavy, and his flavor permeated her mouth, deterring thoughts of fleeing as she might've done if she'd had any sense of self-preservation left.

"Let me loose." He clawed at the bed with the heels of his boots. "Fucking let me go . . . *now!*"

Vash fought to be free of her catsuit, struggling out of both it and her boots in a near-mindless frenzy. Once naked, she fell on his twisting body, wrestling his bucking hips to yank open his button fly.

"Vashti!" He arched violently. "Not like this, damn you. Don't fucking tie me up like an animal."

As always, Elijah was commando beneath his jeans, ready to shift forms at a moment's notice. Nothing impeded her mouth from his cock, which she swallowed greedily, her lips and tongue tightening around his raging length.

"Shit," he hissed, bucking his hips in an attempt to throw her off. "Get your bloodsucking mouth off me!"

She couldn't. If the entire den poured into the room and found her fellating a lycan, she didn't think she could stop. Her hunger for the taste of him was too great, her need to bring about his surrender even greater. Pumping the thick root with her fist, she tongued the wide head, her mouth sucking hard and quick as she drove him relentlessly toward orgasm. He fought the whole way, his powerful thighs bunched with strain, his chest rumbling with furious growls, his torso twisting back and forth to dislodge her.

When he climaxed, it was with a wolven howl that brought goose bumps to her skin. The baying sound was high and plaintive, purely animal with none of the human evident in it. Tears stung her eyes even as she drank him down, something ancient and primal within her ravenous for the heady flavor of his savage virility.

"Damn you." He panted, his chest heaving as she shoved his jeans to his knees. "Damn you to hell, you traitorous— Fuck!"

Her fangs sank into his femoral artery and she lost what tiny bit of humanity she clung to. His blood mingled with the semen in her mouth, creating a blended essence that was the most delicious thing she'd ever tasted. She circled his powerful thigh with both arms, embracing it like a lover, her throat working with each gulping swallow.

"Fucking bitch," he spat. "You goddamned fucking bitch. You're stealing my right to give what belongs to me."

She heard the anchors in the wall creak in protest as Elijah strained against his bonds, a testament to how strong he was, so strong that the silver that incapacitated most vamps wanting a true submissive experience was barely enough to contain him.

Dizzyingly intoxicated, Vash slid her fangs free and closed the punctures with soothing licks of her tongue.

"I can't stop," she whispered, achingly empty and needing him, despite the terrible effort she'd made not to. No lycan could tolerate being caged, and Elijah was no mere lycan. He was an Alpha. As rare as a new angel and in some ways just as fragile.

She crawled over him, putting her back to his enraged face and training her eyes on the door. A door that would see them exiting far differently than they'd come in. His fury was pulsing off him in searing, battering waves. Yet she couldn't stop herself from gripping his still-hard cock and positioning herself over the massive crown.

"Don't do this," he warned in a thick, hoarse voice.

She licked the taste of him off her suddenly dry lips. "I . . . need you."

"Not like this, Vashti. Don't take me like this."

Their intimate flesh touched. The lips of her sex hugged him, flexing gently around him. Her hand gripping him shook like a junky's in need of a fix. "This is the only way I can have you."

Vash sheathed him in a swift plunge of her hips. He roared as she cried out, her body shocked by a penetration it hadn't experienced for over half a century. The cement wall behind the bed exploded with a deafening sound; dust and debris burst in a cloud around her. She was catapulted forward violently, her body thrust toward the door and down, her torso slammed into the mattress with breathtaking force.

She was mounted before she knew what hit her, Elijah's rock-hard body nailing her to the bed with a powerful thrust of his rigid cock into her aching sex. The coils of cable that had failed to contain him thudded to the floor, the sound reverberating through her.

Elijah wrapped his forearm with the spilled length of her hair. Fisting the tresses at the root, he pulled her head back and growled in her ear, "You can't tame me."

He shifted his hips, pulling free of her clinging depths only to drive into her again. "You can't chain me."

Yanking her up by the hips and hair, he brought her to her hands and knees. "And you goddamn can't rape me."

His next lunge hit the end of her, driving his supremacy home with a heavy surge of his hips. She cried out, completely at the mercy of his primal need for her and her own for him. He pounded into her, riding her hard and deep, stroking over and over and over a tender spot inside her that made her shake and moan. She had no leverage, no way to move or participate. Or so she told herself.

It was a lie, of course. He was stronger than she was, but she could fight him off. She could hurt him, make him work for it. They both knew she could. Yet she let him have his way, for reasons she couldn't grasp.

Something broke free inside her.

Set adrift, she clung to Elijah as the only anchor against the storm that whipped through her. Tears fell. Her chest ached. Her body burned with the feverish pleasure buffeting her from all sides, shattering the walls that had protected her for so long.

He gave her no quarter. Elijah fucked her like the animal he was, rutting into her with unmitigated ferocity. She climaxed in a helpless rush, screaming his name because he didn't relent, didn't falter. He kept driving the ecstasy into her, making her take it. All that he was. Everything. Beyond what she could handle, what she'd tried to limit herself to.

He followed her down when she melted into the mattress, her head and shoulders hanging off the edge. "You'll take me as I am," he snarled. "You'll want me as I am. Or you won't have me at all."

His knee shoved her legs wider; his big cock sank a fraction deeper. His grip on her hair pulled her head down toward the floor, forcing her into the most submissive of poses. She felt his teeth sink into the nape of her neck, his canines inhumanly long, his bite firm enough to break the skin but not tear it.

Subdued, mounted, and dominated in every way, Vashti came again and again, sobbing her pleasure, shame, and guilt. Begging him to forgive her. To finish her. To fill her.

Which he did, hours later, pumping his lust and fury into the greedy depths of her body, emptying himself with a serrated groan that sounded like the sweetest agony.

CHAPTER 7

From his vantage point high on a rocky hill, Adrian Mitchell surveyed the blond fledgling vampire attempting to sneak up on three of the most fearsome angels ever created, one of whom was his lieutenant. They stood with their winged backs to her, their focus on the papers spread out on the teakwood patio table in front of them.

Dawn had passed and now the morning sun rose in the east. The soft pinkish golden glow that would have fried any other minion caressed her pale limbs and austerely beautiful face just as his lips had done mere hours ago. Behind her, their house clung to the hill with the appearance of defying gravity, its three tiers jutting out from the craggy rock, its weathered wood and rock exterior making it seem a natural part of the native Southern California landscape.

He watched and waited, his crimson-tipped wings tucked close to his back to avoid catching drag in the wind. He admired the vampress's bravado, even as he acknowledged the futility of it. She couldn't take on even one of his Sentinels; three was impossible.

Crouching, she slunk across his wide deck with a slender blade in her hand. When she pounced, he appreciated her grace and agility, which nearly matched Damien's when he turned at the last possible moment and caught the business end of her blade in his hand, proving he'd sensed her coming.

One might have thought that would be the end of it, but she surprised them all by using the Sentinel's grip to support her weight as she kicked out spread-eagled and knocked the two Sentinels flanking Damien into the table like falling chess pieces, sending papers flying.

Adrian leaped from his perch, his wings extending to their full thirty-foot span to catch an updraft. He soared, then dove, spiraling downward, relishing the rush of air through his hair and over his feathers. He skimmed the wide deck, the tips of his wings touching the planks, before he darted upward again, using the pull of gravity to slow his momentum and pull him back to the earth.

Lowering with effortless strength, he settled into place beside his mischievous mate, landing on the balls of his feet without a sound.

She caught his wrist and squeezed, opening her mind so that her thoughts became his. *Watching you fly makes me so hot.*

"Watching you hunt is similarly affecting." His face and tone of voice revealed nothing of his feelings for her, out of deference for his men, but the way her fingertips slid across his palm told him she knew.

Malachai and Geoffrey straightened from their ignoble sprawls.

"That's cheating," Malachai said, stretching and flexing wings that were the color of sunset—pale yellow that darkened into deep orange tips.

Lindsay's smile was brilliant. "One-on-one I get my ass kicked, but I think I might be able to work with a group. Using one to distract the others."

"That's insane," Geoffrey scoffed, looking disgruntled. He'd recently likened Lindsay to a troublesome cat, one who crouched under couches and swiped at anyone hapless enough to walk by. But in truth, he appreciated her ceaseless efforts to hone herself so that she wasn't as much of a liability. While Lindsay was an expert marksman and bladesman and was working hard on her hand-to-hand combat skills, she was still a fledgling vampire newly Changed. She hadn't yet achieved the power and resilience that would eventually come with age. In the interim, she was unbearably vulnerable and easily broken.

Damien sighed. "No, that's Lindsay. It's our fault we weren't ready for her."

The lieutenant was wary of Lindsay's impact on Adrian and the Sentinels' mission, but he admired her as a warrior. While Adrian's original second and beloved friend, Phineas, had been a strategist and Phineas's replacement, Jason, had been good for morale, Damien's strengths were found in battle and those were the same strengths he most appreciated in others.

Lindsay slid her blade into the sheath strapped to her thigh. "I touched base with all the international packs overnight. The communication blackout is working— you still have one hundred percent containment of the overseas lycan outposts. They have no idea the North American packs revolted."

"Thank the Creator for small favors," Malachai muttered.

"But we can't risk using those lycans to contain their rogue brethren," Geoffrey said. "Even though some of them will do so willingly."

Adrian's gaze lifted to the building set a half mile away—the lycan barracks. Once home to his pack and now home to a mere dozen lycans who'd straggled in over the last week and a half since the outposts had begun falling like a chain of dominos. More lycans returned to him every day, and when he touched their minds, as he did Lindsay's, he felt their fear and confusion—and their loyalty, which humbled him.

The crumbling of the order he'd worked so hard for was part of his punishment for loving Lindsay, he knew—the loss of the lycans, the guilt of knowing others were paying for his mistakes, the strain of holding on to the tenuous balance between vampires and mortals by his fingernails. Although he'd committed the same offense as the Fallen, his penalty was different; he suspected that was because he was too useful to throw away. But he was paying in other ways, every day of his endless life. He'd paid for centuries watching Shadoe die over and over again, and he would continue to pay mentally and emotionally for an indefinite time to come. "We need to reinforce the Sentinels still holding on to their outposts, which leaves us with only a handful here in the States to pull everything back together."

They were outnumbered by a fatalistic margin. He had a firm hold on the Jasper and Juarez outposts, but the others were lost. He looked at the beautiful vampress beside him, once the vessel that carried Shadoe's soul and now the woman who carried his heart in her hands. Her vampirism offered her a better chance of survival than she'd had as a mere mortal, but she was still weak and in need of frequent feeding. And Adrian's powerful Sentinel blood was all she would drink, which afforded her the ability to withstand sunlight but also meant he couldn't be separated from her for too long. As fragile as she yet was, that made her a terrible disadvantage for him.

His hands fisted against the need to touch her, a display of affection she wouldn't welcome, not in front of his Sentinels. She was ever careful to keep from flaunting the love that consumed them both, knowing the risks he'd taken to claim her as his own. Angels weren't supposed to crave or need another to complete them. They were meant to be above the failings of mortals, but he wasn't so perfect. He hungered and ached for Lindsay with a ferocity he couldn't control, and he couldn't regret his trespass because it would belittle what he felt for her. He couldn't profess his love for Lindsay in one breath, then beg forgiveness for it with the other without rendering both pledges worthless. And he couldn't walk away or turn his back to her. She was the very air he breathed, his reason for waking and fighting and persisting against the odds.

Inhaling deeply, he looked to the sky for answers and found none. "We don't have the resources to hunt both lycans and vampires. We have to choose. We know what we're dealing with on the latter front. The lycans, however, are a mystery."

"They could expose us to mortals," Damien said.

"They could hunt us to neutralize the risk we present to them," Malachai suggested.

"They could ally with the vampires," Geoffrey threw in. "I wouldn't put it past Syre."

Adrian nodded, knowing Syre was hurting now, having lost his daughter forever when Lindsay had exorcised Shadoe's reincarnated soul from her body. "That's the most likely scenario of the three."

The three Sentinels didn't know what it was like to lose a piece of one's heart—they hadn't been compromised by human emotions as Adrian and Syre had been. Adrian didn't doubt that the vampire leader wanted to strike out in his grief, and the lycan revolt would give Syre the perfect means to that end.

Lindsay's eyes lost their brightness. She shook her head vehemently. "I can't see that happening. Elijah lives to hunt vamps, and he wants Vashti's head on a platter for what she did to Micah."

"And Syre, Torque, and Vashti want his because of Nikki's abduction," Adrian said, "but vengeance can be postponed with the right incentive." He softened his voice, knowing she considered the lycan a friend. "You never thought he would revolt and he did."

She bit her lower lip, her eyes reflecting her concern. Even now she worried about the Alpha.

Adrian brushed across her mind, a gentle caress to calm her, because he couldn't bear to see her troubled. It wasn't just Elijah's fate making her anxious, but Syre's, too. She wasn't the vampire leader's daughter by blood, but carrying Shadoe's soul inside her had left a mark—she'd been exposed to Shadoe's memories of Syre: fond, sweet recollections of a daughter's love for her father. While they weren't her memories, Lindsay felt the emotion of them as if they had been, and she grieved their loss.

She shot him a warning look, reminding him of her demand that he not "mess" with her mind. His head tilted in acknowledgment, but he didn't cease soothing her because he didn't perceive that as messing with her. At least not to his way of thinking.

Lindsay caught his wrist and imagined sticking her tongue out at him, the thought entering his mind with vivid clarity. He felt a silent laugh move through him. She was so full of vitality and humor despite the many blows life had dealt her. He was so different from her, having been created to punish and imprison, to maim and kill. But she was teaching him a different way, changing him in slow degrees, bringing her light into his darkness. And he made a concerted effort to learn and grow, to be the sort of man who could bring a smile to her face and happiness to her life. Because she was his soul. Who was he if not the man who loved her beyond all reason and self-preservation?

The phone began to ring in his office. They all heard

it despite the distance from where they stood and the glass patio door that closed off his workspace from the outdoors. Lindsay frowned and turned, still growing accustomed to her vampiric senses.

Adrian moved away, rounding the corner. The glass panel slid aside as he approached and he willed his wings away. They dissipated like fog in a stiff wind when he stepped inside, affording him comfortable movement as well as the ability to blend with mortals. The speakerphone was engaged by the third ring and his gaze held Lindsay's as he settled into his chair.

"Mitchell," he greeted the caller.

"Captain. Siobhán here."

He leaned back in his chair, settling in. He'd tasked Siobhán with studying the disease ravaging the vampire ranks, and she had been working ceaselessly on that mission for weeks. It was she who'd inadvertently discovered that Sentinel blood cured the illness when a Sentinel working with her was bitten by one of the infected, resulting in the infected returning to a normal vampiric state. Considering the tens of thousands of vampires in North America alone and the less than two hundred Sentinels left in existence, it was information they couldn't afford to have the vampires discover before an alternate cure was found. "How are you progressing?"

"Slowly but surely. I've got a dozen infected in stasis now. We can keep them alive with steady blood transfusions, but they have to stay anesthetized or they're impossible to control."

Adrian had seen the monstrosities in action firsthand. He knew how mindlessly violent they were. "How quickly do they lose higher brain function?"

"How far do you want me to go to find out?" she asked grimly. "They're already infected by the time I get them. If you want a play-by-play of what happens from exposure to illness, I'll need to deliberately infect healthy subjects."

"Do it. Our blood is a cure, so we can reverse the damage." It was a brutal order and one he didn't enjoy making, but the ends justified the means. When Nikki had attacked him and nearly taken his life, she'd still been cognizant enough to speak to him coherently. How recently had she been exposed? Had she been an example of someone who'd been recently contaminated? Or someone who'd been ill for a while? "Have you been able to spot any patterns in the rapidity of progression?"

Some vamps were dead within a few days, others lasted a few weeks, and still others appeared to be immune. Why?

"I think I'm onto something in that regard." Her excitement came through in her voice. The pixielike Sentinel was ravenous for knowledge. "I'm not entirely positive yet, but it seems as if the advancement varies depending on how far removed the minion is from the Fallen heading their vampiric hierarchy. For example, Lindsay is once removed from Syre. Her infection would advance much more slowly than a minion she Changed, who would be twice removed from Syre. And so on and so on."

He set his elbows on the armrests and steepled his fingers together. "You need to test Fallen blood."

"It would be helpful, yes," she conceded, certainly knowing how difficult it would be to attain. "Then I could see if it at least slows the development of the disease."

"I'm your best chance of getting it," Lindsay interjected. "As a vampire myself, I'd fit right in to any location where they congregate."

Adrian's response was immediate. "No."

Her brows lifted. Her amber eyes challenged him—the distinctive irises of a vampire. One who could move among the others with ease, but who was still frail in many ways. His Sentinel blood would protect her from the illness, and she knew how to fight and wouldn't hesitate to kill, but she'd still be vulnerable and he wouldn't be close enough to protect her. And there was the fact that while most minions would have no idea who she was, some of the Fallen did because of Syre and Shadoe. She wasn't totally anonymous.

He couldn't risk her, couldn't lose her. "No," he said again, pushing the negation into her mind for emphasis.

"Stay out of my head, angel," she growled.

Siobhán's melodious voice floated out of the phone's speaker. "I'm also going to need more lycan blood."

"Not a problem." He had plenty cryogenically stored, for identification and genetic testing purposes. "Anything else?"

"Perhaps . . ." She hesitated a moment. "Perhaps other angelic blood samples. From a *mal'akh* or even an archangel. Preferably both. Perhaps we Sentinels aren't the only ones who carry the cure in our veins."

"You don't ask for much, do you?" Adrian said drily. Even though *malakhim*—the lowest rank of angel in the lowest sphere—were the most numerous, getting blood from one was no easy task. "I'll see what I can do. Keep me posted."

"Yes, Captain. Of course."

He hung up, his gaze never leaving Lindsay's face. She was careful not to openly challenge him in front of his subordinates, a circumspection she'd always displayed and he had always appreciated. But she'd challenge him in private. He would never tell her how much it aroused him when she did so. He'd just continue to show her instead . . .

"We need a plan B, Lindsay. Work on coming up with that."

Elijah shoved both hands through his hair, his heart pounding violently, his gaze on the woman sprawled prone on the bed. Vashti's hair was a crimson cloud around her, the glossy strands lying sinuously atop her back and shoulders. Her face was turned toward him, her lips parted with her panting exhalations. Her clawed hands fisted the fitted sheet, and trails of tears were still visible on her pale cheeks. Not due to him, but to the nightmare she'd suffered that had woken him.

No . . . please . . . stop . . . Over and over in a broken litany. Whimpers and gasps of pain. Moans of agony that ripped through his vitals.

He would never forget the bloodcurdling scream that had sent him leaping from the bed as a man but landing on the floor in his lupine form.

Without his will. His beast had bypassed his control for the first time ever. For her. Because she'd cried out in distress, struggling through the throes of a nightmare.

And he'd been unable to shift back until the beast was certain she was all right. He'd paced the room, sniffing along the cracks around the door and in the corners, growling because there was no other outlet for his helpless fury but to search and find nothing to kill. Once he'd been assured that nothing in the locked room posed a threat to her, he'd padded over to the bed. He had nuzzled against the crown of her head and licked away her tears. She'd calmed then, settling back into a fitful sleep. Only then had he been capable of shifting back.

Everyone was wrong about him—he was no Alpha or he would never have shifted without conscious thought. Which meant they needed to find one who was. Quickly.

In the meantime, he was crazily attuned to Vashti. To the extreme. Their primal mating had brought on more than explosive orgasms. It had altered him and his reactions to her, eroding his control along with his goddamn common sense. He could hardly recognize himself this morning. What the fuck was the matter with him?

He was afraid he knew. Those endless moments when he'd been bound and captured beneath her, helpless to stop her as she took his blood and his semen into her mouth, riveted by the burn of fury and ferocious desire as she sheathed his aching cock in her tight, hot depths . . . they'd shifted him on the inside. And when he had taken over and she'd shattered beneath him, he had accepted the surrender of such a powerful and lethal woman with a possessive surge of awe and gratitude.

Someone's fist pounded against the door, and Elijah yanked it open, scowling at the interruption of Vashti's rest.

"What do you want?" he snapped at Salem, who sucked up all the space in the hallway. Elijah didn't give a shit that he was bare-assed naked. Neither did the vamp.

"Have you seen Vashti?" Salem barked back. Then his nose twitched as he scented the air. His eyes widened as he comprehended just how thoroughly Elijah had seen her.

"Yeah. Go away."

"Where'd she go?"

"She's sleeping. Come back later." Elijah backed up and shut the door.

Salem stopped the latch from catching with a slap of his palm against the metal. *"Sleeping?"*

"You know. Eyes closed. Lack of consciousness. Sound familiar? Go away."

Salem pushed to widen the opening. "Move aside, lycan."

Bored with the conversation and still aggravated by Vash's nightmare, Elijah stepped out to the hallway and shut the door carefully behind him. Then he shoved the vampire across the hall and into the opposite doorway, which Salem busted through to slide into the foot of a heavily occupied bed. Elijah got a glimpse of enough bare limbs and arched necks to make up at least four bodies.

Salem was up and in Elijah's face in a split-second. "You're pissing me off, dog. Vash doesn't sleep."

"She does when she's tired."

Amber eyes glowing, Salem's voice lowered ominously. "What did you do to her?"

"Really?" Elijah asked drily. "That's none of your damn business."

"If you hurt her—"

Elijah laughed at that, a sound with little humor in it. He'd been chained and assaulted, and the vamp was worried about Vash. "She can take of herself."

Salem stared him down. Elijah yawned.

"She hasn't slept in decades," the vamp said finally.

"Well, that might explain why she's so bitchy." Elijah's voice changed, lowered. "But then bitchy is preferable to broken."

The vamp's jaw tightened.

"What happened to her, Salem?"

"Ask her yourself, lycan." Salem's mouth curved with mocking cruelty. "Until she tells you that, you've got nothing but sex with her. You're just a dick with stamina."

Elijah was a second away from slamming his fist in the vamp's taunting face when Salem turned and stepped back into the room he'd crashed into, lifting the warped door off the ground and popping it into the frame with himself inside.

It took Elijah a few minutes and several deep breaths

to rein in his volatile mood enough to return to the room he shared with Vash. He pushed the door open slowly and just wide enough for him to slide in. What he saw inside froze him.

Vashti sat on the edge of the mattress, his shirt in her fisted hands and pressed to her nose. She jerked guiltily when he came in, as if she'd been caught doing something she shouldn't. Her hands dropped into her lap, baring her gorgeous tits.

She stood in an agitated rush. "What time is it? We should get going."

"It's a little after seven." He didn't need a watch to tell him that. His circadian rhythm was instinctively set by the moon, wherever in the world he was, courtesy of the werewolf blood in his lineage. He approached her cautiously, as if nearing a skittish animal.

Her eyes were huge in her face, and even in the dark room they were shadowed. The stench of fear and pain still clung to her skin, which might have been why she'd buried her nose in his scent instead. Or maybe she just craved it, as he craved hers. He could struggle with that craving, even hate himself for it, but he'd learned that ignoring it was too dangerous, leaving him too off-balance and unstable to control himself as he needed to. He was a creature of instinct and she called to that primal part of him in a way he couldn't afford to ignore or marginalize.

"We're already late getting back," she said, attempting to turn away as if to reach for her clothes.

He caught her with a gentle but firm grip on her elbow. The feel of her skin against his fingertips was like satin, and a powerful jolt shot through him. "Come here."

"Elijah—"

Tugging her closer, he gripped her nape and pulled her face into the crook of his neck, where he knew his scent would be concentrated. She inhaled sharply, then sighed. A heartbeat later she was nuzzling her face into his skin, her lips feathering over his rapidly elevating pulse. He wondered if she knew how much pleasure her gesture gave a lycan, then decided she didn't, which was for the best. She didn't need to have any more ammunition to use against him.

Closing his eyes, he absorbed the feeling of her lushness pressed against him and the blessed lack of tension between them. Her height was just right and her curves molded into his harder frame as if they were two halves of a whole. A perfect fit . . . with the absolute wrong woman. "What do you dream about, Vashti?"

She stiffened and tried to pull away, but he'd anticipated that and held tight.

"Let me go," she said crossly.

"Not gonna happen."

"I could make you."

His hand fisted in her hair, pulling her head back to look into his eyes. "You can ask me nicely and I'll think about it."

"Fuck you."

"Well, that's not a very nice way to ask, but okay."

A laugh escaped her and was quickly stifled, but it was breathtaking while it lasted. Deep and husky, it was rusty, but as full-bodied as she was.

He scooped her up and set one knee on the mattress, then the other, until he reached the center, where he laid her out. Joining her, he stretched out along his side and propped his head in his hand. He laid the other on her taut, smooth stomach with his fingers splayed, holding her down without pressure while also anchoring her for his questions.

"Who hurt you, Vashti?"

She shook her head. "It's none of your business."

"Sure it is. I can't kill them if I don't know who they are."

"It's not your problem."

"The hell it isn't."

"We screwed around once. Don't make anything out of it."

"Actually"—he grinned—"it was more like a dozen screws. Give or take a few."

"Leave it alone, puppy."

"Can't do that."

Her gaze narrowed. "Shit. You're a fuckin' Boy Scout, aren't you? Saving the world one problem at a time."

"I'm helping you find the ones who killed your mate, but you won't trust me with those who hurt you? Do I get to you in some way, Vash?" he goaded. "Do I make you feel vulnerable?"

"You flatter yourself."

"So put me in my place."

Vash took a deep breath, her muscular abdomen lifting into his palm. "Syre took care of it."

"Took care of what?"

"I don't want to talk about it, Elijah. It's done and over with. Ancient history."

"You're gonna tell me." He lifted his hand to her mouth, running his thumb across her bottom lip. He slid it inside when she started to protest. "Maybe not today, but soon."

He groaned when she sucked on his finger, her bottom teeth scoring over the pad. His cock lengthened and thickened, remembering what it felt like to have her mouth on him. She'd taken from him by force what he would've given her willingly, but the pleasure had been there nevertheless, his hunger for her so sharp he'd wanted her however he could have her. But what he really needed was to be gentle with her and she needed that tenderness, even though she fought so damned hard against it. Fought enough for both of them.

He parted her lips with a gentle downward press of his thumb and bent his head to lick teasingly inside, barely enough for her to feel him. As badly as he'd wanted to devour her in the parking lot the night before, he wanted something softer and sweeter now.

Her hand wrapped around his wrist. "We don't have time for this. We've got a lot to get done."

Cupping her cheek, he took her mouth in a deep, wet kiss. He kept the pace slow when she tried to speed it up, resisting giving her the swift plunges of his tongue that she begged for with her plaintive whimpers and heated enthusiasm. Instead he stroked and he licked. His lips moved softly against hers.

She gasped, slinging one long, lean leg over his hip. "Stop playing with me."

Elijah rolled over her and pinned her down. Linking their fingers, he restrained her hands on either side of her head. "We need to play, Vashti. I need to. After this last week . . . the last fucking month, really."

She stared up at him, looking younger and more fragile than he'd ever seen her. She was ageless, a fallen angel who'd existed for millennia. She'd killed countless beings, some viciously, as she had Micah, and she would kill countless more. And yet she was soft and lax in his arms, warm and open, exposed for a moment due to a nightmare she'd avoided facing for decades. He wondered if he would ever have her like this again or if she would always be as she'd been last night, brutally determined to objectify him.

And he wondered why he gave a shit either way when he was going to kill her.

"You like me," he murmured, sliding his tongue along her bottom lip, which was plump and swollen from his kisses.

"I *want* you. There's a difference."

"*I* like *you*."

Vash turned her head away from his mouth. "Don't."

"Trust me, I wish I didn't." He settled comfortably in the cradle of her thighs. "You shouldn't be afraid of liking me. I won't use it against you, except when I need my cock in you. You'll like that, too, once I show you how it's really going to be between us, without all the bullshit you pulled last night." He nuzzled his nose between her breasts, breathing in her luscious scent now mingled with his own. "There's no chance that us liking each other will change our agreement. You like that about me, too—that I keep my word."

Her hands lifted to his waist and he hummed his approval. He was a lycan; he liked to be touched. Petted.

"You're *trying* to piss me off," she said, before sinking a fang through his earlobe.

The sweet nip of pain swelled his dick to the point of aching. Provoked, he rocked his hips against hers, nudging against her cleft. "Why would I do that?"

"You k-know why." Her slender arms wrapped around him. "*I* know why."

Because a pissed-off Vashti he could deal with. It was the newly discovered, tormented one that shredded him. She was so strong and fearless. To see such a magnificent woman reduced to cowering fear offended him deeply, made him want to rip something—or someone—apart.

Her fingers walked down his spine, eliciting a soft growl of pleasure. "Thank you for irritating me."

"Actions speak louder than words. Touch me, Vashti."

"Where?"

"Everywhere." The way he needed her to but wouldn't explain, not after the rough night they'd had. He could want her and like her, but needing her was too much. Didn't make any damn sense. But then he wasn't at his best now. In some ways, perhaps, the violent upheaval in his life had left him as raw as she was.

She moaned when he plumped her tit in his hand, then hissed as his mouth surrounded her and his tongue flicked lightly over her hardening nipple.

He also liked to lick.

"Mmm . . ." She arched her spine, pushing her lushness into his working lips. "You're a breast man."

He was a Vash man, but kept that to himself. Instead he wallowed in her, breathing in the cherry-sweet scent of her that drove him out of his mind. She responded by pushing her fingers into his hair and kneading his scalp, holding him close. His eyes closed on a groan. A shudder racked his frame.

"Can you be so easy to pleasure, lycan?" she asked softly.

"Why don't you try and see what happens?"

CHAPTER 8

"Father."

Syre glanced over at his son standing in the doorway and took one last, deep drink from the wrist at his mouth. He licked the wound closed and lifted his head, looking into the dazed blue eyes of the sexy brunette who'd been feeding him. "Get some orange juice, Kelly, and go lie down for an hour or two."

She blinked, coming to a fuller awareness. Her mouth curved as she focused on him, completely unaware that she'd just donated a pint of blood to his diet. "Come with me."

"I'll join you," he promised, looking forward to it. Kelly was hot to get fucked, having come into Raceport for the express purpose of indulging in as much booze and sex as she could get her hands on. He'd carefully cultivated Raceport to become a premier destination for bikers and their babes, needing the adventurous transients to fuel the proliferation of cabals and covens in the area. The abundance of sexual partners was a side benefit he hadn't considered in advance, but was certainly appreciative of now.

Sex was one of the few activities in his life that made him feel . . . human. For a little while.

Pouting, she pushed to her feet and tossed her long hair over her shoulder. Her midriff was bared by her cropped tank and her legs were exposed by super-short cutoff jeans. Her slender arms were covered in sleeves of tattoos, and her navel was pierced with a tiny silver ring. Syre enjoyed the view despite its inability to truly inspire him. He preferred a different sort of female, mature and discerning, but he'd long ago realized what a mistake he was in those women's lives. He could give nothing but physical pleasure, which eventually turned into emotional pain. So he'd learned to ignore what suited him best in favor of partnering with women whom he best suited, even though that was very rarely one and the same.

"The sooner you leave, Kelly," Torque said drily, "the sooner he'll join you."

She turned, realizing they weren't alone in his suite after all. For a moment, she looked irritated; then her gaze swept over Torque, warming with interest.

The resemblance between him and Torque was so slight as to be almost nonexistent. Like his twin, Shadoe, Torque had taken after their mother in his facial features. He was shorter than Syre by half a foot, lean in the waist and hips but thick with muscle in the thighs, arms, and chest. His brutally short hair was spiked in opposing directions, the thick Asian locks dyed a shocking green at the tips. It was a style that suited both his sloe eyes and his sharp-edged lifestyle. Torque managed a chain of clubs that offered haven to fledgling minions while also catering to the hungers of elder vampires.

Licking her lips, Kelly offered, "Why don't you join us, too?"

Torque's face stayed hard, his heart too freshly shattered by the loss of his mate, Nikki, to even think about sex. "Sorry. Sharing pussy with Syre is a bit too incestuous for my tastes."

"Incestuous?" She frowned and glanced at Syre, who appeared to be about ten years older than Torque's mid-twenties appearance. "No way are you related."

Syre caught her gaze and murmured, "Go."

The compulsion settled into her mind and she nodded, exiting the room with a dreamy smile.

"They never believe me," Torque said, coming deeper into the room and dropping into a black leather wingback.

"How are you?"

"You keep asking me that."

"You keep being evasive." He knew his son's pain, had experienced it himself when he'd lost his mate so very, very long ago. And Torque was a naphil, one of the nephalim children he and the other Fallen had created with their mortal mates before their fall. The nephalim were halflings, part angel and part mortal. Unlike the Fallen or minions, they had souls. They felt joy and pain more deeply; Syre's lingering grief was a shadow of what his beloved son felt.

"I'm terrible," Torque said bluntly. "The Alpha told

Vashti the truth: there was anticoagulant in the blood we found at the site of Nikki's abduction, which makes it possible he was set up to take the blame. I'm back at square one looking for whoever took her from me."

"We'll find them," Syre promised, vengeance hot and fierce in his veins. It was the overriding emotion in his life of late, as his carefully constructed world crumbled around him.

"Don't count on it. The cabal in Anaheim has been slaughtered. Every single member."

Syre hissed out his breath. "An angel somewhere is covering his or her tracks. Whose side are they are on? They steal Lindsay from Adrian and deliver her into my hands, then vanquish the vampires who saw to her delivery."

"Who the fuck knows?" Torque's booted foot rapped out a frustrated staccato on the hardwood floor. "Even if it *is* an angel, there's no guarantee it was a Sentinel. It could be a winged class of demon who took her from Angels' Point, for all we know."

"Who else would have access to stored lycan blood but a Sentinel?" Adrian's cryogenic storage facilities were well guarded by Sentinels. Not even the lycans themselves had access to their own samples.

"You're assuming there's only one individual responsible for both Nikki and Lindsay's abductions."

"Occam's Razor," Syre murmured, his mind shifting through the known facts.

"Fuck Occam. I'd like to shove his razor up his ass."

Brows lifting, he refocused on his son. "Use your anger to strengthen your focus."

"None of us have our head in the game, Dad. We're all reeling." Torque took a deep breath. "But the reason I interrupted your afternoon snack is Vash. I just got off the phone with Salem, and he's concerned about the Alpha."

"So am I." He would never forget the sight of Vash pinned to a tree by a bristling, infuriated lycan—a breed she had just cause to revile.

"He fucked her last night."

A long moment passed as Syre's brain struggled to process the impossible. "Be careful how you speak of her."

"How else am I supposed to say it?" Leaning forward, Torque set his elbows on his knees and clasped his hands. "I know how she feels about lycans, and this one is under suspicion for Nikki's kidnapping."

"But we seem to have discovered that he's not responsible."

"Let's not forget the lycan she tortured for information. What are the chances the Alpha doesn't know about that or that she was hunting him when she did it? You ever heard of a lycan not avenging the unprovoked death of a packmate?"

"You think he forced her? Or extorted her cooperation in some way? Is that what Salem said?" Syre's voice was low and furious. The thought twisted through his mind, rousing a murderous ferocity.

He would raze the earth to protect Vashti. She was his conscience, his adviser, his hammer, his ambassador, and countless other extensions of himself. She was the strongest woman he'd ever known, yet he'd seen her shattered into pieces. Utterly broken and defiled. She'd pulled herself together in the years since, but the cracks and fissures remained. While others thought she was harder and more inviolate than she had ever been, he knew she was more fragile. It was why he forced himself—against every instinct—to keep her on the front lines. If she thought he viewed her as diminished by the desecrations inflicted on her, it would be a blow he didn't think she was strong enough to bear. His belief in her strength was what bolstered her belief in herself.

"Salem doesn't know what's going on; that's why he called. He only knows that they had sex and the Alpha wouldn't let him see Vash this morning, said she was sleeping."

Syre pushed to his feet, knowing damn well that Vash hadn't slept in ages.

"She hasn't touched a man since Charron," Torque reminded him unnecessarily. "You really think her first go would be with a lycan?"

"Ready my plane." Syre stalked toward his bedroom to pack. He'd heard enough. "I want to take off within the hour."

Vash blinked against the harsh glare of the sun as she exited Shred. Behind her, Elijah growled at the Vegas heat not yet at its fiercest. Lycans were sensitive creatures, which—if she'd been thinking clearly—might've clued her in to how much Elijah enjoyed being touched. She knew now, and she damned the time constraints that prevented her from indulging him. She'd had him purring at the time Salem came back to pound on the door. Her captain had given them barely thirty minutes between interruptions, just long enough for Salem to get a blow job while he called Torque, taking multitasking to the extreme.

If she could have . . . if there had been time . . . she would have sent Salem away so Elijah could finish what he'd started. She was shamed now to think of what she'd done to him the night before in her fear. Her own astonishing weakness for him made her so vulnerable, which both terrified her and made her blind to his returning vulnerability where she was concerned. That she, a woman who'd long ago learned to use her attractiveness against men, could miss that susceptibility was a sign of how skewed she was. It would have soothed her body and mind to do it over again, to start the day with gentle morning sex to erase the lingering anger of the night before and to reestablish her control of herself and the situation.

Taking a deep breath, she tried to clear Elijah from her mind. She'd reached the Jeep alongside Salem before she realized the Alpha wasn't with them. Turning around, she looked for him and found him circling slowly, his head tilted back to put his nose in the air. Something in the way he held his body warned her. She grabbed one of her katanas and her cell phone from the backseat and returned to him.

"What is it?" Vash inhaled again, but her sense of smell wasn't as acute as a lycan's.

As she shoved her phone into her top, he looked at her, his face grim. "An infected. No more than two blocks over. Somewhere to the north of us."

Yanking his shirt over his head, he toed off his boots and dropped his jeans. In an instant he was wolven, a big and beautifully regal beast. A moment beyond that, he was gone.

She was right on his tail, tracking the scent of him that seemed embedded in her senses. Distantly, she was aware of Salem at her side. They'd been hunting together so long it was effortless. He feinted in counterpoint to her, darting around obstacles like Dumpsters and discarded cardboard boxes. With nary a signal between them, they took to the walls, racing opposite each other down an alleyway. Her hair whipped in the wind, her steel stilettos bit into the stucco, breaking off chunks to crumble to the ground below.

And in the back of her mind she was aware that Elijah had thrown himself into a hunt for a vampire without a second thought. One of her people, as they were all hers. As if it was instinctive for him to do so when in truth he'd simply been well trained. By Adrian.

How could that have slipped in importance in her mind?

The shattering of glass preceded her turning a corner. Elijah's tail disappearing through a broken window directed her along with his scent. It was a building under construction; most of the windows still bore the manufacturer's sticker. Salem bounded through first, widening the opening. Vash sailed through after him, tucking and rolling and springing up onto her feet. And froze.

The construction workers that should have been all over the site were all over the floor instead. In pieces.

Salem cursed. Elijah crouched low and growled.

The bare concrete was covered in blood and entrails. Limbs and heads were scattered across the floor or lifted to ravenous foaming maws of at least a dozen wraiths. Bloodshot eyes glittered, nostrils twitching as they smelled fresh meat.

Vash had seen such carnage before, when a rogue minion, driven insane by the deterioration of his mortal soul, had Changed everyone in his family. Lost to the initial bloodlust of the Change, they'd gone on a rampage, slaughtering their entire neighborhood.

God. It never got easier to bear.

One of the wraiths stood apart from the others. Hunched and shuffling, he darted back and forth swiftly, wearing a semicircular path in the blood. His gaze was riveted to Elijah, who paced with restless energy. With his ears flattened to his head, the Alpha snarled a threat.

The sickened vamp glanced at Vash and Salem. "Go. Away."

The words were uttered in a voice so guttural it took her a moment to figure out what he'd said. "Fuckin' A. Did that wraith just *talk*?"

Just as she processed the possibility of higher brain function, the wraith leaped a good twenty feet across the room . . . directly at her. Startled, she raised her katana, knowing she was a split second too late and steeling herself for the impact.

Elijah blocked the assault in midair, jaws first, catching the wraith in the juncture between the shoulder and neck. A sickening crunch reverberated through the space, inciting an unexpected reaction—the bloodpack abandoned their feast and lunged at the powerful lycan en masse.

Vashti leaped into the fray with a scream of rage, cutting anything that got in her way. Salem waded in bare-handed, cracking heads and necks as he progressed. None of the wraiths came after them. They remained dog piled on Elijah, ignoring the incoming vamps with a complete lack of self-preservation. Tossing his head, Elijah threw one after another over the writhing bodies surrounding him, his growls and barks lost amid the mindless screeches of his attackers.

She sliced through the frenzy toward the center, her heart pounding when she lost sight of him completely. Spurting blood obscured her vision as she hacked her way deeper. She swiped at her eyes, searching for Elijah amid the massacre, yelling his name.

His yelp of pain seized her lungs. His pained howl broke her paralysis. "Salem! Goddamn it. *Help him.*"

"I can't get to him. Shit. I'm fucking trying!"

Yanking heads back by fistfuls of gray hair, she ripped wraiths off her lycan and decapitated them, her stomach knotting at the sight of chunks of bloodied fur clinging to their foaming mouths.

An agonized scream rent the air, followed by another.

Not Elijah. The tone wasn't deep enough. Jesus. The room was spinning around her in her panic.

She hauled another wraith back and saw Elijah in the space she'd opened up. The wraith's body went limp in her grasp, then began to convulse. Another wraith jerked away. Then another.

Suddenly what was left of the bloodpack fell away from the downed lycan. Flopping on their backs like fish out of water, they writhed, foam pouring from their mouths and their eyes rolling back. The one who'd spoken clutched his head, wailing. Abruptly, he ceased, crashing to the ground in a dead faint.

Or just dead, period.

When nothing moved in the lake of blood, Vash dropped her blade and sank to her knees beside Elijah, who lay panting on his side, his fur matted and his flesh torn away in deep gouges. She reached out, wanting to comfort but unsure of how she could.

"Don't touch him!" Salem kicked bodies out of the way as he approached.

Elijah gave a low warning growl.

"He's a wounded animal, Vash. You know better."

Yes, she knew. Lycans were at their fiercest when they were most vulnerable. But as she looked into the green eyes of the wolf, she saw the man. The man who'd mastered her during the long night, then surrendered to her touch in the morning.

"Can you shift?" she asked softly, knowing that the process of shifting forms would knit some of his injuries and staunch the copious amounts of blood draining from his body.

His eyes closed on a shuddering breath. He was still for so long she feared she'd lost him.

"Elijah!" The urgency in her voice made it harsh. Uncaring of the danger, she gingerly touched his head, stroking it. His eyelids lifted slowly, revealing unfocused irises. "Shift. Now. You can do it, you arrogant son of a bitch. You're too fucking stubborn to let a couple of diseased vamps get the best of you."

His rumbling growl was stronger than before, giving her wild hope.

"Vash—" Salem set his hand on her shoulder.

Elijah lifted his head and bared his teeth, snarling.

Salem yanked his hand back. "Crazy assed dog."

"Salem will have to take care of me if you can't do it," Vash goaded, fighting off another spurt of panic. "Raze, too. Maybe even that pretty pincushion I almost sucked on last night—"

Fire lit Elijah's eyes. He began to shimmer, like heat waves rising from sun-scorched asphalt. For a breathless moment he hovered in that in-between state, flickering between human and lupine form. Then, with a rattling exhale, he settled before her as a nude, severely wounded man.

"Get the car," she ordered over her shoulder, pulling Elijah close to cradle his head in her lap.

Salem left so fast, he caused a draft. Around her, the wraith bodies began to gurgle and shake. She watched, horrified, as they disintegrated into puddles of a thick tarlike substance. "Eww."

"Hey. I'm not . . . as bad off as I look," Elijah whispered, his eyes still closed.

"Of course not." But the blood that wasn't his was now clearly demarked by its obsidian coloring, leaving far too much crimson on his ravaged skin. It ran in thin rivulets over her lap and eroded canyons in the black ooze. "You damned heroic idiot. Stop protecting me. I can take care of myself."

"And let you have all the fun?"

Pain twisted in her chest. Lifting her wrist to her mouth, Vash pierced the vein with her fangs and pressed the gushing wound to his mouth. He gagged, then struggled weakly, but she held fast, pinching his nose so that he was forced to swallow. One gulp. Two. Three. His protests gained strength and she ceased, licking her wound closed.

"Turn me into a vampire," he said hoarsely, "and you'll be the first I suck dry."

"You'd have to take me down first." She brushed his sweat and blood-soaked hair away from his forehead. His heart beat too strongly to slip into the Change, but if she'd waited another few minutes . . . ? She pushed the thought away.

"This babying you're doing . . . as good as a verbal admission that you like me."

"Ha!" Her eyes stung, but she told herself that was from the blood spatter on her face. She couldn't stop touching him, running her fingertips over his face and stroking through his hair to his scalp. "You pulled this little stunt just to play on my sympathy."

"Not my fault you'd look hot in one of those naughty nurse's outfits." His chest lifted and fell with a sharp breath.

Their banter was breaking her heart, knowing how much the effort was costing him. But she didn't relent. As bad as it sucked, his pain was keeping his heartbeat elevated, which was helping to pump her healing blood through his veins. It was nowhere near as powerful as a seraph's pure blood, but it would nevertheless speed his healing.

"Who knew I was so damn popular?" he groused. "Must be you, sweetheart. You want a piece of me . . . now they all do."

The one wraith with some active brain cells had baited Elijah. She'd bet her ass on it. He'd goaded the chase that led to this ambush and then provoked Elijah by attacking the woman covered in his scent.

Higher brain function is subverted by pure instinct, Grace had said.

"I wasn't imagining it, was I?" she asked, noting that the brainy wraith's puddle had some shape to it, unlike the others. As if he was deteriorating more slowly. "He did talk, didn't he?"

"Yeah. Fucker."

"I was told their brains are mush. Lights not on and no one home."

"Your friend . . . Nikki . . . she talked."

Vash stiffened. "What did she say?"

"Nothing worth remembering, but it was English."

"Oh." She jerked in surprise when her cell phone rang.

"Your tit's ringing."

Pulling her phone out, she saw Syre's name on the caller ID. She activated video. "Syre."

His handsome visage appeared, scowling. Then he paled. "My god . . . what's happened to you? Where are you? That lycan is *dead,* Vashti. I'll shred him."

"Take a number," Elijah muttered.

Realizing how she must look with blood all over her, she spoke quickly. "We ran into some wraith action in Vegas and it got messy, but I'm fine."

"Tell me where you are and I'll be there in less than thirty minutes. I've got a helicopter on standby now."

"Where are you?"

"McCarran. I just landed."

"Thank god." She exhaled in relief. "Wait there. I'll send Salem to you with Elijah and you can take them to the warehouse. He needs medical treatment and we're set up for it there."

Syre's gaze narrowed. "The Alpha?"

"Yes."

"Where will you be?"

Vash didn't say her intentions aloud, unwilling to jinx her plans. "I've got something to take care of."

"Me," Elijah said, his eyes open and staring into hers.

Yes, she thought. *You.*

CHAPTER 9

Lindsay woke when the steady hum of the car's engine and air-conditioning ceased. Lifting her head from the seat back, she blinked at Adrian, who sat behind the wheel. "I fell asleep."

"You did," he agreed, his blue eyes warm and soft. He reached for her hand and linked their fingers together.

"I'm sorry." She straightened and looked around, noting that they were in the driveway of a two-story peach stucco home in a quiet residential neighborhood. In lieu of grass, white gravel covered the yard, which wasn't unusual in Las Vegas. "Oh man . . . and you drove because you wanted to talk."

Needing to utilize every minute of his endless time, Adrian was usually chauffeured from one place to another, allowing him to work even when he was on the road. In addition to his duties as leader of the Sentinels, he owned Mitchell Aeronautics, effectively giving him two full-time endeavors to manage. It was fortunate that he didn't require sleep, or he'd never get anything finished.

She shoved her free hand through her short blond curls and looked at her lover contritely. Sentinels had astonishingly acute hearing. There was no privacy to be found at Angels' Point. Every word and sound could be picked up by any Sentinel within a mile radius. When Adrian wished to speak to her privately, he took her away, flying her to remote hills surrounding the Point so that eavesdropping would be impossible. He'd suggested they make the five-hour drive to Vegas alone, shunning both a driver and the use of any of his many privately owned aircraft so they could chat at length as they so rarely had the opportunity to do.

He hummed softly and reached out to stroke a fingertip down the side of her face. "Watching you sleep was a joy as well, *neshama*."

My soul. The endearment still astonished and awed her. How could she be the soul of this man . . . this *angel*? Her eyes swept over his beloved features, his dark and seductive beauty tightening her chest. His inky black hair framed a face so savagely masculine just looking at him turned her on. Winged brows and thick lashes framed eyes of a preternatural cerulean—the pristine blue found at the heart of a flame.

Too often she forgot what he was, a powerful winged being not of this world. When her hands and mouth stroked over his impossibly perfect body, worshipping warm olive skin stretched taut over rippling muscles, his abandoned and feverish response made him all too human. His voice when he spoke to her privately, in the flesh and in her mind. The way he touched her . . . nuzzled against her . . . wrapped himself around her when they took to their bed . . . He was simply a man to her. Earthy, sultry, and achingly fervent.

Adrian, my love, she thought, guilt and sorrow tainting the edges of her happiness. He was the greatest gift she'd ever received in her life, her solace and dearest pleasure. And she returned that joy by being a tragedy in his life, a weakness and a sin she feared he would one day pay too steep a price for.

"Stop it." It was the nature of what he was that his voice could be so mesmerizingly resonant while also sharp and furious.

Embarrassed that he'd heard her maudlin internal pity party, Lindsay tried to tug her hand out of his and break the connection. He held fast, his seductively curved mouth thinned into a determined line. "Perhaps I should demonstrate how much solace and pleasure you give me in return. Maybe the memory has faded in the hours since you last wrang me dry. If so, I'll need to work harder to leave a more indelible recollection."

A shiver moved through her and her eyes slid helplessly to the thick vein pumping strong and steady along his throat. She licked her lips, her own blood hot and thick with wanting him. She'd fed from his wrist just before she slept, but her hunger was acute, both for his blood and his rockin' body.

"Sex," she breathed, overwhelmed by her sudden need for it. For him. The rapidly heating interior of the car only increased her desire. The continuing evolution of her Change made her a tactile creature, one who responded swiftly, and often unexpectedly, to external stimuli. Once she matured past the fledgling stage, she'd be impervious to such things as external temperature, but for now everything seemed capable of setting her off.

"Love," he corrected, cupping her cheek with his free hand and leaning toward her. "Expressed physically."

"Repeatedly."

"Oh, yes," he purred, sliding his mouth softly across hers. "You're teaching me every day, in so many ways, how to love. I thought I knew, but I was wrong."

She fought off a twinge of jealousy over Shadoe, the naphil daughter of Syre whom Adrian had loved for ages. Over many reincarnations. The last one being Lindsay herself. And yet faced with the culmination of his endless quest to possess Shadoe, he'd chosen her—Lindsay—instead. She wondered if she would ever truly understand why.

His lips moved against hers. "Because you showed me what love truly is just by giving yours so selflessly. I wasn't made for love. It wasn't weaved into the fabric of my being. I didn't know what it was, what I was looking for, what I needed. I had no point of reference, no examples, nothing. Until you."

Adrian took her mouth in a lush, deep kiss, his tongue stroking along hers, the leisurely rhythm and his total control a blatantly erotic promise of things to come.

She moaned, the sound both a plea and a surrender.

Lifting his head, Adrian watched her with heavy-lidded eyes, his thumb brushing over her swollen mouth and peeping fangs. "Shadoe possessed me. I was consumed by her hunger and her conviction that I was meant to be hers. I was a void, *neshama*. An emotionless being. When you bring something into nothing, it's impossible to know if it's good or bad for you. You know only that losing what you have would leave you with nothing again. She brought me emotional pain and physical pleasure, and I clung to those things even as I wanted nothing so much as to go back and make a different choice."

"Don't say any more." The torment in his voice made her heartsick.

"But you, Lindsay my love, delight me. You fill the hole in me I didn't know was there. The pleasure of your touch is the sweetest agony, because it's never enough. I'll never have enough. As many times as I have you, I always want more. What I feel for you consumes me. I couldn't live without it. Couldn't live without you."

Lindsay pressed her forehead to his. "I'm learning, too. Slower than you, but I'm getting there."

"She made me a man," Adrian whispered, his tongue tracing the curve of her bottom lip. "You've made me human."

She cried at that, tears slipping free. That's what she feared most—that she'd irrevocably damaged something irreplaceable.

You make me stronger than I've ever been. She broke me

down; you built me up. Why don't you know this, neshama?
Tell me how to show you.

"You do. Beautifully. It's the Change, Adrian. It's like premenstrual syndrome times a thousand. I'm having mood swings. Cravings. My sex drive is out of control. God, how do you put up with me?"

"With pleasure." His clever fingertips stroked a circular pattern over the tender flesh behind her ear. "I wouldn't change a thing about you."

She met his fierce gaze and held it. "I love you."

"I know." Adrian's smile was so potently sexual and warmly tender that she grew slick between the thighs.

"And I want you again. Now."

"Always. I'm yours." He glanced at the dashboard clock. "We have just enough time before the others catch up with us."

They'd taken off an hour and a half before the two lycans who would be accompanying them, so they'd be assured of privacy. Then she'd messed it all up by falling asleep only a couple of hours into the drive.

Her nose wrinkled. "How are you going to get anything done once I get to the point where I don't need sleep anymore? I can't keep my hands off you."

He exited the car and rounded the hood to her door before she could blink. His laughter sifted through her mind as he extended his hand to assist her out. "What we'll do with each other during sleepless nights isn't a concern I'm ever going to have."

Looking at the lovely but average house in front of her, she asked, "What is this place?"

"Helena's home."

Lindsay's hand tightened on his. She knew how it tormented him that he'd lost one of his closest and most treasured Sentinels.

"We're staying here? Maybe the Mondego would be better?" she suggested, thinking of the glamorous hotel and casino owned by Raguel Gadara, a man known worldwide as a real estate and entertainment mogul. In celestial circles, he was known to be one of the seven earthbound archangels, his territory encompassing all of North America. Falling two spheres and several rungs lower in the angelic hierarchy than Adrian, Gadara was ambitious in both halves of his life.

"After the stunt he pulled last time? No." While his voice didn't rise, the adamancy in it was unmistakable. "Raguel's more trouble than he's worth. I just want his blood."

A chill rolled down Lindsay's spine. The way Adrian spoke sounded figurative as well as literal, which would be bad news for Gadara. She wondered if Adrian's enmity had anything—or everything—to do with Gadara helping her flee Adrian and her forbidden feelings for him so many weeks ago.

"Raguel makes enough trouble for himself on his own," Adrian answered. Linking their fingers, he led her to the front door.

The strengthening of his grip on her hand wasn't an indication of disquiet, but she knew visiting this place must be hard. Helena had been special to him. She'd been a Sentinel Adrian considered pure of purpose and unshakable in her faith. She had been his proof that the Sentinels weren't destined to fail their mission as a rule, that his transgressions with Shadoe and herself were unique failures of his.

But Helena had fallen in love with her lycan guard and she'd given up her life trying to be with him, shattering that tender hope.

Adrian unlocked the door and they stepped inside. As he typed the access code into the beeping security system keypad, she frowned. "Is someone staying here?"

His gaze raked the room. "Good question. Nice and cool in here, isn't it?"

"Yeah, my thought exactly—why is the air-conditioning on?"

Skirting him, Lindsay moved deeper into the living room. A glass walkway bisected the vaulted ceiling, connecting rooms over the garage with a room over the kitchen. Square windows near the ceiling allowed light to flood the space, creating an open and airy feel in the small, welcoming home.

Her nose twitched and she caught his wrist, pushing her thoughts at him. *Doesn't smell musty, like you'd expect a closed-up house would. The plants are looking healthy, too.*

Sleek tendrils of smoke unfurled from his back, taking on the shape and substance of wings. Gorgeous, bloodstained wings. They were soft to the touch, but deadly, capable of slicing through anything with the precision of the finest sword. If she was ever inclined to forget how dangerous he truly was, those wings would remind her—she'd watched him deflect bullets with them. He was a being created for war, an enforcer of such power he wielded the fist of God.

I'll take the upstairs, he said. *Please be careful.*

Not for the first time, Lindsay wondered if he knew how much his trust in her ability to defend herself meant. He was a possessive man and one who was ferociously concerned for her well-being, yet he knew that to hold her back or smother her would only lead to resentment and unhappiness. She wasn't equal to him and never would be, but she couldn't hide behind his wings and still look at herself in the mirror. As disparate as their skills and natural weapons were, they had to face their battles side by side or there would be no hope for them as a couple. Adrian understood and made concessions for that tenuous balance between them, even though she knew it cost him dearly to do so.

Concentrating hard, she got her fangs and claws to extend. She was still getting used to what she was—a monster; one of the bloodsucking creatures she'd trained herself to kill in vengeance for her mother's murder. Making peace with her new identity was difficult at the best of times, but there were occasions— such as this one—when she appreciated the benefits.

Adrian moved quickly and silently, one moment at her side, the next on the glass walkway above her. If transients had holed up in the house, they were about to receive the fright of their lives. Perhaps that would teach them not to squat in someone else's abode.

Lindsay entered the combination family room/ kitchen through an open archway. The space was small but cozy. A dinette filled the alcove in front of a backyard window and a couch faced a flat-screen TV hung over a small gas fireplace. A homey fragrance hung in the air, soothing her enough that her claws retreated without her volition. She was trying to process her lack of control over her body when a photo of Adrian and Helena on the mantel caught her eye, momentarily distracting her. It was a costly lapse.

"Hello, Lindsay."

An agonizing shard of pain in her shoulder dropped her to her knees with a sharp cry. Dizzy, her flesh sizzling, she looked at the small throwing knife embedded in her shoulder. Then she lifted her head to meet a face that haunted her nightmares. "Vashti."

Lindsay's memories of her mother's killing were hazy at best—more like impressions and feelings than true pictures—but Vash was a hard woman to forget. The vivid red hair and penchant for painted-on black clothing made her almost a caricature of a comic book superhero. But when Lindsay had bitten into Vash's throat and swallowed the vampress's blood, she'd been exposed to the memories that blood carried and Rachel Gibson's brutal slaying was absent from them. Vash was the spitting image of her mother's killer, but that was all. Still, Lindsay couldn't fight the terror and revulsion she felt every time she saw the vampress.

Residual fear gave her the strength to yank the blade from her arm, but she moved too slowly. A mere split second and she found herself on her feet with Vashti pressed to her back and another silver blade—a dagger—held to her throat.

"Let her go, Vashti." Adrian's voice was chillingly modulated, his face impassive as he suddenly filled the threshold between the kitchen and living room.

Lindsay wasn't fooled by his calm demeanor. With her heightened senses, she felt his turmoil and fury roiling through the air—a tempest barely leashed.

"An unexpected surprise finding you here," Vash said, speaking over Lindsay's shoulder, their faces nearly cheek to cheek. "I was waiting on Helena, but you'll more than compensate."

"Let her go," Adrian repeated, taking a step into the room. "I warned you, Vash. I won't do so again."

"She's as weak as a babe." Vash shifted, positioning her body so that both Lindsay and the kitchen island stood between her and Adrian. "Fledglings are like infants, you know. Floundering in their own bodies, overwhelmed by their senses, easily damaged. She really should be with the rest of us. We can teach her how to survive."

"What part of 'she's mine' don't you understand?"

"As much as you hate it, she's also mine and she's presently a rogue minion. I have the right to take her life. We police ourselves, as you know."

"And do a piss-poor job of it."

"We have to leave you something to do."

His chest lifted and fell with a deep inhalation. "What do you want, Vashti?"

"And so the fierce and mighty Adrian bends . . . for a vampire. I so wish I had time to enjoy this." Vash snatched something off the counter and tossed it at Adrian, who caught it deftly. "But I'm in a hurry. Fill it up."

Lindsay began to struggle when she saw what it was.

A blood bag.

"Don't do it," Lindsay said, realizing just how dangerous this confrontation had become. If Vash had sniffed out the effects of Sentinel blood on the infected vampires and wanted to test the cure, the resulting discovery endangered every life on earth. As few Sentinels as there were, they still managed to keep the vampire population in check, sparing countless mortal lives. If they were hunted to extinction for their blood, the whole world would suffer.

"How noble and self-sacrificing," Vash murmured scornfully. "And monumentally stupid. The helpless fledgling sacrificing herself for the powerful Sentinel. You two are so sappy you're making me nauseous."

Adrian took another step toward them. "You used to know what it was like to love."

"Not a step closer or I'll have to kill her." The flat of the blade sizzled against Lindsay's neck, making her squirm. "Don't think I won't. My life means nothing to me—you know that."

Lindsay stared hard at Adrian. "Don't do it."

Vash's lips pressed to her ear like a lover's. "Isn't Elijah worth it to you? Or is your friendship so fickle?"

Stiffening, Lindsay's breath quickened. The familiar scent that had sent her claws into retreat was Elijah's. And it was all over Vash. "What have you done to him?"

"What's been done can still be undone . . . with a little Sentinel blood."

A tremor racked Lindsay's frame. She hadn't spoken to Elijah since he mutinied. She had no idea what had prompted him to revolt or whether his doing so made them enemies.

But it doesn't matter, she thought grimly. What she and Elijah were to each other now might be a mystery, but what they'd been to each other before was not. He'd been a friend and trusted companion when she needed one. She couldn't bear to think of him suffering.

"He might die," Vash prodded. "This could be the one thing capable of saving him."

Swallowing hard, Lindsay continued to stare at Adrian, who would've heard every word with his powerful Sentinel hearing.

"Your blood is damn near as good as mine, Vash." Adrian's wings flexed, a sign Lindsay recognized as agitation. "If you want to save him, do it yourself."

"I've given him what I can."

"If that wasn't enough, he's dead already."

Lindsay's stomach knotted. "Take me. I'll be your blood bag. I'm easier to transport and no spillage."

"Lindsay, no." To the casual observer, Adrian appeared unmoved by her statement. But the compulsory resonance in his words hit her like a Mack truck, sending a racking jolt through her body.

Vash's grip loosened a fraction. "When's the last time you fed from him?"

It took her a moment to squeeze an answer past Adrian's compulsion. "Three hours ago."

"Vashti." Adrian's voice rumbled through the room like thunder.

The world exploded in a shower of glass. Lindsay was thrown outside the house and into the street . . . or so it seemed. When the world shuddered back into place, she realized Vash had leaped with her through the glass door and over the wall . . . into a waiting convertible. They tore off like a bullet with Adrian directly behind them.

Lightning split the sky and hit the asphalt in front of the car.

Cursing, Vash jerked the wheel to the left and punched it around a corner, tires squealing as they nearly careened up the side of the curb and into a streetlamp.

"Better grab the wheel when the time comes," the vampress hissed. "You'll be the only one who dies if you don't."

Lindsay, feeling ill from the lingering effects of the silver, clung to the door handle and tried to kick her rattled brain into gear.

Adrian landed on the trunk with a violent thud, his feet sinking deep prints into the metal.

"Now!" Vash yelled, deflecting Adrian's grasping arm and lunging at him between the two front seats.

Throwing herself across the center console, Lindsay snatched at the wheel. Her sudden grab jerked the car right, then left as she tried to steer a straight line while lying on her side. Adrian was thrown free.

Vash tumbled into the backseat with a curse. "Drive straight, damn it! Get to the Strip. He'll have to back off."

A massive shadow darkened the sky over the car as Adrian swooped in again.

It didn't escape Lindsay's mind that she was fleeing

her very reason for living, the one individual she couldn't live without. But that's why she was doing it. Adrian's blood was too precious—and the ramifications too great—to risk what Vash demanded.

"Red light!" Lindsay shouted.

"A little busy!" Vash shot back, straightening to fight off Adrian's dive bomb. "You're making a spectacle of yourself, Sentinel!"

Lightning struck the vampress square in the chest, knocking her unconscious. She slumped into the corner of the backseat like a broken doll.

"Move, Lindsay," Adrian ordered, dropping wingless into the driver's seat and taking over the wheel. He turned into a strip mall and parked with a squeal of rubber over pavement. Twisting in the seat, he faced her with burning irises. "What the hell are you doing?"

"It's best this way."

"Fuck if it is."

"You know it is," she argued, looking at Vash to make sure the vampress was still out cold. "We can't risk you."

"You're doing this for Elijah."

"Partly," she admitted. "But that benefits you, too. You and I both want to figure out what happened with him."

"I don't give a shit what happened with him. I give a shit about you. Maybe you haven't been paying attention—I can't live without you. Damned if I'll risk you."

"Elijah won't let anything happen to me. You know that, or you would never have made him my guard."

Adrian's knuckles whitened with the force of his grip on the steering wheel. "Elijah's half dead, apparently."

"Not if I can help it."

"We don't know if you can. Your blood has a negative effect on some beings. Don't forget I watched you slide a knife into a dragon's impenetrable hide just by coating the blade with your blood."

"Siobhán thinks that's because I was carrying two souls inside me," she reminded, "and the creatures that were affected by it were demons."

"That's a guess. We don't know, and Elijah has demon blood in him."

She nodded, knowing that demon blood—werewolf blood—is what had turned some of the Fallen into lycans rather than vampires. "I'll tell him the risks and let him decide."

"Think of the reasons he'd be incapacitated in Vashti's keeping. One, she fucked him up because of the Nikki incident or because she's looking for Charron's killers. Two, they're working together and he got jacked in the process. You're either reviving him to put up with more torture or reviving him to collude with the vampires against us. Nothing good is going to come out of doing this. In the meantime, you'll be among the very people who need me weakened to achieve their aims. You're cutting out my heart and handing it to them."

"Adrian." She cupped his cheek in her hand. His jaw was tight beneath her palm, the teeth grinding together. "I would do that and more to save your life."

He set his hand over hers and squeezed. "My life is nothing without you."

"Then let me do this for your Sentinels. You'll be putting their welfare ahead of mine and I think they need to feel like you would, at least under certain circumstances. And what will it say to the lycans that you've done this for Elijah? More may come back to you because they won't be afraid that you'll kill them on sight. And the vampires . . . if they ever considered the thought that having me in their possession would weaken your mission, they'll see that's not the case. Everyone knows what I mean to you. You'll make a powerful statement by using me this way."

He exhaled harshly. "Damn you."

"You sweet talker, you." Lindsay reached into the medical supply store shopping bag on the floorboard between her feet and pulled out a blood bag from an open multipack. "Here's your opportunity to get the Fallen blood Siobhán needs."

"Can you please stop being so fucking rational about this?"

"Love you," she retorted. "More than my life. More than anything."

"You have your cell phone on you?"

She shook her head.

He pulled his out of his pocket and began tweaking the settings on it. "You'll check in every hour on the hour. I want to hear your voice. Something goes south and you can't say it aloud, call me Sentinel instead of my name and I'll know. You miss a call by more than ten minutes and I'll raze the desert looking for you. I've set the alarm to remind you."

"I won't forget."

Climbing over the seats, he grabbed Vashti's biceps with enough force to act as a tourniquet and slid the needle attached to the blood bag into her vein.

The vampress jolted awake to find the crimson tip of one of Adrian's wings curled inward and pressed to her throat—the slightest resistance and she'd lose her head.

"Asshole," she growled, glaring.

"You have twelve hours," he said with icy impassivity, watching the bag fill. "You'll bring her back to me without a scratch or I'll stake you to a wall and make you watch as I disarticulate every one of the Fallen and shove their severed limbs down their throats. Without Lindsay I've got nothing to lose. Do you understand? *Nothing* will stop me."

"Fine."

He withdrew the needle, then his wing. "She's going to call me every hour and you're going to let her."

"Jeez, Adrian," Vash muttered, sitting up. "One would almost think you didn't trust me."

CHAPTER 10

"How's the shoulder?" Vash asked Lindsay as the helicopter lifted gracefully into the scorching desert sky with Raze at the cyclic. The car she'd stolen was whipped with sand scattered by the revolving copter blades, but that probably wouldn't matter as much to the owner as the dents Adrian had left behind.

"Good as new." Lindsay's voice betrayed her irritation. "Are the blindfold and restraints really necessary?"

"I could knock you out," Vash offered, smiling because the other woman couldn't see it.

"Gee, you're so helpful," Lindsay muttered.

"I try."

"Doesn't sound like that worked out too well for Elijah, considering he's on his deathbed."

Vash took the hit with clenched fists. She felt guilty and worried, her mind racing ahead of her common sense. She'd risked more than her own hide by going after Sentinel blood. That she'd done so for a lycan who intended to kill her made no damn sense at all.

Leaning forward, she tapped Raze on the shoulder. "How's the Alpha doing?"

"How do you think? He's like a wolf in a bear trap—he's snarling and snapping at everyone. Not that the lycans seem to mind. They're tripping over themselves trying to take care of him. I thought they were going to riot when he was unloaded from the chopper, but they calmed down when he told them he was jumped and you saved his ass." The Fallen captain looked over his shoulder at her. "He won't stop asking for you. I tried to distract him with a hot little honey named Sarah, but that's not doing the trick."

Her lip curled as she remembered the demure lycan who'd been so eager to tend Elijah's injuries and remain by his side.

Vash fell back into her seat with a heavy exhale, struggling to find her balance. She was an emotional disaster.

The helicopter was landing fifteen minutes later. The moment Raze cut the engine, Vash shoved the door open and hopped out. "Get her. Keep her eyes covered until we've got her in a room."

Her heels clicked across the parking lot and she entered the warehouse to find an industriously working crew. Van Halen blared on the radio as various groups went about unpacking and moving in. Salem stood before the map of contagion, explaining its significance to a mixed group of minions and lycans. Syre stood in the center of the vast space, clearly the orchestrator of activity.

Dressed in sleek black trousers and a gray silk shirt, the Fallen leader was drawing the eye of everyone in the room. Elegant, powerful, compelling. A crazed minion had once called him the antichrist, the dark prince who would mesmerize the world and bring about its destruction. A ridiculous assertion if one knew Syre's heart at all, but she conceded that his charisma was fierce and seductive enough to bend the wills of even the most contained of individuals. Even Vash, as used to him as she was, was drawn to him inexorably.

"Commander," she greeted him as she approached. "Your visit to Vegas is an unexpected surprise."

"An appreciated one?" he queried smoothly, his whiskey-warm gaze searching her features.

"Depends on whether or not you're here for the fun of it or because you think I need a hand."

"Would the latter be so terrible?"

She sighed. "I'm not fragile."

"You don't like to think so." He held up a hand when her mouth opened in protest. "Fragility isn't always a weakness, Vashti. It happens to be one of your greatest strengths."

"What a crock." Her mouth twisted ruefully. "Sir."

He shook his head at her, then froze, his gaze locked on something over her shoulder.

"Lindsay," she said, knowing without looking. Damn it, she'd been so scrambled over Elijah, she had forgotten Syre would be present to see the mortal shell that once housed his daughter's reincarnated soul.

"What have you done?"

"No more than Adrian allowed me to do. Lindsay offered to come when she learned Elijah was injured."

"Why?" he said tightly. "What purpose does her presence serve?"

"She's a Sentinel blood source, in lieu of Adrian—" She gasped when Syre cut off her breath with a crushing hand wrapped around her throat. Her boots dangled two feet off the floor.

His eyes burned into hers, his fury stunning and frightening. "You went after *Adrian*?"

"H-Helena . . . actually," she managed, fighting the urge to claw at the constriction that impeded her ability to speak.

He threw her thirty feet across the room at Salem, who caught her deftly. The warehouse fell into silence as someone hastily shut off the stereo; then the growls of agitated lycans rumbled through the air like war drums.

Vash struggled free of Salem's hold, embarrassed at being so publicly chastised and worried about Syre's cracked control. He didn't use physical force as a rule; he didn't need to. He could mesmerize like a snake charmer to get his way.

She was his fist. At least she had been until now.

Brow arched, Raze had stopped his progress across the warehouse floor halfway between the main door and Syre, his hand gripping Lindsay's elbow. She was still bound at the wrists and blindfolded . . . by her choice. Her vampire strength could easily break the rope. She could lift her hand and push the blindfold up at any time. Her continuing cooperation was starting to make Vash suspicious.

"Where's Elijah?" the blonde asked sharply. "I want to see him. That was the deal."

The lycans responded with low rumbles. The ones who were seated rose to their feet, while those who stood sidled closer.

Unsure of whether their support lay with Lindsay or Elijah, Vash caught Raze's gaze. "Take her to him."

Raze glanced at Syre, who stood unmoving for a long moment before giving a curt nod. All heads turned to track Lindsay's progress. The smell of fear became thick and oppressive.

No one in the room doubted that her well-being was tied to theirs. Adrian's wrath was something no one wished to incite.

When she disappeared through one of the office doorways lining the rear wall, the room as a whole seemed to exhale in a rush.

Syre pivoted and disappeared behind another door. The latch engaged with a quiet click, but the sound struck everyone like a gunshot report.

"What the fuck were you thinking?" Salem snapped behind her.

She shoved a hand through her hair. "I wasn't."

The tension in the room was so brittle it scraped along her skin. Making a beeline for the locker room and a much-needed shower, Vash fled the consequences of her inexplicable actions.

Elijah stirred from a half-conscious state when the door to his makeshift infirmary opened. "Vash?" he croaked through a dry throat.

"No."

He stilled, his nostrils flaring. Opening gritty eyes, he tried to blink through the fog of pain. "Lindsay?"

"Hi, El," she said softly, lifting his hand from the bed and gripping it. "You look like shit."

Fuck. Had the Sentinels rooted them out so quickly? He pushed the concern aside, finding he cared less about that than Lindsay's welfare. He lifted his other hand to scrub at his eyes. Trying again to see, he looked toward her voice and found worried vampire irises glowing down at him.

"Jesus. You *are* a vamp," he managed, taking some comfort in the fact that he smelled Adrian all over her. The Sentinel really hadn't turned his back on her when she was returned to him as something different from what she'd been when she was taken.

"Yeah, imagine that." Releasing him, she picked up the water cup on the table beside the bed, twisting the straw around to offer it to him.

He drank deeply and gratefully, soothing his parched throat. When he'd emptied the cup, his head fell heavily into the pillow. "What are you doing here?"

"I'm overdue for blood donation and I heard you were in line for a transfusion."

His chest tightened as the import of her words sank in. "Lindsay . . ."

She glanced over her shoulder at Raze, then offered a small smile to Sarah. "Would you two give us a minute, please?"

Both Raze and Sarah hesitated.

"It's okay," Elijah said, hating that he was so weak the others feared leaving him alone. "She's a friend."

Once the door shut, he studied Lindsay's face. Her hair was still styled in short blond curls that framed a breathtaking face. Delicate brows and dark lashes framed eyes that had once been chocolate brown but were now the honey hue of a vampire. Her generous mouth was curved in an affectionate smile that revealed no fangs at present, but he could imagine them there.

"Kinda weird, right?" she said wryly. "I'm still getting used to it."

"I was told you wanted the Change. Was I lied to?" Nothing would save Syre if that was the case. Elijah would kill him the moment he was strong enough to do so.

"It was the only way." She settled into the seat by the bed. "There were two people inside me—two souls—and one of them had to go. That's why I had that crazy inhuman speed as a mortal. That's also what I need to talk to you about."

He listened to Lindsay's explanation of the possible hazards to accepting her blood before he asked, "How the hell did you get here? Where's Adrian? How did you find me?"

"It was Vashti who brought me." All the warmth left her face. "What did she do to you, El? If she's just going to hurt you again, healing you isn't going to be enough. You have to tell me what I'm dealing with here."

"Vash found you?" His eyes closed on a shaky exhalation. Christ. "Why?"

"She came after Sentinel blood. She said she needed it to save you, but she wouldn't tell me why you were hurt in the first place." She gestured toward the door. "I smell other lycans out there. Are they using you to control the others?"

Fuck . . . He'd do just about anything to not disappoint Lindsay. Anything except lie to her. "She didn't do this to me, Linds. We were working together and I got jumped by a pack of vamps. She tried to get to me, but she couldn't."

"Working together," she repeated. She slumped back into her seat, her gaze stark and sad. "What about Micah's death? Was that part of some plan between you two?"

"No! For fuck's sake. You know me better than that. We're working together in spite of Micah's murder, not because of it."

She looked him straight in the eyes, then nodded, as if she saw the truth of what he said on his face. "Tell me honestly. Are we enemies now? Are you gunning for the Sentinels?"

"Never. I'm just trying to save as many lycan and mortal lives as possible." He thought of the wraith ambush and a chill moved through him. What kind of world would they be living in if such attacks were commonplace? "The vamp infection we saw in Hurricane is spreading. Vash is trying to stop it."

"Why couldn't you stop it with us?" Straightening, she set her elbows on her knees and leaned in close. "Why did you have to revolt?"

"I didn't want this." He pled for her understanding

with his gaze. "But once it happened, I couldn't *not* step up. Those who want to work with the Sentinels will find their way back to Adrian. The rest need an Alpha or they'll die. I couldn't just turn my back and let that happen."

The door opened and Vash walked in. "How cozy. I'm not interrupting an intimate moment, am I?"

Elijah felt the knot in his gut loosen at the sight of her. She was fresh from a shower, dressed in her trademark stark black with her damp hair pulled back in a ponytail. Her skintight pants barely clung to her hips, while her short sleeveless vest was small enough to pass for a bra. It was a testament to how incapacitated he was that his dick couldn't muster more than a semi in appreciation.

"You're a crazy bitch," he said gruffly. He glanced at Lindsay. "You, too. Adrian can't be happy about this. Shit, I'm not entirely happy about it. You're too exposed here."

"What was I going to do?" Lindsay shot back. "Let you die? Couldn't do it, El."

Vash gave an exaggerated sigh and rolled her eyes. "My god, the way women fawn all over you."

Lindsay snorted. "So says the vampress who fought off Adrian to get blood for him."

The ringing of a cell phone had Lindsay pushing to her feet. She dug it out of her pocket and answered. "Adrian . . . Yes, I'm fine."

As she moved into a corner to talk, Vash stepped closer. She put her hands on her hips and glared at him. "How do you feel?"

"Like hammered shit."

"You look like it, too."

"So I've been told."

Muttering to herself, she reached out and pushed her hands through his hair, brushing the strands back from his face. He nuzzled into her touch, moved by what she'd done for him. He was a man sworn to kill her, yet she had risked her life to save him. "You went to a lot of trouble, Vashti. Put a lot on the line."

"Don't read anything into it," she muttered. "We need the lycans, and you're a package deal."

"Hmm . . ."

"That's all this is," she insisted, scowling.

"We don't know what this is," he said softly. Somewhere along the way, in an impossibly short span of time, their higher reasoning in regard to each other had been subverted by impulse.

Lindsay returned. She gave Elijah a searching glance. "Are we going to do this?"

He knew what she was asking, whether or not he wanted to risk the possible hazards of her blood. After what she and Vash had gone through to get it for him, it was a no-brainer. "Yeah, let's do this."

Needing air, Syre left the building. It was dusk now, the desert sky painted in shades of orange, pink, and purple. A streak of lightning arced through the sky, then another. Out of place, he thought, but beautiful.

The sizzling heat of the day had abated, as had the fury of his earlier mood. His second-in-command had put every vampire at risk by her actions, but part of him was secretly relieved to see her fighting for something beyond her vengeance. She'd been twisted by bitterness for so long. Long enough that it had become the only thing she lived for.

He pulled his phone out of his pocket and dialed Adrian. When the call went to voice mail, he left a message. "Adrian," he said darkly. "Vashti's actions today weren't sanctioned. Nevertheless, I'll go to the wall for her. If it's vengeance you want, you know where to find me. Leave her out of it."

Killing the call, he rounded the corner of the building and came to an abrupt stop. Raze leaned against the metal siding of the building's exterior, his arms crossed and massive biceps bulging. His gaze was riveted to the slender female silhouette just a few yards away. She was pacing, as if agitated, and speaking on a phone. To Adrian.

Syre waved the Fallen captain away and shoved his hands in his pockets, taking up the watchful position he'd dismissed Raze from. Syre's emotions were a morass of pain, guilt, sorrow, grief, and anger. As he watched the woman who'd supplanted his beloved daughter in every way—the woman who was the greatest vulnerability of his oldest adversary—he realized he had no idea what to say to her . . . or do with her. If anything.

"I can tough it out," she was saying. "I'll be home soon, *neshama*. Please don't worry . . . Yes, I know that's impossible. That's why I'm here, isn't it? Because I'm worried about you . . . I will . . . I love you, too."

Ending the call, she stared down at the phone in her

hand and sighed. There was something in the sound, a note of regret and weariness that struck a chord in Syre.

Pivoting, she faced him and saw him standing there. She froze, her eyes blinking in the waning light. She was a fledgling, still growing into her new senses.

"How are you feeling, Lindsay?"

She shoved her hand through her curls, a habit he remembered she fell into when discomfited. Her mouth opened, then closed. She shrugged. "Not so hot."

He stepped closer, slowly, approaching her in a non-threatening manner. As he neared, he saw the fever brightness of her eyes and her rapid, shallow breathing. "How much blood did you give the Alpha?"

"A pint. Maybe a little more."

"It's too soon after the Change," he murmured, lifting his hand cautiously toward her face. "Can I?"

She nodded.

He found her skin burning hot. "How often is Adrian feeding you?"

"Every few hours."

"How long has it been?" He caught her chin when she looked away. "How long, Lindsay?"

"Six. Maybe seven."

"You need to eat."

She shook her head.

Syre remembered how the act of drinking blood had so horrified her. She'd almost died by refusing to feed. He was surprised to find that he was relieved she'd survived after all.

He blew out his breath. "Come inside."

Reaching into her back pocket, she pulled out a bandana and began to tie it around her head, covering her eyes.

"That's not necessary," he said.

"It's safer for me. And for you. If something happens to me, Adrian will go ballistic. The less risk I pose, the better for everyone."

"All right." Gripping her elbow, he steered her back into the building and toward the office he'd commandeered as his own.

As they crossed the vast space, lycans who'd been sitting at various points around the open warehouse pushed slowly to their feet, eyeing him with hostile suspicion. Old habits die hard, he thought. Going head-to-head with Adrian and the Sentinels wasn't something they were willing to risk yet. They weren't going to let him incite a war with Adrian over Lindsay.

Syre shut them out by closing his office door, then tugged the bandana off her face. Although his night vision was excellent, he was struck by the sight of her in the harsh glare of the fluorescent overhead lights. She was nothing like Shadoe, but still . . . he felt oddly soothed in her presence. Something that had been vibrating with disquiet inside him settled down. She sank into one of the two chairs positioned in front of the utilitarian metal desk and he took the one beside it.

She studied him boldly.

His brows rose in silent inquiry.

"I was scared the first time I saw you," she explained. "Afterward, I was distracted and then very ill."

"You're not scared now?"

"You're being very careful that I won't be."

His mouth curved and her breath caught.

"You're . . . very attractive," she admitted. "I'd forgotten how young you appear."

Leaning forward, he set his elbows on his knees and got to the most pressing point. "You drank from me once before. Will you do so again?"

"Why?"

"You need to eat. Fledglings are easily damaged by lack of blood. It's been too long between feedings and you've given some of your blood away."

"That's not what I meant. I know why I should want to, but I don't know why you would."

Syre looked down, gathering his thoughts. "I don't know. It's a combination of things, I suppose. You're as close as I'll ever be to Shadoe. Until I pass on."

"I'm not Shadoe." Her voice was soft and compassionate, earning his appreciation and respect.

"I've heard some families of organ donors keep in touch with the transplant recipients." He glanced up at her. "There's a bond there, whether it's real or imagined."

"Is that healthy?"

It was his turn to shrug. "Who can say? There's something else, though, that would lead me to make this same offer. I Changed you, Lindsay. In that respect there's no doubt I sired you."

The space between her brows was marred by a frown. "How long does that sense of obligation last?"

"I really can't say. I've only Changed two individuals in my life: Shadoe, who didn't complete the transformation, and you, who won't if you don't feed."

Her eyes widened. "Only two of us? How is that possible? There are so many vampires."

"If each vampire infected just one other person, our numbers would be great. Of course, there are those who Change far more than one." His mouth curved wryly. "Are you disappointed I'm not more evil?"

"Not disappointed, but I'm struggling with it. Not just about you but about all vampires in general."

"Adrian's brainwashing."

"Adrian has nothing to do with it. Vampires killed my mother in front of me. They held me down . . . made me watch as they brutalized her." A violent shiver moved through her, followed by the immediate stiffening of her posture. "My feelings about vampires are my own, based on my own truths and experiences."

Syre reached for her hand and was pleased when she let him take it. "There are minions who lose their sanity with the Change. They're the most responsible for the spread of vampirism, not the Fallen."

"We were on a picnic in the park on a cloudless day. They were either Fallen or the kept pets of one—or more—or they couldn't have tolerated the sunlight."

He inhaled sharply. "Tell me everything."

"Why? I'm not Shadoe," she said again. "Still, I feel . . . a connection to you. I have memories of you and her together that feel like they're mine. It's messing with my head."

"So is blood loss." Sinking his fangs into his wrist,

he stood and came around her, setting one hand on her head and lifting his bleeding wound to her mouth.

She might have been able to refuse him if he'd expected her to make the punctures herself. But with the coppery scent of blood filling her nostrils, her instincts kicked in and she was too much of a fledgling to fight them. Cupping the back of his wrist with both hands, she drank greedily, her eyes rolling back in her head before she closed them.

He would've preferred she ingest more than she did, but somehow she found the fortitude to pull away. He admired her strength of will. Most fledglings that hungry would've had to be ripped away for the safety of the donor.

"Better?" he asked.

Nodding, she licked her lips. Already the unnatural brightness of her eyes was softening and a healthy flush stained her cheeks. "Thank you."

"I'm glad you accepted." He leaned against the desk and crossed his arms. "I would be even more grateful if you'd trust me with what you remember of the attack on your mother."

He listened as she described a trinity of vampires who sounded remarkably like Vashti, Salem, and Raze.

"It wasn't them," he said quietly when she finished, having no doubt as to their innocence.

"I know that now. When I bit Vash—"

"Ah, yes. I won't forget that." He smiled inwardly, recalling how infuriated Vashti had been at being bested by a fledgling. His second hadn't fought back, of course, out of deference for his paternal feelings.

Which only made it more concerning that she'd brought Lindsay to heal the Alpha. It seemed Vashti had been focused on the lycan's health to the exclusion of every other consideration.

"Adrian searched through my mind and he concurs with my description, but says the memory is faulty. Too murky. More of an emotional impression than a photographic one."

He settled in his chair again. "I'd see for myself if you hadn't lost enough blood already. I could've looked when I drained you for the Change, but I didn't want to personalize you. I know how cold that sounds."

"I appreciate the truth." One side of her mouth lifted. "Hot or cold."

"But it doesn't matter whether I see the memory myself or not. I believe you. I'll investigate and see what turns up."

"I— Thank you, again. For obvious reasons, I'd love to know who they are." She took a deep breath, then released it in a rush. She looked away quickly when he caught her gaze, but he'd seen how her eyes were shadowed and haunted.

"What else is troubling you, Lindsay?" he asked softly. "Will you tell me?"

There was a long hesitation before she said, "I lost my father recently. The day before I met you. It's hard, you know . . . feeling this way about someone else. Even though I know they're Shadoe's feelings— knowing doesn't change how it affects me."

Syre nodded grimly. "Yes, it feels somewhat disloyal, doesn't it? I'm warring with the same thing. I don't want a replacement for my daughter; I want *her*. But I can't help the sense of affinity I feel for you. If there's one thing I've learned in all my years on earth, it's that certain events change our lives for a reason and that certain paths cross because they're meant to. We don't have to be enemies, Lindsay. Or even allies. Perhaps you and I can just . . . be ourselves. Perhaps we can just accept that we have a bond and not fight it or try to analyze it. Perhaps we can even come to nurture it, if we decide we want to."

A knock came to the door a second before it opened and Vash stepped in. "Syre, I— Oh. Sorry."

Lindsay's mouth twisted ruefully.

"It's all right, Vashti," he said. "What do you need?"

"I'd like a word. Elijah wants to see you, Lindsay."

"Okay." Pushing to her feet, she moved to pass Syre and paused abreast of him.

He glanced up at her and was startled when she bent down and pressed a quick kiss to his forehead. She left without another word.

Syre was glad Vashti had enough to say on her own. It was many moments later before his throat loosened enough for him to speak again.

CHAPTER 11

It was on a rooftop under the light of the moon that the phone call was made.

"Someone fucked up," he said without preamble. "Adrian arrived almost two hours earlier than I was told to expect him."

There was a short pause. "Has he discovered that you're still alive?"

"No. I had the interior of the house taken care of. There's nothing of me to be found in there."

"Then there's nothing to worry about."

"The hell there isn't!" Agitation forced his wings to unfurl and stretch, casting a massive shadow on the lawn below. "If he's got any of his brain left, he'll figure out someone's been staying there."

"I'm not prepared to say that's a problem."

"Because you *want* the shit to hit the fan. It's what you've been working for all these centuries." He heard the familiar creaking of Syre's desk chair and his fists clenched. *While the cat's away, the rat will play . . .*

"It's not time yet, and Syre and Adrian are both focusing more on the virus than I expected them to. I assumed they'd concentrate on each other and the lycans. Anything that distracts them is a good thing right now."

"Easy for you to say, you're not out here hanging in the wind. I told you staying in Helena's home was a bad idea."

"Any other option would have left a trail in money, paper, or blood."

The hardness of the voice on the other end of the line fired his temper further. He was a Sentinel. The vampire on the other end of the line would do well to remember that. "You didn't seem concerned about those things when you talked about infecting entire neighborhoods with the pathogen."

"Did you have a reason for calling me? Or did you just want to bitch?"

Gritting his teeth, he asked, "Any suggestions on where to hole up now?"

"The cabal in Anaheim has been eradicated. No one expects Torque to deal with it while both Syre and Vashti are in the field. You can have the entire compound to yourself. That'll put you close to Adrian, but you know how to stay out of sight. Your only concern now is to live the mortal life you've been coveting. Go get laid or kill something for the hell of it. I'll be in touch when it's time for you to rise from the ashes."

The line went dead. He crushed the burner phone to

dust in his fist, his gaze trained on the lights blazing from Helena's home across the street. Perhaps it was time to build his own army.

As he lifted into the air and flew away, the thought twisted through his mind . . . and found fertile ground in which to take root.

The sky was an ebony blanket of stars as Elijah drove Lindsay back to Adrian. As crappy as he'd felt just hours ago, he felt like a million dollars now. Life was good at the moment. The cool desert night air was whipping through the lowered windows and beside him sat one of his dearest friends, a woman to whom he owed his life . . . yet again. Her Sentinel-laced blood was amazingly powerful, its regenerative properties astonishing.

"Hey, you okay?" he asked, noting her staring pensively out at the desert. "You're not mad about the blindfold, are you? I went along with it only because it was safer for you. I trust you, you know. Always have."

He'd only made her wear the damn thing until they were out of sight of the warehouse. Then he'd tugged it off her himself and thrown it out the window.

"I wanted to wear it. I thought the same thing—the less of a threat I am, the better." She sighed. "I was thinking about my dad."

Remembering her heartbroken sobbing when she'd heard the news of her father's death, his chest ached with sympathy . . . and guilt. He'd handpicked the team of lycans tasked with watching over Eddie Gibson and keeping him safe. "Wanna talk about it?"

She twisted in her seat to look at him. "I want to talk to the lycans who were picked to guard him. I would've asked you back there, but I want to question them away from the vampires."

"I've got questions, too, but they haven't checked in since then."

Lindsay stiffened. "They disappeared?"

"I wouldn't put it like that. My guess? They're working their way to the West Coast on foot, trying to stay under the radar. What do you want to know?"

"That they're one hundred percent certain, without a shadow of a doubt, that his death was an accident."

"And you'll believe them?"

"If you do, I will."

Nodding, he asked, "Why do you doubt it?"

"Cars were his life, El. He was pure poetry behind the wheel. Honestly, I'd be more likely to buy a random drive-by shooting than I am a single-car accident. I've been with him when creatures have wandered into the road. He avoided a buck, for chrissakes, on a two-lane highway with oncoming traffic and didn't get a scratch on his car. It's damned hard for me to believe he overcorrected for an unknown obstruction on an isolated rural lane."

Hearing the pain and grief in Lindsay's voice, he set his mind to doing whatever it took to help her put the past behind her. She'd lost both parents before their time and he knew she was haunted by their deaths. "I'll find Trent and Lucas and bring them to you."

"Thank you." She leaned her head back into the

headrest. "You and Vashti . . . Correct me if I'm wrong, but there's something there, right?"

A dry laugh escaped him. "Don't ask me to explain."

"She went to a lot of trouble to save you. I take it she doesn't know you intend to avenge Micah?"

"She knows." He stared straight ahead, his gaze looking beyond the swathe of the headlights into the darkness beyond.

"But she saved your ass anyway?"

"She needs my help."

"Oh, El." Lindsay shook her head. "I'm sorry."

He glanced at her. "For what?"

"For the position you're in. I saw the way you look at her. For a guy who avoids trouble like the plague, you're deep in it now. It's not your style."

"Didn't realize I had a style."

"Don't be flippant about something that's bothering you. You've got my undivided attention between here and Vegas—take advantage of it. If you keep everything bottled up, you'll go nuts."

Elijah knew she was right. He couldn't talk about Vash with anyone else. No lycan or vampire would want to listen to him hash out what he was feeling for Syre's second. Shit, he didn't want to listen to it himself— would prefer to ignore it altogether—but the path that had seemed so clear in the beginning was now dark and murky. He could use someone else's input to help him find his way.

"If I have a type," he said finally, "she's it. Physically. I was hot for her the first time I saw her. You were tossing knives at her and I was thinking about doing something else with her entirely."

Lindsay choked out a laugh. "Jesus, El."

"Yeah, well . . . when she came to ask for help researching this vampire disease—they're calling it the Wraith Virus—I knew who she was and what she'd done to Micah. And she realized I was supposedly responsible for her friend Nikki's death. We straightened that out right away, but her guilt over Micah was never in question. We laid out our terms—I help her with the wraiths and she keeps the Sentinels off our backs; I help her find the lycans responsible for the death of her mate and she sets up her demise in a way that keeps Syre off my back."

Pinching the bridge of her nose, Lindsay sighed. "What a fucking mess."

"There was no way in hell I could concentrate with the sexual tension between us, so I threw that into the mix, too. But when it went down . . . it was rough. And a lot more personal than we were counting on."

"Is she your mate?"

"I told you before—it's not like that with lycans. Yes, there's an inherent level of instinct and physical chemistry that comes into play, but it doesn't dictate how things go. I'll choose my mate when the time comes, just like a mortal would."

"Mortals don't choose who they fall in love with. I would never have chosen to fall in love with Adrian, knowing how dangerous it is for him to be with me."

"We're not talking about love, Linds. This is physical."

She shot him a wry look. "You didn't see Vash in ac-

tion today, El. She went after Adrian. *Adrian*. I don't
believe she did it because of a pact with you or the need
for a booty call. She was too desperate and worried.
And if her big concern was info about her mate's killers, she could've asked Adrian while she had me with
a knife at my throat."

His grip tightened on the steering wheel. Vash had
been suicidal in her efforts to save his hide. In too deep.
Both of them.

Pulling her left knee up onto the seat, Lindsay adjusted her position so that she angled toward him.
"You're awfully quiet after what I just said."

"Like you said, there's something there. It's . . . complicated."

"Are you friends?"

"I wouldn't have called us that." Yet they'd put their
necks on the line for each other. Supported each
other . . . "But maybe. I guess."

"Can you let your anger about Micah go? If she cares
about you, just knowing you're hurting over what she
did could be punishment enough."

"I'm gonna have to let it go or stop screwing her. But
we've still got nowhere to take this."

"So you've thought about possibly continuing a relationship with her?"

"Only just now. With you pushing me to think about
it. I won't again after I drop you off." He didn't have
time to waste on impossibilities. "Ideally, I'll hit up
Adrian for the info she wants; he'll have it; Vash and I
will deal with it; and our association will end. Second
best scenario is us wrapping this up quick even with-

out Adrian's help. If we could just put some distance between us—"

"Didn't help with me and Adrian," she reminded. "Absence made the heart grow fonder."

"You're not helping. You're supposed to knock some sense into me. You hate her guts. Make me hate her guts, too."

"Next time. She saved your life today. I owe her for that."

"You saved my life, too. And not for the first time." As the light pollution of Vegas appeared in the distance, he said, "I don't want to lose touch with you, Linds. Promise me that won't happen."

"I promise you that won't happen."

He nodded, his mouth too dry to say anything in reply.

"I won't give up on you, El," she said firmly. "Don't you dare give up on me, or I'll hunt you down and bite you with my fangs."

Elijah was still smiling when they reached the city limits.

Vash crossed her arms and studied Syre's face. His posture was different, his carriage lighter. His eyes were less shadowed than they'd been just that afternoon.

"You look better," she said.

"I feel better." From their position just outside of Syre's warehouse office, they watched minions quietly make the necessary preparations for the sleeping lycans to head out at daybreak. They'd work in the field the same way—the lycans taking the day shift and the minions the night. "Are you certain it was a good idea to allow Elijah to escort Lindsay back?"

She shifted on her feet, hating to hear her own concern voiced aloud. "I can't allow or disallow Elijah anything. And if he's going to have second thoughts about this alliance, better he has them now instead of later."

"Hmm . . . the Vash I know would kill a lycan she couldn't trust rather than test him."

"Ha! If that was true, they'd all be dead. Besides, we don't have that option. He's the only Alpha around."

"You want him to choose you."

"Isn't that why you sent me to him to begin with?"

Syre turned so that he stood directly in front of her, forcing her to look at him. "I sent you to strengthen our position. Instead, you very nearly kicked off a war today."

She met his gaze, letting him see her disquiet. "The Sentinels aren't in any position to attack us. There are too few of them."

"You believe they'd wage a battle instead of a war. You're wrong. They won't come at us in a swarm. They'll pick away at us, hitting strategic targets and individuals, excising the most valuable players with surgical precision. What's left of us will be chaotic and easily overwhelmed."

"You're guessing," she shot back. "Adrian isn't at the top of his game now. He attacked me in full daylight on a public street! He's reckless and emotional."

"Yet he risked his most valuable possession, putting his mission first yet again—something I've always relied on you doing . . . until today."

"Elijah is pivotal to our plans. You said it yourself."

"Your responses are making me wonder if the Alpha is more of a liability than an asset," he said softly.

Vash schooled her features to show no emotion, even though the elevated rhythm of her heartbeat gave her away. "It's not the Alpha you're worried about—it's me. If you think I'm compromised, you should assign someone else to deal with him as I suggested in the beginning."

His arms crossed. "You misunderstand me, perhaps deliberately. I don't want to separate you from anything that makes you happy, and frankly, the Alpha's fascination for you works to my benefit. His hunger for you is a weakness. If we can control him with it, we'll have an even stronger advantage. But I can't allow anything or anyone to jeopardize the vampire nation, including you. Enjoy your lycan, Vashti, but don't forget where your priorities lie. Like you said, the time to have second thoughts is now."

Pressing the heels of her palms against her eyes, she cursed under her breath. Everything was screwed up. *She* was screwed up. Her priorities had shifted at some point, from the past to her present. Now the thought of manipulating Elijah like a puppet made her sick.

She dropped her arms and looked at him. "Pair him with Raze. It'll be best for everyone."

"Thank you," he said softly, pressing a kiss to her forehead. "Perhaps a bit of distance will clear your perspective and you'll be able to revisit. Do you want to tell him or should I?"

That Syre made the offer told her how shaky the

ground was that she walked on. For him to step up personally rather than delegate meant he gave the matter serious weight.

"No, I'll do it."

"He won't take it well." It wasn't a question.

Remembering how Elijah had responded the last time she tried to gain a little space, she smiled ruefully. "I don't know, but probably not."

"Use me if you need me." He dug into his pocket and she heard the rattle of keys. "I'm heading to Shred with some of the others. You're welcome to come."

"No, thanks. I'll see to the final prep here. I want to get this entire crew out tomorrow, so we can get the next wave in and debriefed. Hopefully we'll pick up some strays while we're out in the field; we need more than one outpost's worth of lycans."

"We'll dig into that in the morning. See you then."

Remembering something she should never have forgotten, Vash called after him. "Commander. Adrian took my blood."

He turned slowly back to her. "Why?"

"I don't know."

"We need to know. Something with the Wraith Virus, perhaps?"

"What else?"

"Find out." He left, his stride clipped with repressed violence.

Vash got to work on the composition of the teams she'd be sending out into the field in the morning. She'd hoped to tap Elijah for assistance with that, but he was still gone and they were already a day behind schedule.

Sitting at one of the computer workstations, she started creating groups based on physical characteristics, trying to create well-rounded teams of short and tall, big and small, heavy and slender.

The moment El returned, she felt it. The air in the room became charged with his energy . . . and the stirring animosity of the vampires who smelled him approaching.

He came back.

A shiver of excitement coursed through her, along with a flood of relief that nearly made her dizzy. She watched him approach with eyes that devoured every breathtakingly sexy inch, eyeing his confident stride and the sleek fluidity of his movements. And she wasn't the only one awed by the air of command that clung to him. His path across the open space between them was tracked by everyone, but his eyes were locked on her. Hot and fiercely determined. Filled with admiration, but nothing close to deference.

God, he was gorgeous. Beautiful, really, although she'd never call him that to his face. He was too fiercely masculine to be even remotely pretty. And his body . . . so hard and strong. Defined by slabs of powerful muscle. She remembered how it felt to have all that power against her. Over her. Inside her . . .

The other vampresses in the room eyed him with equal avidness, lust burning along with distrust and lingering resentment. She wasn't completely off her rocker for being sexually attracted to a lycan, but the quantity of female attention Elijah received was beginning to chafe. He wasn't available for that kind of interest and she wanted everyone to know it. To respect it.

He paused by a table of vamps putting together travel packets of cash, debit cards, IDs, and cell phones. He thanked them for their hard work, offered to help, and smiled genuinely when it was refused with less hostility than had been displayed when he'd walked in.

The smile stayed in place as he headed toward her, but it took on a wicked, sexy edge that sizzled through her.

"Hey," he said when he stopped beside her. He looked at the computer screen and shook his head. "You can't put Luke and Thomas in the same group. They'll fight. And Nicodemus has a thing for Bethany and so does Horatio. It's best if you don't put her in a group with either one of them."

"Fuck it all." She pushed back from the desk. Of course he knew such personal details. He took the time to know everyone. "I've been working on this for over an hour."

"You got the vamps lined up straight? Then don't worry about the rest. I'll make the adjustments to the lycans."

"By morning?" Studying him up close, she noted the exhaustion that rimmed his eyes and mouth. "You're beat."

"I could use sleep," he agreed. "But it won't take much."

She stood and rocked back on her heels. What she really wanted to do was step forward into him. He smelled delicious. She knew he tasted that way, too. All over. Inside and out. "Can I talk to you a moment?"

She led the way to one of the offices. It was dark inside, as was most of the warehouse, to accommodate the sleeping lycans. Neither she nor Elijah required light to see, which was working to her benefit now. By keeping the lights off, he would be less likely to read anything on her face she didn't want him to.

The door had barely shut behind them when she found herself in his arms, his lips cool and firm on hers. Caught at the waist and nape, she was held immobile against him. Claimed. She gasped in surprised pleasure, and the kiss swiftly heated. His tongue slid deep and slow into her mouth, thrusting in a steady unhurried rhythm that made her ache for more. Much more, damn it.

She slid one hand through his hair and the other up beneath his shirt. He arched and groaned at her touch, as responsive to her as she was to him.

"Thank you," he whispered huskily against her parted lips.

Vash swallowed, trying to hang on to the wits that would enable her to tell him about their altered working relationship. The exquisite taste of him sidetracked her, scattering her reason.

He nuzzled his nose against hers. "I brought back some news that might make you happier about keeping me alive."

She was *too* happy about that. Already she was dreading his getting on a separate plane from her tomorrow, one that would take him to the opposite side of the country from where she'd be. She was glad now that she hadn't plugged either of their names into her outlined groups. He would have seen straightaway, and they might be arguing now instead of kissing. Elijah was a damned good kisser. He took his time with it, as he did with everything, savoring the act as if he didn't care if anything more intimate followed it.

But *she* cared. Sixty years without sexual desire and suddenly being naked with Elijah was damn near all she thought about.

"I want you." The words were out of Vash's mouth before she realized she'd thought them. Mortified, her head fell forward to press her forehead into his shoulder. She just had to get through another six hours until they parted, a few of which he'd sleep through. "Forget I said that."

"Why?" His hand at her waist dropped to the curve of her ass and molded her into the thick ridge of his erection.

Her entire body lit up like a live wire. He was hard and ready for her, and she craved him—one last time before she sent him on his way with Raze and got her head back in the game. "You need to take it easy and get some rest. Tomorrow, we hit the ground running."

"So you do all the work. I'll just kick back and come."

She bit him in the pectoral with her fangs.

"Ow! Damn it." He shoved her back. "Go easy on me. I'm in recovery."

"Which is why you need sleep, not sex." But god, he tasted good. She licked her lips, making sure she didn't miss a drop.

His eyes glittered in the darkness. "You've revved me up. Now the sleep won't come without the sex."

"Cry me a river. Listen, I have something to tell you."

He covered her mouth with his hand. "I called mine first."

Vash growled. His grin flashed before he released her.

"Get on with it, then," she snapped.

"Can't." There was nothing even remotely apologetic in his tone. He popped open the brass snaps holding her vest together and took possession of a heavy, tender breast. "All the blood has flowed into my other brain. Have to take care of that first."

The sheer audacity of his statement stunned her silent for a moment. "What's gotten into you?"

Whatever it was, she liked the effect it had on him. He was a serious guy by nature; this more relaxed version was hitting many of her hot buttons.

"I'm about to get laid by the hottest woman on the planet. That tends to cheer a guy up. Plus, I've got a present for you. It may not be quite as lifesaving as the one you brought me today, but hopefully it'll turn out that way."

Warmth twisted through her, along with shards of near-painful delight as he tugged on her nipple with his thumb and forefinger. "What is it?"

"I've got a lead on Charron's killers."

Her breath clogged behind a tight throat. "What . . . ? How . . . ?"

"Adrian." Elijah pulled her closer. "I asked him

what he knew. He'd heard the rumors about your mate and sent Jason to investigate. The lycans who admitted to being involved were interviewed. He doesn't recall their names or what their story was, only that they didn't relay the events the way you told them to me or he would've terminated them himself."

"Sure he would have."

"Vashti, he was never told Charron had been slaughtered in the manner you described. He knew only that your mate was dead and lycans were involved. If he'd heard differently, he would've had the matter looked into more closely. I believe that."

"He wouldn't give a shit."

"I think you're wrong."

"Whatever. I've known him a hell of a lot longer than you have." She blew her hair off her face and pushed away. Refastening her vest, she began to pace. "I need names, El. I don't care what those lycans said. I *know* what I saw and I know Char. He would never have done anything worthy of a death like that. He was a kind, gentle-hearted man."

"The interviews were recorded on tape, then later transferred to disk and uploaded to a backup cloud."

"Did he give you copies?"

"No. And he doesn't have the password to access them."

"Bullshit. He's lying."

He crossed his arms and looked straight into her eyes. "No, Vashti. He isn't. Each outpost has a separate log-in to the cloud. It was a safety precaution that prevented a full-system breach at the outpost level. I know he's right because Stephan broke into the system at Navajo Lake. There was no access to information about the other outposts."

"So who has the password?"

"Jason and Armand. Unfortunately, Jason was at Navajo Lake and Armand was still at the Huntington outpost—where the interviews were taken—when the revolt happened. Both Sentinels are presently considered missing in action."

She strode up to him and gripped his belt loops. "*You* can get the data."

"If there's anything left of the place, yes. But regardless, the names of those lycans are in the cloud. So even if Huntington is trashed, it won't be the end of the road."

Taking a deep breath, Vash struggled to get her emotions under control. If pressed, she wouldn't have been able to identify them. Elation, maybe. Fear, certainly. More than a little confusion, as well. Where did one go when they reached the end of the road? And twining through the mess of her mind was her acute awareness of the man she held on to. She was working on something for Char while in a compromising position with another man and she didn't feel guilty. She searched for the sense that she was doing something wrong . . . being disloyal . . . but she didn't find it.

"I can't tell you what this means to me, Elijah," she said quietly.

His warm hands encircled her wrists. "Then show me."

CHAPTER 12

Amused by his very male one-track mind, Vash scoped out the furnishings in the small room. "The choices are limited here, sex fiend: desktop or the floor. I'm lacking a penis, so I can't nail you against the wall. And every chair in this room has arms, so straddling you is impossible."

"Where's your imagination?" Letting her go, Elijah tugged his shirt over his head. She was so focused on looking for any lingering injuries that she missed him toeing off his boots. Her hands were sliding over his torso, feeling for wounds she might have missed with her night vision when his jeans hit the floor.

The full force of his nudity hit her and she hissed, riveted by his blatant masculinity.

"Say it again," he demanded.

She unstuck her tongue from the roof of her mouth. "Huh?"

"What you wanted me to forget you said."

Her gaze lifted to his, found his eyes feverishly bright. She wanted those eyes on her, sliding over her with their heat and hunger. No one had ever looked at her quite that way, with a desire that was untamed and wild.

She shrugged out of her vest and tossed it aside. Balancing on one foot, she unzipped one boot, then followed up with the other. As she pushed her pants down her legs, he sank into a chair, settling back and watching avidly.

"Say it, Vashti." The rumble lacing his words was almost a purr. It drifted over and around her like warm tendrils of smoke.

Straightening, she kicked her pants aside.

"I want you"—she deliberately paused— "to let me do all the work. You were torn up good today."

"I'll promise not to overly exert myself and we'll call it square."

"Not good enough."

"Don't trust me?"

"I could tie you up again, maybe. But you'd fuck us both to death for it."

"You can't top me, Vashti," he said harshly. "That's not what you need. Not what you want. Don't ever try again."

She approached him. Gripping the back of his chair, she lowered her lips to his brow and breathed him in, letting the scent of his skin slide through her. Soothing her.

He *knew* her, saw *through* her. She didn't know how, but he did . . .

Whatever. It didn't matter. This was the last time they'd have this; their association was coming to a close. Soon she'd be the Vashti *she* knew, the one everyone needed her to be. Once she had Charron's killers beneath her boot heels, she'd honor her end of their bargain. They'd both have what they really wanted, which—contrary to the way things were going at that moment—wasn't each other. "Tonight will be slow and easy."

The fingertips of his right hand skimmed lightly along the outside of her thigh. The caress was barely there, yet it reverberated through her in waves of warmth and need. That he didn't do more, didn't take over, gave her the chance to wipe the slate clean between them.

I need that, too, she thought. Needed to leave him with a different memory than the one from Shred.

"Show me how to work around this damned chair," she muttered, although just the thought of wriggling and squirming over his hard body made her wet.

"Stand back first. Lemme look at you."

She straightened slowly. Stepping back, she thrust her hands through her hair and piled it on top of her head. Arching her back, Vash posed like a '50s pinup.

He breathed roughly, his hands fisting around the ends of the armrests. "My god, Vashti . . ."

It was the note of awed pleasure in his voice that pierced her, slicing through her defenses to strike the tender places within. A shiver moved through her.

"You're so damn gorgeous," he growled. "Lush and curvy. Fucking perfect. And you're so strong. Strong and tough."

There was possession in the way he spoke. And she relished that, which confused her. She was a woman who took care of herself. Always had been. Char had known that about her and hadn't been territorial. She had a job to do, one that outranked his, and he'd stayed to the side and let her do it, following her commands when she gave them to him. That's what she needed from her mate, what she wanted . . . Support. Acceptance.

Yet Elijah's dominant streak turned her on like crazy.

Turning slowly, she hid how shaken she was by presenting him with her back.

"Come closer. Back up to me," he ordered, reminding her that he'd never stand to the side. He would always require her surrender, even as he praised and admired her strength and toughness.

His splayed hand caressed the length of her back, gentling her. "Bend over."

Knowing how exposed she'd be in the position he wanted her in, she leaned forward slowly, widening the spread of her legs to better support her canted weight. His hands cupped the backs of her thighs in the crease just below the curve of her buttocks. His thumbs rubbed gently over the lips of her sex, parting her, opening her to his gaze.

"Mmm . . . you're wet and soft already."

She swallowed hard, then bit her lip to stifle a moan. His breath fanned hot and humid over her most sensitive flesh. Her hands went to her knees, adding support to keep her from toppling onto her face.

"I'll make you wetter," he promised darkly, the moment before he licked leisurely across her swollen cleft.

She gasped, the sound overly loud in the quiet room. It was exciting to be willing and ready for him. Bereft of control.

His tongue swiped over her again. The texture was rougher than before, like wet velvet, and the reach longer. She moaned in delight, wondering if he'd made that slight shift in form for her pleasure or his. Either was equally arousing. The last time they'd been together, he'd arranged her the way he wanted her and *taken* her. Taken what he needed, how he needed it, and expected her to find her pleasure in giving it to him. Which she had. She'd never come so hard or often, never experienced ecstasy so fierce and wild. No boundaries. No limits.

His groan vibrated against her. "Your taste drives me insane. I could eat you for hours. Days. Lick up every sweet, creamy drop of you."

The next glide of his tongue teased her slick opening, rimming it in leisurely circles that had her straining toward him. He kept her in place with his easy grip, nudging her clitoris with the tip of his tongue and humming a soft chastisement.

"Elijah," she complained.

"Elijah . . . what?"

Her teeth grit. "Elijah, please."

"Please . . . what?"

She couldn't stop the frustrated noise that escaped her. "Please don't be an ass."

"But I can't rush," he said smoothly, "or I might overly exert myself and break my promise."

"Using your *tongue*?"

When she attempted to straighten, he kept her in place with a hand at the small of her back. "Is it so difficult, letting me take the lead?"

"Yes." No. That was what chafed the most. Sure, he was an Alpha, but he wasn't *her* Alpha. And for her people, *she* was damn near the Alpha. What would they think if they could see her now?

"Even though doing so brings you pleasure?" he prodded.

Vash looked at him over her shoulder. He was looking right back at her, not at the slick hot flesh quivering for more of his attention. Prurient interest would have soothed her, oddly. His focus on her reactions and her emotions was far more intimate.

"I'm not one of the countless bitches sniffing around after you," she snapped. "Subservience isn't in my nature."

"Good. Women without backbones make me twitchy." He kissed her, right on the ass. "You've got a great rack, but even your spectacular tits wouldn't be enough to keep me interested past the first screw. That must mean I'm in this for your charming tendency to bark orders and run everything around you . . . except for me, of course. Now, finish your damn sentence: Elijah, please do what? You want me to do whatever I want with you? Say so. You want to give me some direction, go for it. I'm open to suggestions."

Her gaze moved to the floor. Damn it, she wanted to direct him *and* she wanted him to do whatever he wanted. She didn't know which one she wanted more.

So she split it down the middle.

"Elijah." She exhaled in a rush. "Please lick me until I come. Then do whatever the hell you want with me."

"Thought you'd never ask, sweetheart."

If the hand at the small of her back hadn't reached around to clasp the front of her thigh, Vash would have fallen over with his first deep lick. He used his mouth as only a creature who relied on it as much as he did his hands would. The stroking of his crushed-velvet tongue was rhythmic and precise; the tempo of his thrusts into her needy sex had her rocking back on her heels, trying to capture the perfect pressure that would push her into orgasm. She could see him between her legs, see how thick he was. How rigid and long. The heavily veined length so brutally beautiful. Just like the man himself. She wanted it . . . wanted him . . .

Christ. She wanted so fiercely, it hurt. Her breath soughed from her lungs; her nipples were hard and tight. Her stomach concaved with her helpless writhing, desperate whimpers escaping her as he massaged her clitoris with the roughened pad of his tongue.

"Please," she begged, when she couldn't take another minute.

"Yes." He gave a fierce, quick suck, and she climaxed with a relieved cry, shuddering violently as the pleasure broke over her in rippling spasms.

As her legs shook and threatened to collapse, Elijah drew her into his lap and urged her to lean against his chest. Her head lolled on his shoulder, his scent filling her nostrils and intoxicating her already floating senses. The feel of him against her back, so solid and warm and strong, made her never want to move. His arms came around her, one hand cupping her breast while the other caught her knee and widened the spread of her legs.

"Guide me," he whispered against her cheek. "Put me inside you."

Swallowing past a dry throat, she fisted him in her hand, pumping his cock from root to tip. Once. Twice. Then more. He was so hard, and she was enamored with the feel of him and the effect she had on him. He was rumbling his pleasure in her ear, his chest vibrating against her back. Her hand grew slick with his semen as his excitement built, her own body responding to his hands on her breasts. With practiced skill, he kneaded the heavy flesh, his talented fingers rolling and tugging on the sensitive tips.

"You're gonna make me come," he warned, his teeth scraping along the top of her shoulder.

"That's the goal, isn't it?"

"If all I wanted was an orgasm, I'd have skipped the long walk across the warehouse and taken the offer I got in the parking lot."

Her fist tightened on him and he made a noise that was half groan and half laugh. Damn him, he knew she hated how females salivated over him. He was deliberately pushing her in the direction he wanted her to go and she complied anyway. Because she had the right to take what other women could only hope for.

Rising, she gained the height needed to position the wide crest of his cock against her. One deep breath later and she was lowering onto him, her eyes closing as he filled her, stretched her. She was tight in this position, squeezing down on him, making him work to claim her.

His low groan of pleasure was so erotically charged she almost came from the sound of it. It was laced with a whisper of his own surrender, reminding her that they were equally captured by their all-consuming desire. Equally helpless to fight the pull of attraction between them.

With his hands caging her ribs just below her breasts, he controlled the speed and angle of her descent, increasing her awareness of every ragingly aroused inch of him as he possessed her. As she possessed him in return. Her hair fell over his shoulder, and her hips began to circle without volition. Her arms came up and behind her to push her fingers into his thick, dark hair.

"Mmm . . ." She moaned. "Feels so good."

"There's more."

"Yes . . . more." Vash went lax in his arms and let him have his way.

He eased her lower, effortlessly supporting her weight. She wasn't a small woman. She was tall, with an overabundance of curves. She'd never in her life felt delicate, but Elijah made her feel more feminine than anyone ever had besides Char. It was a feeling she relished—to be something other than a vampire, someone other than Syre's lieutenant.

Once he was to the hilt in her, he embraced her from behind. His arms reached around her and crossed over her chest. Sweat coated the skin between them, sealing them together. Her thighs splayed along the top of his; his teeth nipped at her shoulder. Inside her, he throbbed. She was utterly claimed. She felt it, even though he didn't say it.

Elijah reached between her legs, found her exposed clitoris and massaged gently with the pads of two fingers. She climaxed with a breathless cry. His soft growl of satisfaction spurred her hunger, kept her on the edge so that she wanted more. More of him and the way he made her feel.

"I love the way you squeeze me when you're coming," he whispered. "You tighten around me . . . milk me . . . Do it again."

Her hands fell to the arms of the chair and she straightened away from him. As her body leaned forward, he pressed even deeper, the sensation so exquisitely sublime she almost came again. She couldn't explain how or why he was such an aphrodisiac to her, but there was no denying he was. Everything about him was a delight to her senses, keeping her primed and ready.

His lips slid gently over her back, the tender gesture making her throat tighten. "Ride me, Vashti. Fuck me until I can't take any more."

She did, starting out the first half-hour slow and easy as she'd promised, relishing his white-knuckled response. She lost herself in the rhythmic flux and flow, in the steady lift and fall of her hips . . . the in-and-out glide of his body into hers . . . the rush and ebb of need as she timed her movements to the sounds of his breathing. Slowing when he gasped, quickening when he quieted.

She could have gone on like that forever, but the feel

of his fingers between them, circling the base of his cock, brought her scattered mind into focus. He stiffened a moment, then a ferocious orgasm tore through him. He shook so violently, the chair quaked as if rocked by an earthquake, his teeth grinding audibly, the claws of his free hand piercing the solid metal armrests as if they were made of tinfoil. He came long and hard . . . yet he didn't. The expected wash of heat never followed.

Oh, no, you don't, she thought grimly, determined to break his steely control.

Vash took his knowledge and skill, his ability to hold back ejaculating even while he climaxed, as a challenge. He was too contained. Too reasoned. While she'd been damn near insensate with pleasure.

Setting her hands over his, she pinned them down with her weight.

Then, *she* took *him.* Not like the first time. Never again like that. This time, she chained him with desire, his and hers, and the delights of her body. She drove him hard and fast, giving him no quarter, forcing him to the precipice at a speed he couldn't back away from.

"Vashti," he gasped, then he cursed viciously. Swearing at her, telling her to slow down, hold on, give him a minute.

When he came this time, it was harder than before, his breath heaving from his lungs, his legs straining beneath hers as he shot hotly into her. She felt him go off, relished his shout of her name. Feminine satisfaction pumped through her, kicking off her orgasm to catch the tail end of his.

His arms banded around her, crushing her tightly against him. They succumbed to their desire together.

As the sun rose over the desert sands, Elijah found himself greeting the new day in the best shape of his life. No mean feat, considering he'd been on his death-bed the day before. His wounds had healed without scarring, and his strength was back in spades. Whether that was due to the Sentinel blood pumping through him or the lingering charge from a night spent with a warm and passionate Vashti, he couldn't say.

Fuck me until I can't take any more.

Hell if Vashti hadn't taken him at his word. He'd tried to hold back, tried to make it last. For her sake as well as his. She'd been enjoying him so much, taking her plea-sure with unabashed delight, instinct driving her into a primal state of animal need and desire where her body had silenced the doubts and anger in her mind . . .

"Alpha."

He looked over his shoulder at Raze, who wore black dress slacks and a gray silk shirt, the quiet ele-gance of his attire making him almost unrecognizable. Pivoting to catch the mini-duffel the vampire threw at him, Elijah asked, "What's up?"

"Let's go. You can change at the airport after we check in."

Brows raised, he glanced at Syre's office door. Vashti had disappeared behind it about twenty minutes be-fore, leaving him to get the last few teams on the road while she updated the vampire leader about her per-sonal plans to visit the Huntington post.

"Her orders." Raze had the decency to refrain from gloating. "She put you with me last night."

Ah. Now he knew what she'd wanted to talk to him about before desire distracted them, just as he knew she'd changed her mind and planned on heading out to Huntington with him instead.

Shaking his head, he adjusted his grip on the bag in his hand and grabbed his shades from the desk. Changed mind or not, they had a few things to work out. She needed to learn that making decisions and giving orders relating to him—relating to *them*—required both of them. "Let's roll."

They walked to the door abreast of each other.

The hell of it was, Elijah understood why she'd want the distance, and he understood that it was the information he'd dug up about Charron's killers that had altered her plans. If she'd bothered to talk with him about it, he would've told her he didn't care if she was attracted to him for info, sex, or access to the lycans—anything could serve as a foundation for a relationship between them, something he'd decided he had to pursue because he couldn't keep his hands or his mind off her.

What troubled him was the hour or so they'd spent together after they'd sated their hunger for each other. An hour during which they'd gone over the composition of the teams. An hour during which she hadn't said a goddamn word about shoving him off on someone else. He'd even asked her point blank what it was she had wanted to talk to him about and she'd evaded the question with a breezy reply.

As Salem had said, they had nothing if she wasn't going to talk to him.

"Where are we headed?" he asked as they stepped outside.

"Seattle."

With an earsplitting whistle, Elijah stopped two Jeeps that were pulling out of the lot. He approached the first driver and asked for her team's orders, then switched them with the team in the car behind them. He tossed Raze's orders into the mix so that all three teams were reassigned. Then he reminded the lycans that his cell phone number was programmed in their contact lists.

"Don't hesitate to call me," he said to each team, "for anything. Even if you just want to talk, I'm here for you."

As the two SUVs resumed their exit from the lot, Elijah glanced at his new partner. "Now we're going to Shreveport."

Which was apropos, since it was Nikki's abduction from the city that had first brought him to Vash's attention and vice versa. Micah had been mortally wounded there, tortured by Vash in an effort to glean Elijah's identity and location.

"You think she'll come looking for you," the vamp surmised.

He tossed his duffel in the backseat of the Jeep Raze selected. No reply was necessary, so Elijah didn't give one.

"You're holding yourself in high esteem, Alpha."

Raze slid behind the wheel. "But after what she did for you yesterday, I guess you have a right to."

"Mind your own business," he warned without heat. "She's safe with me."

The vampire pulled out of the lot, leaving a small sand cloud in their wake. "There's an off chance I might come to like you."

"I won't hold my breath."

"Yeah . . . I wouldn't recommend it."

"We need to get that cooler to Grace." Vash jerked her chin at the red and white ice chest on Syre's desk.

He lifted the lid and frowned at the contents. "What's all this?"

"The stuff we used to transfuse Lindsay's blood into Elijah."

Syre's gaze met hers. "You're suspicious. Because Adrian sent her instead of a bag of blood?"

"I saw his eyes when I had a knife to her throat. He'd bleed for her and wouldn't think twice. So why didn't he?" She paced. "I wish I knew what she'd said to him while I was knocked out in the back of the car."

"You think she talked him into letting her come. Why?"

"I know she did. And she did it for him, of course. Hasn't everything she's done been for him?"

"But wasn't this as much about the Alpha?"

"Yeah, she came for Elijah, too." Her hands fisted and she clasped them behind her back to hide the tell-tale movement. "But that wouldn't have been enough for Adrian to let her go. There's something else. After all, what she gave us was pretty much Adrian's blood, filtered. Why was that acceptable and not the pure stuff? I'm hoping Grace can figure it out."

Closing the cooler, Syre leaned back against his desk and tracked her movements with his gaze. "Grace is busy researching the Wraith Virus."

"Then we get someone else. We need more lab rats anyway. Every day that passes, the infection spreads. If we don't get a lid on this, we're going to give Adrian the excuse he needs to take us all out. We need to test lycan blood as well. The wraiths were all over Elijah. They completely ignored me and Salem, but ingesting El's blood killed them. I know we want a cure, but we may not have the luxury of one. We may need to take the infected down for damage control, and if lycan blood is poisonous to them, we should know that."

"I'll look into some suitable 'lab rat' candidates. As for lycan blood, it could be the touch of demon in them that's the culprit."

"Well, there's an endless supply of demons. If we need to test them, too, I'll round some up when I get back."

"You're heading out?"

She stopped pacing and told him about Elijah's queries to Adrian.

"And Adrian just gave up this information voluntarily?" Syre crossed his arms. "To the very lycan who's weakened his position so drastically?"

"I'm sure Lindsay argued on Elijah's behalf. Again."

"She's that close to the Alpha? Is there something between them?"

Vash exhaled harshly. "Friendship. Adrian would've killed him if it was anything else. Actually, maybe they're more like family—siblings or close cousins. She gave up her mortal life to be with Adrian; I can't imagine she had many close ties to be able to do that so easily. And Elijah . . . he's somewhat of a lone wolf. He's a hands-on leader, but he doesn't share so much as he supports. What few friends he has are valuable to him."

He'd kill for them. Was planning on killing her for one of them. That Lindsay was one of the rare and fortunate people to occupy that inner circle in Elijah's life irritated Vash to no end. Knowing there was nothing romantic involved didn't stem her irrational jealousy. And thinking about just how much Micah must have meant to Elijah sent acidic surges of guilt through her. She'd learned long ago not to nurse regrets. It was too dangerous to do so when living an endless life. But hurting Elijah as she had . . . for a crime he'd turned out to be innocent of . . . it ate at her.

"So you're taking him with you to Huntington?" Syre asked.

"Yes. I told you my price in the beginning—I'd round him up for you, but I get what I need from him, too."

His mouth curved. "I haven't forgotten."

"I'll check in and keep you apprised. It shouldn't

take long." She was eager to get going. Not just to get the task done but to work alongside Elijah. In the tasks they'd tackled together so far, he'd balanced her. Leveled her out. And she'd done the same for him. They worked well together.

It was his more intimate effect on her that knocked her off kilter.

"Be careful, Vashti. And watchful for traps. His authority is still being established, and he'll be challenged often. I don't want you caught in the crosshairs. No one wants to see what I'd do if something happened to you."

She caught his hand and squeezed, grateful for him and his faith in her, something that must have been hard to maintain in the years since Charron died.

Opening the office door, she strode out into an eerily quiet warehouse. Not a soul moved in the cavernous space and while it might have been possible that Elijah was in one of the offices, she knew right away he was gone. She felt the void, and her stomach knotted, a reaction that set off her temper. She wasn't mad that he'd left—it didn't take a genius to figure out what must have unfolded while she was distracted—but it infuriated her that it rocked her to find him gone. It stung that he had been able to leave without a fight after she'd struggled with just the thought of it.

Grabbing a set of car keys off the wall rack, Vash was halfway to the door when it opened and the next busload of lycans poured in, brought to her courtesy of Salem, who'd headed out before dawn to pick them up.

"Fuckin' A." She was trapped until she and Salem

could get the new teams squared away. Elijah had plugged in his suggestions for team compositions that morning, which would save her time, but there was no way she'd catch him before his flight left the ground.

Her anger simmering, she hung the keys back up and got to work.

CHAPTER 13

Elijah knew something was off the moment he turned his rental vehicle onto a residential street in a suburban neighborhood on the outskirts of Shreveport, Louisiana. Although it was early evening, he thought there were too many cars in evidence, especially considering how few lights were on in the homes. When he unfolded from the economy sedan, his sense of unease deepened.

It was too quiet. Almost deathly so. No birds chirping, no dogs barking, no television sets or radios. With his hearing, he should be hearing toilets flushing, people chatting, dinner simmering.

Rolling his shoulders back, he repeated what Lindsay had said when they'd first arrived in Hurricane, Utah, moments before they'd found a nest of wraiths: "This place crawls."

"Shit." Raze looked at him over the roof of the car. "I was hoping it was just me."

"Bound to catch a snag at some point."

"Thought we'd already done that," Raze groused.

Elijah grinned. They'd hit the ground running, renting a car at the airport and heading immediately to the home of the vampire who'd first called in a concern to Syre. That visit had introduced them to a very pretty male vamp who went by the name of Minolo. The leggy blond had buzzed them into his UV-blocked apartment and proceeded to serve lemon cookies and tea in floral cups with saucers. Minolo had taken an instant shine to Raze, and over the hour they'd stayed to conduct the interview, the vamp had flirted and fluttered his mascara-coated lashes at Vashti's captain with warm invitation.

"Not interested," Raze had growled finally.

"I can fix that, sugar," the blond shot back with a saucy wink.

Elijah had stepped in then, just to avoid bloodshed, redirecting Minolo's attention to the reason they'd come. They'd learned it was an interview conducted by the local authorities that first roused Minolo's suspicions. He'd waylaid the investigation into the disappearance of a former lover with a bit of vampire mind compulsion; then he'd started digging around on his own. Minolo was the gossip center of the area's vampire community, and it hadn't taken more than a couple of days to ascertain that several vampires he was familiar with were no longer being seen around town.

Elijah and Raze's subsequent five-hour canvas of the city had turned up enough information to let them know there was definitely a problem in Shreveport.

They'd worked their way outward from Minolo's residence in an ever-widening circle, interviewing the neighbors of vamps gone missing.

Most of the minions they'd inquired after worked nights, so their neighbors had scant opportunity to observe their comings and goings. In those cases, he and Raze would appear to drive away, only to return shortly after to enter those residences on the sly. They checked out the interiors and found empty homes, which led to a grim conclusion—there were too many minions whose whereabouts were unaccounted for in the bright light of day.

But the subdivision they'd just driven into was by far the most concerning.

"We'll need backup," Elijah said. "At the very least, the two minions we've got coming in on the red-eye to take the nightshift, but ideally more than that. I'd say a team of a dozen or more."

"Want to reconnoiter? We've got a bit of daylight now."

"Won't help. We had daylight in Vegas and three of us."

Raze rubbed a hand over his shaved head. "I hate walking away. Makes me feel like a pussy."

"I don't like it either, but it's best. Trust me." Elijah got back into the car. "We'll hit up the tech team to access the layout of this subdivision and we'll get a plan in place for tomorrow."

"Fuck." Raze took another look around. "All right."

Elijah didn't discount how easily the vamp had ceded to the advice of a lycan. Whether that was because he was banging Raze's commanding officer or because of his own merits, he couldn't say, but he'd take it for now. Eventually they would all trust him. Because he'd earn it.

They headed back to the motel, changed into jeans and T-shirts, and decided to make dinner easy by hitting up the adjacent restaurant on foot. They'd chosen to stay in a rural area, far from the city. Pine forest surrounded the uninspired motel they were bedding down in, which Elijah found soothing, something his mood needed after hitting a road bump with Vash. Every minute that passed brought him closer to their inevitable confrontation. He was ready for it now, on edge because of a fruitless hunt and the aggravation of separation.

Settling into a booth, he ordered two of the house special and a beer. As the waitress walked away, he and Raze leaned back to size each other up, something they'd avoided doing earlier because the job came first.

Elijah took special care with his examination, having learned that Vashti rarely went anywhere without Raze or Salem—usually both—in tow. Both vampire captains were big for their kind; the Fallen were usually slender and elegantly built, their bodies having been made for flight. Salem was the bigger of the two, towering at a good six feet six inches and easily two hundred and fifty pounds of pure muscle. Raze was similar to Elijah's size of six feet three inches and a solid two hundred and twenty pounds.

But Vashti was a powerful woman, tall and leanly muscular, a renowned expert with all weaponry. She didn't need bodyguards. And from a resources stand-point, it didn't seem wise for Syre to tie three of his best Fallen together.

"So what's your story, Alpha?" Raze drawled. While Elijah wasn't much of a judge when it came to male attractiveness, he'd noted the number of female glances that followed the vamp when he had stepped outside to take a call.

"I'll tell you mine, if you tell me yours."

Raze snorted. "I suppose you want me to focus on my story as it relates to Vash."

He didn't deny it. "She carries a lot of manpower in you and Salem, but she's strong and smart. She can take care of herself."

"She's still a woman."

Elijah took a long pull on his beer and absorbed that. He knew damn well Raze and Salem had a healthy re-spect for Vashti or they wouldn't be taking orders from her. Which meant the mention of her sex wasn't gender bias.

Women were vulnerable to attack in ways men rarely were.

Syre, Raze, and Salem were all fiercely protective. And the way she'd first had sex with him . . . restrain-ing him . . . trying to maintain total control . . .

"Lycans?" Elijah asked tightly, fury simmering in his blood.

"I don't know what you're talking about."

So . . . Raze wouldn't discuss Vash outright, he'd only allude. Elijah respected that, even as he hungered for more information.

Raze draped his arm along the window ledge. "You know what we were before—Watchers. After we fell, we had to figure out what to do with ourselves. We all had different areas of knowledge, and that's where we focused our efforts. Vashti specialized in armaments—how to create them and use them. Even as a scholar, she was a warrior."

The note of affection in Raze's voice tightened Elijah's grip on his bottle. "I can see that."

"At the time, we thought maybe we just needed to earn our way back into the Creator's good graces. Pay a penance of some sort. Make amends. Vash took to hunting demons, which came in handy later on when they started fucking with us. We were the throwaway angels, the ones they thought they'd have carte blanche to screw around with." Raze exhaled audibly. "Syre wanted to take a more diplomatic approach, while Vash was more aggressive. Since she was the one in the field, her way prevailed. It's a fuckin' major understatement to say she wasn't popular in the demon community."

"Jesus . . ." Elijah fell heavily into the booth back. He'd seen the leavings of demon attacks. Just the thought of that sort of damage in any relation whatsoever to Vashti made his stomach knot.

"And demons like to kick you when you're down. The death of a mate is one of those perfect times for them."

Teeth grinding, he bit out, "She said Syre took care of it. Is that right?"

"Yeah. He took care of it. When he was done with

them, he dumped their ashes into a trash can and sent them back to their liege."

Elijah bitterly regretted that he wouldn't be able to exact vengeance of his own. The feeling of impotence was so sharp it was painful. "What was your specialty?"

"Triage."

Scrubbing a hand over his face, Elijah pulled everything together and created a picture that gnawed at his gut. "Jesus," he said again, remembering how roughly he'd taken her in Vegas, how completely he'd dominated her.

Raze smiled at the waitress when she returned with Elijah's food. She smiled back, her eyes bright with interest. She asked Raze twice if he was sure she couldn't get him anything and he replied that he was just waiting for her to go on break, if she was of the mind to share it with him. Which she was, of course.

"Sex will limber you," Raze said to Elijah once she'd walked away. "You might want to grab a piece of ass before tomorrow, especially considering how close you came to croaking yesterday. This might be your last chance to get laid."

"I'm touched you care, but my sex life is none of your business."

"You like redheads, right? There's a honey of a redhead that just walked in. You might get lucky." Raze whistled. "Damn, you didn't even look. Vash must have you wrapped around her little finger."

Elijah finished chewing his first bite of an excellent rare tri-tip. "Is that supposed to make me feel like a douche? I don't see any problem with knowing when you've got it good and sticking with it."

"Just 'cuz it's good, doesn't mean you can't get better."

"Christ, man." He popped a hush puppy into his mouth and decimated it in two bites. "You lost your wings over a woman. You can't have forgotten what it feels like."

A shadow passed over Raze's features, erasing all levity. "It wasn't like that for me. I wasn't as noble as the others. I was banging everything that let me."

Chewing his steak, Elijah wondered if that made Raze feel more culpable than the others or less.

The vamp shrugged off his sudden dark mood. "Anyway. There was one later on . . . not too long ago . . ."

Elijah set aside the now-empty bowl that once held collard greens and dropped a cleaned rib bone into it.

"Holy shit, Alpha," Raze muttered, watching him mow through his second platter. "You can put it away."

"What happened to the one?"

"She deserved someone without fangs." Raze smiled at the waitress, but his eyes were flat. He slid out of the booth. "There's my dinner bell. I'll catch you later. Good luck with the redhead. Looks like she wants a piece of you."

"Take her, too," Elijah shot back, unfolding the wet nap next to his plate to clean his hands. "Make it a party."

Raze laughed and headed out.

Picking up the check sitting on the edge of the table,

Elijah noted the total and reached into his back pocket for his wallet.

"What the fuck are you doing here?"

The sound of Vashti's irate voice nearly made him smile, but he restrained himself. "Eating."

"Don't be coy." She dropped into the seat Raze had just vacated. "What are you doing here in Louisiana?"

"Working."

Her amber eyes were hot with fury, her cheeks flushed and lips red. With her long mane of crimson hair and her sleek black bodysuit, she was so damned delicious she made his mouth water. He wouldn't change a thing about her, except the pain in her past and her evasive tendencies in the present.

"You're deliberately trying to piss me off, lycan."

He pushed to his feet. "Let's take this next door."

Tossing cash for the bill on the table, he gestured his bristling vampress toward the exit.

When they stepped outside, she rounded on him. "We had a deal."

His brow arched. "That's the way you wanna play this?"

"You know I want that information, and you owe it to me."

"You'll get it." Elijah sidestepped around her and headed to his room.

"I'm talking to you!" she yelled at his back, followed by the rapid click of her heels along the cement walkway.

"No, you're not. Your gums are flapping, but you're not actually saying anything."

"You're an asshole."

His temper began to heat. He opened the door to his room and stepped inside.

Her palm slapped against the closing door and pushed it open hard enough to bounce off the wall. "You deliberately switched around the assignments so it took me all damn day to find you!"

"Really? Since you put me with Raze, I would think a quick phone call to him would've cleared things up."

"I *thought* about putting you with Raze. I was going to talk to you about it last night, but you wouldn't let me. You just had to talk first and then the next thing I knew, I was fucking your brains out."

"Right. Talk *to* me, not *with* me. You'd already made up your mind. I'm not your pet. I'm your partner. I have a say."

"You didn't give me a chance to bring it up," she repeated obstinately.

Elijah reined in his temper with effort. "And this morning? When we were working on the composition of the teams? You could have talked about it then. I asked you."

She glared, her face a mask of righteous fury. "We already had other plans by then."

"Did we? We never talked about the first plans. I figured we'd be getting around to that after we got the teams dispatched."

"Well, you figured wrong."

"And before?" he countered tightly, having trouble deciding if he should throw her out or throw her on the bed and fuck her. "You want to toss our deal in my face, let's talk about it. You agreed to stay with me. Then you made plans that reneged on our agreement."

"I agreed to stay with you while we investigated lycans who might possibly be involved in Char's death," she shot back. "Last night, that wasn't the immediate item on the agenda. The hunt was, and I made a strategic tactical decision."

"And how were you planning on feeding?"

Her hands fisted. "You can't feed anyone now. You're still recovering."

"Coward."

"Fuck you." She stalked closer.

"Is that why you're here, Vashti? Wanna get laid? That's all you want from me, right? And information."

"Whatever. The reason I'm here is obvious."

"Not to me. If you wanted to chew me a new one, you could've done it on the phone. If you wanted to deal with the business in Huntington, I could've met you there tomorrow."

Her chin lifted and her arms crossed. "I like to deal with things directly."

He barked out a dry laugh. "Well, you've accomplished that. Now you can go."

"I'm not done."

"Oh?" Deliberately baiting her, Elijah pulled out the chair tucked into the desk and sat down. "Then by all means, go ahead."

She stared at him for a long moment, a muscle ticcing in her jaw. "Why didn't you just ask me what was going on?"

"Why didn't I ask you to talk about something you went out of your way not to talk about?"

She threw up her hands. "For god's sake, the plans changed. It was a moot point."

"Not to me it wasn't. You want to put distance between us. This was a way to do it, until I came up with information that was more valuable than recovering your skewed peace of mind."

"You're making this personal when it's not."

"The hell it's not." He'd had enough. Irritated with himself as much as with her, he hit her with the truth. "You risked your life and a Sentinel war to save me. You flew fourteen hundred miles just to bitch at me. We've been fucking each other's brains out—as you so eloquently put it—for the last few days. Don't tell me it's not personal when you decide we're better off working on opposite sides of the country!"

Her chest heaved with angry breaths. "There are bigger things going on here a whether or not you got your feelings hurt over a reasonable decision. It doesn't make sense to tie up both of us together. We're too valuable. We need to spread some of that muscle around."

"Fine. Done." He stood. "Get the fuck out of my room."

"You're not throwing me out! What about our deal?"

Elijah caught her elbow and dragged her to the door. "I release you from the deal. I'll get your damned information and you'll have it as soon as I do."

"I want to go with you."

"Too bad. We're too valuable to risk as a unit. We need to keep ourselves spread around."

Yanking her arm free, Vashti spun and shoved at him. She cursed when he didn't budge an inch. "You're being an asshole."

"So you said. Lucky for you, you're not going to have to be around me anymore."

Her eyes widened when he opened the door, as if she really couldn't believe he was throwing her out on her ass. "What the hell do you want from me?"

"Respect. Honesty. Trust. A little consideration for the feelings you just spat on." With an exaggerated sweep of his arm, he urged her to leave. "Out."

"Fuckin' A." She held her ground stubbornly. "How are we going to work this out if you give up? I'm trying to have a conversation with you and you don't want to deal with it."

"No, I don't want to deal with bullshit." He leaned into the edge of the door. "Did you rehearse what you were going to say? Were you thinking about it all day? Trying to come up with ways to justify and spin your way through this discussion so you're on the high ground and I'm wrong in every way?"

"Don't be ridiculous."

"Look who's talking. You're crazy about me, Vashti. You don't know why . . . It doesn't make sense . . . But you can't stop thinking about me. Can't stop wanting me. Can't stop wishing you were with me when you're not. Right now, as pissed off as you are and as righteous as you've convinced yourself you have a right to be, you're hot and wet and aching for me. The last thing you want to do is leave, because you've been busting your ass all day to get to me."

"Oh my god." She tossed her hair over her shoulder. "Conceited much?"

"But, of course, you're not going to admit it. You're not going to *really* clear the air and confess that you were putting me with Raze because I'm getting too close to you and you think you need space. You think you want it. That it'll be safer for you when you have it because then I won't be able to get to you the way I do." He shoved a hand through his hair. "I don't have time for this. And I damn sure don't have time to work with someone I can't trust to be honest with herself, let alone be honest with me. So you can either walk out of here on your own two feet or I can pick you up and toss you out. How do you want it?"

Her throat worked on a hard swallow. The yearning in her eyes almost broke him, but he held his ground. He wasn't going to be satisfied with her the way things were. Last night had shown him that he was moving beyond the sexual attraction phase into something deeper. He wasn't going to wade into those waters alone. Too many people were depending on him. He couldn't afford to get all twisted up over a woman who didn't feel the same pull he did. Or at least wouldn't admit to it. Accept it.

Vashti moved toward the door slowly, all the anger she'd hit him with seeming to have drained away. It no longer stiffened her spine or propelled her steps. She paused on the threshold and looked over her shoulder at him. "Elijah . . . don't be like this. It was a tactical decision that was best for the mission. Let's talk it through."

"No need. Raze and I get along fine, things are moving forward, and I'll get to Huntington before the end of next week. All's right in your world, Vashti. Leave it be."

She stepped outside.

"For what it's worth," he said as he swung the door closed, "I was crazy about you, too."

Vash stared at Elijah's closed door and didn't know what to do with the vibrating anxiety that rattled through her. Everything inside her rebelled at the realization that she was on the outside and he was locked away from her. Closed off in every possible way.

Christ, she'd come all this way with the thought that she would be with him tonight. She'd been pushing toward that all day and now she had nothing at all . . .

She'd never seen him so furious. He was livid. And his anger was more terrifying for its quiet strength. If he'd yelled or hit the wall . . . *anything* . . . the passion of his response would've given her something to hang on to. But his chilly fury had been emotionless. His parting comment had been made without any inflection at all. And spoken in the past tense.

Cursing, she ran both of her hands through her hair.

"Fucked it up, didn't you?"

She glanced at Raze, who sauntered toward her, flush with the healthy glow of a vampire who'd just fed.

His gaze darted over her face and he sighed. Pity

shadowed his eyes. "Ah, Vashti. Maybe it's for the best."

She nodded violently.

"You got a room?" he asked.

"I should head back."

"Nah." He tossed an arm around her shoulder. "We've got a big day tomorrow and we can use you. Wanna stay with me? I have two beds."

"What about the waitress?"

One thickly muscled shoulder lifted in an insolent shrug. "What about her?"

Vash leaned her head in to him. "Still hung up on that med tech in Chicago?"

"Just not in the mood for anything complicated. You know what that's like."

"Sure." Only she didn't, not really. She'd connected with Char and, to a certain extent, Elijah. Raze had only ever connected with one woman, a mortal who'd drifted through his life as quickly as all the others but somehow managed to leave an indelible impression behind. Raze had been a man whore as long as Vash had known him. But when he'd come back from Chicago not too long ago, he'd gone from barely keeping his pants on to never dropping them at all. Aside from his fangs, he kept his body parts to himself.

When she had the time, Vash intended to look up Kimberly McAdams in the Windy City and see if she could get a handle on what it was about the woman that had so drastically altered one of her best captains.

He changed the subject. "I have to head to the airport in a couple hours to pick up the night shift and backup crews we have coming in. If you want to tag along, you still have time to feed. Plenty of selection in the restaurant—a couple truckers, the bartender, a handful of locals. You'll feel better."

No . . . she wouldn't. Her head turned involuntarily toward Elijah's door. He had to hear their conversation with his lycan hearing, yet he didn't come storming out with his demand that she not feed on anyone but him. He'd really washed his hands of her.

Still, she couldn't do it. Didn't want to, even though she was now two days out from when she'd last drunk from Elijah.

"I'm good," she said instead. "Why don't you fill me in on what you picked up today and what you've got on the agenda for tomorrow?"

"Where's your stuff?" His mouth curved. "You brought an overnight bag, didn't you?"

"Yeah. I've got the Explorer over there." He handed her his keycard and she tossed him her rental keys. As embarrassed as she was that she'd been kicked to the curb, at least no one knew she'd been hoping for some after-fight, make-up monkey sex when she'd hopped on a plane a few hours ago.

A girl had to have her pride.

Then she looked over her shoulder at the worn blackout curtains that blocked Elijah's room from her gaze and wondered if maybe she had a bit too much of it.

CHAPTER 14

Vash's brows rose when she saw Syre exit from the private plane.

"Damn. We got the big gun," Raze murmured before stepping forward to clasp forearms with their commander. "Syre."

"An entire subdivision?" Syre asked without preamble. He stood on the tarmac with the wind blowing gently through his hair, his head-to-toe black attire making him nearly one with the darkness.

A beautiful and deadly dark prince, Vash thought whimsically. Regal, powerful, and lethal.

"That's Elijah's take." Raze glanced at the three lycans and four minions disembarking. "Good thing we brought two cars."

"Where is the Alpha?"

"Snoozing. It's damn near two in the morning. Unlike us, he needs sleep."

Syre acknowledged that with a nod. "What's your take, Raze?"

"Same as his. Place gave me the willies. It's like a ghost town."

Syre looked at Vash.

"I haven't scoped it out yet, but if Elijah says it's squirrely, then it's squirrely. We've never faced a cleanup of this magnitude before," she said grimly. "How do you keep a lid on an entire neighborhood vanishing overnight?"

"UFOs."

They all turned their heads toward the minion who'd spoken. Vash placed him in his mid-thirties when he'd gone through the Change, and by the brightness of his smile and his twinkling eyes, he hadn't been a vampire long enough to become world-weary. He wore his dirty-blond hair in a shaggy style, which gave him a laid-back and youthful appearance.

"Seriously," he said. "We snag a few of the video cameras that we're bound to find when we enter the houses and film the rest of you running around with flares in the darkness. You'll look like streaking lights. Then let the government cover it all up."

"Fuckin' A," Vash said, deciding to run with the absurdity. "I'll man a camera. Syre, you're the fastest. You can run around with the flares."

The look on Syre's face was worth the cost of admission. Grinning, she asked the minion, "What's your name?"

"Chad."

"Don't talk around Syre, Chad," she suggested. "He might kill you."

Chad laughed, but she was only half kidding.

He was definitely a newbie. One who hadn't been around long enough to figure out what his moniker would be. Most minions changed their names a century or two into their new lives, when everything they'd once known and loved had burned through the finite days of mortality and passed away. Vamps often chose names that represented who they'd become. Like Raze, who leveled every opponent in his path, and Torque, who tweaked, finessed, and applied pressure to situations as necessary. Contrarily, Vash had kept her angelic name, as a reminder of the woman she'd once been, one who'd been worthy of Charron's love. She'd changed a lot since then. She wondered what Char would think of who she was now, whether he'd want her as much as he had before, whether he would want her as much as Elijah did.

Syre held out his hand. "I'll drive. Chad, ride with Raze."

"Gee," Raze muttered. "Thanks, sir."

Vash took the three lycans with her and Syre; Raze took the four vamps. They hit the road with Vash resetting the GPS so Syre knew where they were going.

"I'm surprised to see you here, Vashti," Syre said, glancing at her.

"No, you're not."

"Yes. I am."

"Not as surprised as I am to see you."

He adjusted the rearview mirror. "I've yet to see one of these wraiths in the flesh and it's high time I did so."

She hit the button to lower the window and rested her elbow on the frame, relishing the cooling kiss of the breeze on her face. "I feel like you're checking up on me. Again."

"Maybe I am," he conceded. "You're valuable to me and I'm concerned that you're . . . conflicted."

Great. Pretty soon everyone who mattered would know she was a mess. "There's a lot on our plate right now. I'm worried we won't be fast enough."

"We'll know more once the other teams check in." His voice was low and soothing, wielding his ability to mesmerize and charm.

"And if they all come back with reports of entire neighborhoods taken over by wraiths? What then?"

"Ah, my eternal pessimist. Then I guess we'll stock up on zombie apocalypse movies and try to pick up some pointers."

She didn't want to smile, so she turned around and looked at the crew instead. The males were dark haired and big. Beautiful male specimens really, but mere shadows of Elijah. The female was blond and petite, pretty in a wholesome homespun way with her stick-straight hair, green eyes, and pink bow lips.

Vash briefed them. "Elijah will be able to zero in on the aspects relating to lycans better than I will, but I'll tell you to be careful regardless. Wraiths seem to have a hard-on for you guys, and our alliance is new enough to be a liability. We haven't fought alongside each other long enough to dance together without stumbling. A stumble with these guys can get us killed. Watch each other's backs more than usual."

All three glared at her with mute hostility.

"Names?" she asked, lacking the energy to get into a pissing match now.

John, Trey, and Himeko, she was told. Turning back around, she called Raze. "Hey. How's the sleeping situation going to work at the motel?"

"I picked up three additional rooms, aside from the one Elijah's got. I wasn't expecting you, Syre, or a five-man backup crew. Hopefully, we can snag another room for the commander; the motel isn't exactly in high demand. If not, we'll put you with Syre and I'll take one of the vamps in my second bed. The other two rooms have multiple beds, so we'll have them bunk up."

"Sounds good. Thanks."

But when they arrived at the motel, they found the place sold out, thanks to a popular band playing at the restaurant next door. Vash claimed her backpack from Raze's room and exited out to the sidewalk to wait for Syre, who was grabbing his bag from her rental on the other side of the lot. Raze was in the front office, taking care of getting keycards for the new arrivals.

She stood alone, feeling inexplicably lonely.

Drawn to Elijah, she sidled closer to his room. Her stomach knotted with every step she took, her mouth watering with the need to taste him. Not just for blood and sex, but the sound of his voice, the beat of his heart beneath her ear, the warmth of his arms around her. It struck her that she was terribly afraid he might open his door and she would plead for him to stop shutting her out, forfeiting all her dignity and pride.

She was shaken by the depth of her craving. She didn't understand why he had to make their . . . *association*—she wasn't going to call it a relationship—so complicated. Couldn't they just take what they needed from each other, give each other what they had to give, and take it one day at a time?

She was formulating an argument to hit him with when a suspicious sound caught her ear. When she heard it again, her lungs seized and an icy lump settled in her gut.

"No, no, no," she growled, stalking closer to Elijah's door. Her blood heated and her heart began to pound.

Horrified and disbelieving, Vash stared at the number on the door, willing it to change when she blinked. The unmistakable sounds of enthusiastic sex emanating from Elijah's room twisted her stomach into a hard knot. A shard of white-hot pain speared through her chest.

A woman's breathless pleas for more . . . rhythmically squeaking bedsprings . . . the growl of a man pumping his way to climax . . .

Her bag fell from her nerveless fingers to the ground. For a moment she stood shattered, something inside her broken into pieces. Then fury took over. Lifting her foot, she kicked in the door. The woman's high-pitched scream only spurred her bloodlust. The smell of sex hit her hard, propelling her across the room toward the big figure rising up from the mattress.

"I'll kill you!" she hissed, backhanding him so hard

he flew from the bed and crashed into the dresser. Her head swiveled toward the cowering nude woman on the mattress, her hand rising and clawed to strike.

Her wrist was caught in a steely grip midair. "Vashti."

Syre's voice, low and furious behind her, penetrated her wrath. She glanced at him. "Let me go."

What the fuck is going on?

Her spine stiffened at Elijah's barked question. Her gaze shifted to the silhouette in the doorway—the familiar broad shoulders, tapered waist, and long legs. He was shirtless, barefooted, his jeans unbuttoned and barely clinging onto lean hips.

The woman on the bed was still screaming like a banshee. The man who'd been fucking her moaned from where he was sprawled on the floor.

Yanking her arm free of Syre, Vash rounded on Elijah. "This is *your* goddamned room!"

His eyes glittered in the semidarkness. His arms crossed, taunting her with the sight of his gorgeous biceps and lickable abs. He was hard all over, precisely cut and built. And she wanted him. Desperately.

Sudden silence descended as the woman abruptly ceased her caterwauling. Syre's soothing murmurs registered in Vash's brain, then faded beneath her roaring blood.

"It *was* my room," he corrected silkily. "Obviously, I moved."

She bit off a scream of frustration. His mouth twitched as his gaze took in the scene behind her.

Mortified at her lack of control, she got in his face.

"Don't smirk. If that guy had been you, you'd be swallowing your severed balls right now."

He set a hand over his heart. "I feel so loved."

Her mouth opened on a retort when Raze sauntered up with their reinforcements in tow. He looked at the crumpled metal door, the warped frame, and the situation inside. Then he looked at Vashti with one brow raised.

"Don't say a word," she warned him. "Not one fucking word."

Syre came out of the room like a shadow, sinuous and silent. His face was impassive, but his eyes were deadly. "The mortals won't remember this incident, but damned if I'll let you forget it, Vashti."

His chin lifted. Elijah stepped forward, positioning himself in a way that put him between her and her commander. The gesture was a protective one. And undeniably challenging.

She didn't need a shield with Syre, but that didn't stop her throat from tightening over Elijah's willingness to be one for her.

Himeko stepped up behind her Alpha, her smile too damn intimate for Vash's tastes. "Does your room have two beds, El?"

His gaze never left Syre's face. "It does, yes. It's open to whoever wants it."

Vash fought with herself, wondering if he'd reject her publicly if she jumped at the chance to share a room with him. She didn't get the opportunity to find out.

Himeko pounced first. "I'll room with you. I know you don't snore."

Vash scowled. *How the hell did she know that?*

"Come on, then." Elijah gestured down the hallway. "We need to crash. We're gonna have a hell of a morning in a few hours."

Which, Vash suddenly realized, was why she needed to be with him so badly. She'd very nearly lost him once. Every minute she wasn't with him was a minute wasted. The fact that she even thought of her time with him in those minuscule terms was telling, considering how long she'd been alive and how much longer she had yet to live.

Needing something else to focus on, she turned to clean up the mess she'd made. Damn it. The poor bastard inside was probably hurt real bad. She'd hit him with the thought that he was a lycan and therefore could take the force of her strength.

"I took care of it," Syre said grimly. "His wounds are healed, but he'll have a hell of a headache."

Wincing, she nodded. "Thank you."

"Take care of that door," Syre ordered Raze, before collecting Vash's bag from the ground and grabbing her by the elbow to steer her away.

The door to their room hadn't yet shut behind them when Syre went off. "What the hell are you doing, Vashti?"

Her spine stiffened at his icy tone. "I . . . I don't know."

"You're a mess. You're a danger to yourself and everyone around you."

Her chin lifted, accepting the hit. She was hungry, hurt, bewildered . . . "I am, yes."

Cursing, he shoved a hand through his hair. "And I can't do a fucking thing about it besides stick close and clean up after you."

Guilt humbled her. He had so much on his plate. He needed her running at one hundred percent. Everyone did. "I'm sorry."

Syre looked at her and she winced at the torment in his eyes. "No, I'm sorry. After all the times you've been there for me . . . all the ways you've helped me over the years . . . the fact that I can't do one goddamn thing to help you is killing me. You're falling apart, and I can only stand here and pick up the pieces."

"Samyaza." She didn't realize she was crying until she felt the wetness on her cheeks.

He opened his arms to her and she walked into them. Fisting her hands in his shirt, she poured out her confusion in a storm of tears.

Vash entered the motel's restaurant at eight thirty in the morning and found the lycans eating breakfast. John and Trey sat in one booth, Elijah and Himeko in another. The striking beauty was laughing at something Elijah had said; her sloe eyes were bright and her smile warm. When she reached out and set her hand over El's, Vash knew they'd slept together at some point in their history.

The bruised feeling in her chest bloomed with a deeper pain and her claws extended, piercing her palms.

Sucking in a deep breath of courage, she did what she'd come to do.

She approached Elijah's table, meeting Himeko's gaze when it lifted to hers. "Beat it."

"Excuse me?"

"Get lost. Take a hike. Go away."

The lycan visibly bristled. "Now, just a minute—"

"Himeko." Elijah's calm, quiet voice settled the matter. "Please excuse us."

Himeko looked at him, searching his face for something. With a jerky nod, she grabbed her plate and shot Vash a look of pure unadulterated malice.

And they were supposed to fight alongside each other today. Terrific.

Vash settled onto the vacated bench seat and kept her clawed hands clasped under the table.

"That was rude," he said, slicing into a slab of ham and shoving it into his mouth. "They want to kill you enough as it is. Stop making it worse."

"She wants you."

He swallowed. "She's had me."

Jealousy dug its green talons into her, shortening her breath.

"Not recently," he qualified, "and not seriously."

"It wasn't enough for her."

"It was for me. We had a mutual itch and we scratched it. End of story." He dumped a pat of butter onto his hash browns and mashed it around. When she didn't say anything else, he asked, "Was there something you wanted?"

"You look tired." His eyes were dark and shadowed, his sexy mouth bracketed with deep grooves.

"Do I? You look drop-dead gorgeous, as always." He

delivered the compliment in so dry a tone she couldn't take it seriously.

"I'm sorry."

He looked at her then, arching a brow when she didn't elaborate.

She exhaled in a rush. "I should've made a greater effort to tell you about the plan to pair you with Raze. I didn't think you'd like it, and I chickened out instead of arguing with you. Later, when the plans changed, I avoided the argument altogether by burying it. *Trying* to bury it. I apologize. I'm not proud that I was a coward about it."

Elijah studied her, his gaze so intense she nearly squirmed in her seat. It was driving her crazy to sit so close to him with such a yawning gap between them. Every inhale brought his scent into her nostrils, making her heart pound. She knew he heard it, knew he'd sense her hunger just as he had when they'd first met in the Bryce Canyon cave.

He resumed eating, his gaze on his plate. "Apology accepted."

Relief filled her so quickly she got dizzy. That was probably why it took her a heartbeat or two to realize she wasn't going to get any more from him.

"That's it?" she demanded when it settled in. "That's all you're going to give me?"

"What more did you want?" he asked coolly, scooping his sunny-side-up fried egg onto a triangle of buttered toast. "You apologized. I accepted."

Her eyes burned. Coming so swiftly on the heels of

relief, her disappointment blew the lid off her already volatile mood. "I think I hate you."

His knuckles whitened on his utensils. "Tread carefully, Vashti."

"What the fuck do you care? No, don't answer. You already have, loud and clear." She slid out of the booth and walked away.

There was a moment of terrible silence.

"Damn it, Vashti." His silverware clattered onto his plate behind her. "God-fucking-damn it."

She raced the distance to the Explorer, desperate to get away before he saw her crying. God . . . she really *was* a hot mess. And for what? A sexy lycan who strung legions of panting women along for kicks? Stupid. The whole thing was stupid. She'd been way better off with a dormant sex drive and the lycan working for the Sentinels.

He reached the driver's-side door just as she locked it with her safely inside.

"Vashti." He'd never looked more furious. His eyes were wild and glowing, his voice guttural. "Open the door."

Flipping him the bird with her left hand, she turned the ignition with her right. "Enjoy your breakfast, asshat. I'm going to grab a bite to eat myself. Fuck if I'll starve myself for you."

His palm slapped against the window, sending hairline fractures exploding through the safety glass. "Vashti. *Don't run.* I won't be able to control myself if you run."

She gunned the vehicle into reverse, sending gravel flying from behind the tires. She was on the road a second later, having no idea where she was going and grateful that there wasn't another soul on the winding rural road.

Pine trees crowded thickly against the serpentine ribbon of asphalt, casting shadows over the highway that perfectly suited her mood. Tears coursed down her face. So many goddamn tears. She'd thought she cried herself dry during the night. It infuriated her that there were more yet to be spilled.

Gripping the steering wheel in both hands, she screamed to purge the sick, roiling tension inside her. Then she screamed again as she hugged a curve in the road and came face-to-face with a massive chocolate-colored wolf. In the split second it took her to realize she was going to barrel right through him, her world ground to a shuddering halt. She stood on the brakes, distantly felt the antilock system vibrating the pedal madly beneath her feet. The wheels didn't lock. The car didn't slow nearly fast enough.

Bracing for the impact, she stiffened into a board . . .

. . . and nearly lost her sanity when Elijah leaped onto the hood, scrambled over the roof, and jumped off the back.

The Explorer slid into a cutout on the side of the road and came to a jerking stop. Vash slammed the transmission into park and hopped out.

"Are you fucking *insane*?" she screamed with fists clenched at her sides.

His wild green irises were aglow above a vicious

snarl. All animal, with none of the man in them. He *was* absolutely crazy.

And she was in big trouble. Huge.

She was faced with the choice of fighting or fleeing. Holding up both hands, she forced her restless body not to move. She debated her options—tearing into him with teeth and claws, ripping him to pieces physically as he'd done to her emotionally, or just running as far and fast as she could. She'd outrun lycans before; she could do it again.

Ears flat to his head and teeth bared, Elijah slinked forward, owning the center of the highway. Vash swallowed hard, as riveted by his lupine beauty as she was by his human form. He was stunningly majestic, his thick fur as glossy and rich as his human hair, his movements lethally graceful. His growl was a deep warning, a rumbling sound of danger that made the hair on her nape stand on end.

Something perverse inside her burst free, fueled by her simmering fury and pain. She'd chased him across the country, then chased him down at breakfast. By god, it was time for him to see what it felt like to pursue. She'd been too damn easy. Just like all the other bitches that fell all over him.

With her eyes on his, her mouth curved in a slow, taunting smile. One of her upraised hands lowered to intersect their line of sight. All of her fingers curved into her palm except for the middle one. "Fuck you."

Vash leaped over the hood of the SUV and darted into the woods.

CHAPTER 15

F resh from a shower, Lindsay tightened the belt of her floor-length satin robe and went downstairs in search of Adrian. It was barely dawn and she knew just where to find him. She moved swiftly and quietly, not wanting to wake the two lycan guards in the guest rooms.

It was time for her to get Adrian to talk.

Being here, in Helena's former home, was difficult for him, but he wasn't sharing his pain. And working without Phineas—his second-in-command, whose death had brought them together—was like working without his right hand. Yet he remained reserved and contained, rigidly so. It was the way he needed to be to hold his command, she knew. It was the way he'd been created. But it wasn't healthy for him. He was adrift and hiding it, shielding her and everyone around him.

Lindsay didn't fully understand how Adrian had come to be. Unlike her, he hadn't been born or raised.

He'd been brought into existence just as he was—a fully mature male angel with a single purpose: to serve as an implement of punishment against other angels.

She couldn't begin to grasp what that would feel like. She'd been raised by adoring parents. She had been hugged a lot. She'd laughed a lot. Not a day went by when she hadn't heard "I love you." In contrast, Adrian had been created to be void of emotion. In time, surrounded by mortals, he'd learned to covet and desire. As a creature built to be hard and merciless, it was the edgier feelings that had manifested first. Later he'd learned to feel loyalty and respect. He had established friendships. Now he was learning how to love her, learning how to give. But the guilt and remorse he was feeling over Phineas's and Helena's deaths were beyond his experience. He didn't know how to express his turmoil, and bottling it up was hurting him more than she could bear.

"My wounded angel," she murmured, her heart aching for him.

She'd fallen in love with a killing machine, one who was slowly but surely becoming a warmhearted, red-blooded man. There were bound to be trials and growing pains in the process, and she would help him as much as she could. But she needed him to open up to her to do so.

He'd lost so much in such a short time. He felt that he'd betrayed Helena's trust, that he hadn't been there for her as he should have been. Not as a commanding officer, but as a friend. Just as Phineas had been a friend, the closest one he'd had, someone dear and precious to him.

She exited through the kitchen door out to the back-yard patio. The enclosed space was small, no more than a postage stamp really, with a circle of mosaic tiles in the center of the rectangle of grass. For some people, the spot would have been perfect for a birdbath or a couple of lawn chairs. Here, she knew it was a landing pad, a place from which angels could lift to the sky and return to the earth.

The air crackled with the electric energy of an approaching desert storm, a storm that was brewing inside Adrian. One he was keeping at bay by sheer will alone. And it was costing him. Greatly.

Tilting her head back, she spoke softly into the dawn breeze. "Adrian, my love. I need you."

A moment later he appeared, his brilliantly white wings with their crimson tips a shock of shimmering alabaster against the pinkish gray heavens. She'd known he would be close, never too far away to be there for her should she need him. His landing was impossibly graceful, the tips of his extended wings nearly touching the stucco walls that separated the yard from their neighbors. The ball of one foot touched the tile first; then the full weight of his body settled firmly onto the ground.

As was his custom, he wore only loose linen pants. His powerful chest and arms were bare and beautiful, his caramel-hued skin stretched over lean, rippling muscle. His black hair was tousled by the wind, framing his gorgeous face. And his eyes, with those gorgeous flame-blue irises, slid over her face with love and tender passion.

Her heart sighed at the sight of him. Her blood heated and flushed her skin.

And he knew, of course. His mouth curved in a sensual smile. "You could have called me from the bed, *neshama*. I would've heard you and come to you there."

"That's not why I need you."

"Oh? Are you sure about that?"

She sucked in a deep breath. "I always want that, but there's something else."

His wings dissipated like mist as she closed the distance between them. She walked right in to him, pressing her face in to his chest and wrapping her arms tightly around him.

"Lindsay." His resonant voice was threaded with concern. "What is it? What's wrong?"

"Do you know how much I need you, Adrian? How dependent I've become on having you near? Not for blood or sex, although I won't deny that I need both of those things from you. It's like you're the force that makes my heart beat and, when we're apart, it forgets how to function."

He crushed her so tightly against him, she couldn't breathe. She was grateful her vampire lungs didn't really need to because she didn't want to pull away. One of his hands fisted in the curls of her hair. The other arm banded around her waist, ensuring that every inch of her was pressed tightly to him. "*Neshama sheli.* You destroy me."

"I love you. So much that I feel your pain as if it were my own."

His chest expanded beneath her cheek. "I would never hurt you."

"Is that why you're bottling it up?" Lindsay pulled back to look up at him. "Is that why you're not letting me in? You should know I didn't shield you."

He pulled her head back and looked at her.

"You're torturing yourself over letting me go with Vash," she said softly. "You're wondering what that says about your love for me. But what are you comparing it to? What we have is something no one else will have. Not just because of who we are as individuals, but because of the obstacles we're facing together. We're going to have to take risks—with ourselves and with each other."

His irises were flickering blue flames, alien and ancient. Tormented. She wondered how he carried all that roiling emotion inside him, how he hid it behind the smiles he gave her and the stoicism he gave to his Sentinels, how he leashed it when he made love to her and fought battles with clearheaded precision. How she could get him to let it out.

"I manipulated you, Adrian."

He stiffened.

"I know you're feeling guilty about Helena." She tightened her embrace when he jerked against her. "I used it against you to get you to put your Sentinels first and let me go with Vashti to help Elijah."

A long moment passed. "The weakness was mine to exploit. I made it possible."

"There's no excuse for what I did, only for why I did it."

"Why are you telling me this?"

"Because I have to," she said simply, lifting her hand to push his hair back from his forehead. "Because we're strongest when we're one unit. I'm trying to remember that this is all new to you. That you're trying and you've come really far from the man I met in the Phoenix airport. But I need you to come farther, step closer, let me in. You're keeping me out."

"I don't . . ." He frowned. "I don't know how to do what you're asking."

"Think out loud. When the thoughts are swirling around in your head, give them a voice. Let me hear them. Let me be your sounding board."

"Why?"

"Because you love me and you need me. I know you have to be strong for the other Sentinels. They lean on you, and if you fall, they fall. But you need to lean on someone, too. That's where I come in, if you'll let me."

"I'm fine."

"Physically, yes. Damn fine. Emotionally, you're a wreck." With her hand at his nape, Lindsay pulled his mouth down to hers and brushed her lips across his. "You couldn't have done things differently with Helena, Adrian."

His hands flexed convulsively against her. "She came to me for help."

"No. She came to you for permission. And you told her the truth—you weren't the guy to ask for it. You broke a law by falling in love with Shadoe, then me. Helena wanted you to say it was okay for her to break the law, too, and you couldn't do that. Honestly, it wasn't fair for her to ask you."

"She was in love, Lindsay. I know how irrational that makes us. I should've been more sympathetic."

"You can't tell me you weren't. I *know* you. It broke your heart when she told you that she'd fallen in love with a lycan. I heard your voice when you called me and, later, when you told me what happened."

"I was going to separate them. Break them apart."

"That was the plan," she agreed. "But you might've changed your mind once you saw them together. Or you might have gone through with it. We'll never know. *She'll* never know, because she took the option away from you. That was her decision. You can't go around regretting the actions of someone else."

"Even if I forced her hand with *my* actions?" he shot back, his voice clipped and icy.

"What did you do, Adrian? She asked you for permission to have a romantic relationship with one of her guards and you told her to ask the Big Guy Upstairs. Then she ran away and they killed themselves. Where in that series of events are you guilty of forcing her hand?"

"She knew me. She knew what I'd do."

"Bullshit. *You* didn't even know what you were going to do. No . . . Hang on . . . Hear me out. You took your time getting to her. You were thinking. Debating. Reasoning with yourself. It's not your fault that we'll never know what could've happened if you'd had a choice." She cupped his face in her hands. "It's not your fault. And if Phineas were here, I'm sure he'd be telling you the exact same thing."

A tear clung to his thick bottom lashes. It slipped

free. He swiped angrily at it, then stared at his glistening finger with something akin to horror. Another tear fell. He whispered brokenly in a language she didn't understand. When his gaze met hers, Lindsay saw shock. And fear.

She wondered if he knew that he'd cried the first time they'd made love.

"*Neshama*," she breathed, hugging him tightly. "It's okay. Let it out."

"I—" He swallowed hard.

"You miss them. I know. You miss them and it hurts."

"I failed her."

"No. Shit. No, you didn't. The system failed. The stupid rules and laws. And your Creator, who's left you all on your own down here for too long without any guidance or reinforcements."

A drop of hot rain splattered on her cheek, another sign of his breaking control.

He pressed his face into her throat. "Hold on to me, Lindsay."

"Always," she vowed. "Forever."

Adrian's wings snapped open and they surged into the air, his powerful body flexing against hers as he forced their combined weight into a steep vertical ascent. The effort was nothing for him, no strain at all for muscles he religiously honed for battle. From the cloudless sky, fat drops of sizzling rain struck her like tiny needles, drenching her in seconds.

Terrified of heights, she buried her face in his chest and hung on, clinging to him so tightly she couldn't miss that he was sobbing silently. Her heart broke for him, even though she knew he needed to purge in this way. His grief had been pent up inside him, festering, weakening him. She twined her legs with his, clutching at his back beneath his wings and licking the raindrops from his throat and jaw. She murmured nonsensical words of comfort, soothing him as best she could.

"Lindsay." His mouth sought hers; his lips sealed firmly over hers. His taste was salty from grief, the faint tinge of tears blended with the wet of the rain. The wind whipped through their hair and her heavy, soaked robe.

They lifted higher and higher.

Her returning kiss was meant to console, but he wanted more. Needed it. Took it. He ravaged her mouth, his tongue thrusting swift and deep. The clothes between them disappeared, willed away by his incredible power. She should have been cold, but he was feverishly hot. And when his hand cupped her breast, her hunger rose to match his, perversely spurred by her terror of heights and her pain over his torment.

They spun as they rose, twirling in the air. Adrian's chest heaved from the surfeit of emotion pouring out of him; his lips across her throat were desperate and greedy. He shifted her, positioned her, slid inside her. She cried out, the pleasure so sharp and unexpected. The rain stopped instantly. His head fell back, their ascent slowed until they hovered for a moment, gently turning in the soft light of dawn.

"*She's mine!*" he roared to heavens, his gaze trained skyward. "My heart. My soul."

Her eyes stung, her vision blurred. Then he twisted and turned, aiming them downward.

They plummeted.

She screamed and locked her legs around his waist. They fell with dizzying speed, spiraling madly, his wings tucked against his back to give no resistance. Her torso was plastered to his, his steely embrace keeping her immobile. But he wasn't. His hips were circling, grinding, screwing his cock into her. Fucking her.

The orgasm slammed into her, the shock of it rippling through her body from head to toe. *"Adrian!"*

He groaned, coming hard and deep. Purging his pain and sorrow with hot, wrenching spurts.

He's mine, she thought fiercely, as they plunged to the earth in the most intimate of embraces. *My heart. My soul. I won't let you break him.*

Adrian spread his wings and they soared.

"Grace. It's good to hear from you." Syre leaned back in the motel's vastly uncomfortable desk chair and managed a smile at his iPad, which was streaming a live feed of the doctor and her report. He was sorry to see that she looked haggard and weary, a rare feat for a vampire.

"That may actually be true this time," she said with a quick flashing smile and a hand shoved through her poorly hacked blond hair. Syre suspected it was a haircut accomplished without the aid of a mirror, just to get it out of her face while she worked.

Through her camera's lens, he saw the rows of hospital beds behind her. "I'm always appreciative of good news."

"Well, how's this? The blood you sent is a breakthrough." Her amber eyes brightened. Haircut aside, she was an attractive woman, petite and delicate in feature. "I blended it with samples of wraith-tainted blood and there was a short period of reversal."

"Reversal?" From Lindsay's blood. No, he corrected himself. Adrian's blood, filtered through Lindsay.

"Temporary," she qualified, "but that's the first ray of sunshine to pierce the doom and gloom around here. We could use more—more sunshine, more blood. We got just enough to get excited and not nearly enough to test properly."

"That may prove difficult."

"I'll leave that end to you. As for my end, we're going balls to the wall. But we'd do a hell of a lot better with an epidemiologist or virologist on board. Got any of those hanging around anywhere?"

"I'm looking into it."

She nodded. "Vash already hit you up, didn't she?"

"Of course." There were very few tricks his second-in-command missed . . . when she was on her game. "And the lycan blood?"

"Twelve subjects' vials. Brilliant, by the way. One or two wouldn't have been enough."

"I'll pass along the kudos to Vash."

"Of course. Quick as a whip, that one. She's a credit to you."

"Yes, she is." He'd trained her well, having seen the kernel of greatness in her from the very beginning. She was bright and thorough and filled with a restless energy that fooled many into thinking she was reckless. She never had been . . . until the Alpha came along.

Syre was watching that situation closely. He wouldn't tolerate Vash's upheaval for long. A day or two more, and if the lycan didn't rectify what he was doing to her, Syre would kill him. It would be a waste of a prime hunter, but the Alpha was less valuable if he wasn't firmly beneath Vashti's thumb. There was also the possibility that now that the lycans were settled in the warehouse and most were already out in the field, they could turn to vampires for leadership and protection if they lost their Alpha. If not for Vashti's turmoil, the death of Elijah Reynolds might be ideal . . .

"The majority of the samples had no effect whatsoever," Grace went on. "However, Subject E is another matter altogether. Whose idea was it to anonymize the samples? Vashti's?"

"Of course." He slid his iPhone over and tapped into the cloud, finding the document that linked donor with sample. But he knew who Subject E was before it was confirmed—the Alpha.

"Well, Subject E is known as FUBAR around here. You want to knock out the wraith population for good, FUBAR's your man. Or woman. His or her blood is like the Hiroshima bomb to wraiths. *Boom*, game over."

"Why? How?"

Grace snorted out a laugh. "I'm good, but I'm not that good. I got these blood samples yesterday evening. I've had just a little over fourteen hours with them. I can give you a 'what,' but it's going to take more time to work on the rest."

"Vashti ran across a wraith with enough brain function to speak coherently. He appeared to be leading a group of other wraiths."

"What?" All levity left her face. "Every wraith I've seen has cotton for brains."

"I need more than that, Grace."

She scrubbed the back of her neck. "Perhaps the subject had only recently been infected, within a few hours maybe. Not enough time to fry the synapses. Or maybe he'd been infected long enough to kick-start his brain cells again. I honestly don't know. I haven't run across anything like that here in the lab."

"Too many questions, Grace."

"And not enough answers. I know. I'm doing the best I can."

"Keep me posted."

"Absolutely. And if you can get me more of that blood, it would really help. Totally the other end of the spectrum there. One annihilates; the other is a possible cure. Knowing you, you'll want both in your arsenal while dealing with this, and I've got a friend here I'd like to have back."

Syre thought of his daughter-in-law. It was too late for Nikki, but hopefully others could be saved. "I'll work on it."

"And the virologist, please. I've got skills, but this is really outside my field of expertise."

With a nod, he ended the call and exhaled harshly.

"What do you know, Adrian?" he murmured softly to himself. "And what will I have to do to get you to tell me about it?"

Vash raced through the trees, darting and weaving, her heart and limbs pumping strong and steady. Her body was a machine, built for her existence as an angel and sculpted by her life as a warrior. Although she heard the pounding lunges and heaving breaths of the lycan hot on her trail, she didn't look back. There was no point. It would only slow her down, and knowing where he was or how close he might be wouldn't make her run faster.

She'd never been outrun by a lycan. Never. She was too quick, too nimble.

But she knew Elijah was different. He'd proven that back on the highway, and even while she thought of that, he proved it again.

She leaped agilely over a fallen log, but he vaulted past her. His front paws dug into the earth and he pivoted, his tail end whipping around 180 degrees.

"Damn it," she hissed.

Faced with a wild beast she didn't have the heart to injure, she sprang and flipped over him. But the leaf-littered forest floor gave her no traction. Her feet slipped out from under her. She hit the ground on her belly and skidded forward, her fingers and toes scrambling for purchase.

He was on her in a heartbeat, straddling her and catching her by the shoulder with his teeth. His breath was hot and fast, a growl rumbling in his chest. When she tried to move, he shook her gently, his teeth dug in but not breaking the skin. He snarled a warning.

Vash melted into the ground, completely pliant. Her stomach quivered with something she began to suspect was delight. Perhaps triumph. Certainly relief.

He'd chased her. Captured her.

Her heart rate kicked up, as did her breathing, reactions her exertions hadn't been capable of eliciting. She lay prone beneath him, absorbing his warmth into her back, her fingers digging restlessly into the dirt.

It took several moments before Elijah released her. When he did, it was with another growled admonition to remain unmoving. He gave her a few moments to prove that she would do so without his interference; then he nuzzled her cheek with his wet nose.

The surprisingly tender gesture had her lifting her head to meet his gaze. "Elijah . . ."

His lip curled in a snarl. His eyes still had that primal light burning inside them.

"Okay. All right." She exhaled and relaxed again, her mind trying to work out why she was submitting so meekly. She submitted to no one but Syre and only in certain respects. In many others, she was the dominant. Yes, because he allowed her to be, but still . . . even Char had known to give her the lead.

She jolted a little when Elijah settled his weight carefully on her, his belly curving into her spine. He didn't give her the whole of it, which would have crushed her, but he gave her enough to pin her and make sure she didn't forget he was there. As if that were possible.

Vash couldn't say how long they lay like that—he atop her and quietly panting, gently sniffing her and nudging with his snout. She couldn't say why it soothed the jagged edges of her mood, edges that had been ripping at her from the inside since he'd shown her the door the day before. She couldn't say when she realized those edges had been tearing her up for years. She knew only that the equanimity she found in the forest with Elijah exposed an inner torment she hadn't been aware she was carrying. Anger and hunger for revenge were her constant companions, but the pain had been buried beyond her awareness of it, an ache not noted until it was gone.

When he shifted forms, she felt the power of it, the ripple that displaced the very space around her. The softness and warmth of rough satin fur morphed into rock-hard muscle and scorching skin. He continued to rub his cheek against her. He continued to pant as if he were exerting himself to his limits.

Her palms grew damp when she felt the unmistakable length of his erection resting in the seam of her thighs. "Elijah . . . ?"

"Vashti." His voice was still guttural. Rough. Sexy as hell. "Isn't enough . . . Sorry."

She stiffened, disappointment piercing her like a blade. She wasn't enough? What they had—whatever it was—wasn't enough?

CHAPTER 16

"Don't tense," Elijah gasped, grinding his hips into the plush swell of her buttocks. "Don't fight. Let me . . . have you. Make it good . . ."

Vash had no defense against the shiver of arousal that rippled through her. "You want sex? *Here?*"

Just the thought made her slick and hungry, the idea that he was so hot for her he couldn't wait, that he would take her on the ground in a forest like an animal in rut . . .

He adjusted his position, his thighs bracketing hers. Then he straightened, pulling her up with him. One hand slid between her breasts, a strong hand gripping her throat and pulling her tight against him. The other reached for the waistband of her stretchy black pants, shoving them down to her knees.

"Sorry." His words were a tormented moan in her ear. "Can't stop. Don't run . . ."

Her head fell back into his shoulder when he cupped

her between the legs with a shaky hand. She couldn't stop the circling of her hips into his touch.

His forehead pressed into her temple. "Wet. Thank god . . ." Bending forward, he urged her back down.

Her arms stretched out, her palms breaking their fall. With her on her hands and knees, he reached between them and fisted himself, sliding the thick crest of his cock through the moisture coating her cleft . . . up and down . . . nudging her clitoris . . . his body trembling behind her.

Every muscle in her body was strung tight as a bow, the expectation so thick Vash thought she might snap. She'd wanted this, her hunger for him as elemental a force as her thirst for blood.

"Need you. *Now*," he growled, rocking her backward to meet the thrust of his entry.

She screamed at the stretching depth of his possession, the pleasure so fierce her vision blurred. He gave her no time to adjust or steel herself, launching into a primal pounding fuck that used her as a vessel for his lust. A dozen wild thrusts were all it took. His roar reverberated through the forest, sending birds screeching in panicked flight from the trees. He came so hard, she felt it inside her, pulsing hot and thick as he emptied himself in fiery pulses. Her thighs were wet with him when he straightened to his knees, bringing her up to sit in the cradle of his spread thighs.

He was parting the lips of her sex and rubbing her aching flesh before she could catch her bearings or her breath. Vibrating with the ferocity of her arousal, she shattered into climax with a drawn-out moan of relief, her body clenching and rippling around his spurting erection.

Then his wrist was at her mouth, offering his franticly throbbing vein. Still shuddering in orgasm, Vash turned her head away. "No . . ."

Elijah buried his face in her hair. "I'm sorry."

She sincerely wanted to reply, but her synapses were fried. And he was still massaging her clitoris, keeping her hot and needy and so damn ready to come all over again, if she'd ever stopped coming.

"Couldn't get a grip." His teeth ground audibly together. "You ran. I couldn't think . . . You have to know, I'd cut off my arm before I hurt you."

Something vital welled up inside her, twining with the understanding of what he was apologizing for—he'd lost control. She shouldn't have been pleased that his beast responded by marking her in the basest, most animalistic way possible, but apparently she was perverse in that way. Oh well. If their fights always ended with him coming inside her, she could live with it.

But his guilt had to go.

When he pushed his wrist at her again, she shoved his arm out of her face, insulted. "Stop that."

Elijah lifted her carefully off of him, no easy task when he was still hard and thick. She let him. Let him throw himself backward into the leaf litter with a forearm tossed across his eyes. Let him ramble hoarsely about her needing to eat and him finding some way to let her do that, since she wouldn't drink from him . . . not that he blamed her . . . he was out of control, losing his mind—

As he muttered to himself, Vash swiftly and silently pulled off her boots and her clothes. Until she was naked. In the woods. With a lycan. What the hell was the world coming to?

"Elijah," she purred, crawling over him. "Shut the fuck up."

She watched his breath catch, then heard it leave him in a rush as she sank back onto him, seizing the intimate connection she craved. His cock was slick with semen cooled by the air, making him cold and hard as marble inside her. He jackknifed upward with a growl, and she caught him with her arms around his neck, meeting him eye to eye.

"I see shrinkage isn't a problem for you," she said drily, noting how his eyes were still feverishly bright. He was savagely gorgeous. Flushed and disheveled and glistening with sweat. She could still smell the animal on him and her sex tightened in primitive appreciation. It was so similar to the scent she'd loathed viciously for so long, yet none of her painful past touched him. She stopped debating why and just . . . accepted it.

"Vashti, I—"

"—offended me. Oh, not with the wild animal sex," she assured him, seeing the torment that crossed his features. "For offering me your wrist, which—if you didn't know—is the most impersonal way to give blood to a vampire. I'd like to think we're beyond that. And if we're not, we need to work on getting beyond it."

His arms tightened around her like steel bands. "Beyond ditching me when you're scared? Beyond apologizing for some stupid shit instead of the real issue?"

"Wow." She pushed her fingers into his hair because she knew how much he enjoyed it. Also because she needed to soothe the beast so she could work things out with the man. "You bounce back quick. I think I liked you better contrite."

"All or nothing."

"Do I have a choice? I'm thinking you'll just chase me if I run."

His gaze narrowed, studying her. After a moment, his nostrils flared and he accused, "You *liked* it."

"I never said I didn't. You're the one who kicked me to the curb."

"Who started it?" Elijah's voice was ominously neutral.

She swallowed, her eyes sliding away to find the powerfully steady pulse in his corded neck.

"Vashti." He shook her a little. "Talk to me. What are we doing here?"

Her gaze shot back to his and she scowled. "Are you kidding?"

"If sex is all you want, I'll point out that there are other options that aren't such a pain in the ass."

"Like Himeko?"

His grin was slow and purely male. "Feeling territorial?"

"How fabulous that you're enjoying my confusion and misery," she groused. "Listen, I've already screwed this to hell and back trying to pick my way through on my own. You need to tell me what you want from me. Then I can tell you if I can give it to you."

"A commitment."

There was a fluttering panic in her stomach. "What kind of commitment?"

"Something beyond being a joystick you like to ride when the mood strikes you."

"Whatever." Vash tried to refocus after feeling Elijah's "joystick" flex inside her when referenced to. "You're one to talk. I know you're just into me for my tits."

"So we'll deal. I'll grant you exclusive and convenient access to what I've got in return for the same from you."

"That's it?" she asked suspiciously. Exclusivity and convenience tied in a lot of different things, she knew, but she still had to ask.

His gaze was steady, all human, and infinitely patient. "What more can you live with?"

"Well . . ." She ran a hand through her hair. "I *can't* live with the cold shoulder. Made me crazy. You were such an ass yesterday."

"*I* was the ass?"

She sighed and knew she had to lay it all out there or risk losing him. The beast might be infatuated, but the man wasn't the type to be strung along. "I want you. Not just for the sex, but for you. I respect you. I respect how you are with your people. But that's exactly why I can't keep you. And I'm afraid to want you more. I'm afraid to get hurt again."

He reached up with both hands and brushed her hair back from her face. "You're thinking about my responsibilities as an Alpha."

"Tell me you're not," she shot back. "And if you aren't, you should be."

"At this point, I'm wondering if there hasn't been a big fucking mistake. This makes twice now I've lost it over you."

Vash frowned. "When was the other time?"

"Doesn't matter when. It happened." His firm, beautifully shaped mouth brushed across hers. "The hunt began the moment I first saw you. It won't end until you admit you're mine or I stop breathing. That's what the beast wants and what I want it to have. As for the man, I admire your strength and your courage. I'm grateful for your advice and that you've always been willing to share it with me. I'm addicted to your body, but I also enjoy just being with you. You're the perfect amount of crazy for me. There's never a dull moment with you, sweetheart."

She leaned into him, something inside her cracking open at what he was saying. Her body tightened around him, hugging him from the inside.

He growled softly. "I could come again just like this. Just holding you and being held by you. Even if I go on as the Alpha, I couldn't pretend to take on a mate now. The thought of being intimate with another woman repulses me."

Her eyes closed as relief and tenderness flooded her. "There was only Char. Then you. I want this to work. I want to *make* it work."

"So commit to this, Vashti—sleeping together, working together, staying together. None of which is anyone else's business. We just have to talk to each other and make each other a priority."

"There isn't a lycan alive who doesn't want to kill me, including you sometimes."

"And there are very few vamps who wouldn't put me down if they thought they could get away with it. Every relationship has its problems and hostile in-laws."

"Ha! You're a riot."

"And I'm stubborn and arrogant." He nipped her lower lip between even, white teeth. "You're mine, Vash. I dare anyone to challenge me otherwise. Even you."

"You suck." Her mouth tingled deliciously; the flavor of him spread richly across her tongue. "You knew what you were doing to me yesterday and last night. You knew it would break me down to lose you, that I wouldn't be able to take it."

"I hoped," he corrected. "And kicked myself with doubts about drawing a line I wasn't sure you'd cross. When I offered my room last night and you didn't take it, I could've strangled you. You tore into a hotel room in a territorial rage, but you wouldn't take that one step I needed you to take. I started to think there was no way to have you the way I need you. Then you came to me at breakfast and I was too damn close to telling you I'd take whatever I could get."

"I was too damn close to begging you to stop punishing me." Her vision blurred and she turned her head. "You shut me out. It . . . hurt. I hate hurting. It makes me crazy. Crazier."

He exhaled and leaned into her. "You're damned stubborn."

Stung by the truth, she said, "And you're rolling over and exposing your belly without much of a fight, puppy."

"You've been here before, with Charron. Of course you'd be wary of putting yourself out there again and making yourself vulnerable. This is new to me. I've never had this, and I want it. I can't imagine not having it. Not having you."

Vash pressed her palm over his strongly beating heart. "Has it occurred to you that I might be seducing you and making you care so you won't be able to kill me?"

He covered her hand with his. "What kind of asshole do you take me for? Think I could nail you six ways from Sunday, then nail you again with a stake? I let that go before we went at each other in the warehouse. Micah's dead. What you did to him was wrong, because your assumptions about me were wrong. But I can't say I would've acted differently. If I kill you on his behalf, I'd just be doing exactly what you did to him for Nikki's sake. It's a vicious cycle that won't bring either of them back, but would destroy both of us."

She nuzzled into his neck, breathing him in. "Some will ask that question and ascribe that motive to me. More will think about it."

"Fuck 'em."

"Nooo . . ." she crooned, nibbling behind his ear.

"We have a deal: exclusivity and convenience. You fuck no one but me."

Elijah's hands cupped her shoulder blades, keeping her close. He tilted his head to the side, giving her total access to the thick artery in his neck that carried his life's blood. Such a submissive gesture by so dominant a male—one that came at great cost, she knew—stirred her blood. The hunter in her stretched in anticipation, while the woman in her melted.

With perfectly gauged strokes of her tongue, Vash expertly plumped his vein. She felt him swallow hard and she smiled. "Did you know a vampire's bite can give the sweetest sexual ecstasy?"

"Why do you think I won't let you feed off anyone else?"

"I was too far gone to see to your pleasure in Vegas. I'm sorry for that. I want to please you, Elijah. I want to make you happy."

"Trust me. I got mine in Vegas." His hands, those warm and wonderful hands, slid down her back and cupped her buttocks, rocking her onto his raging erection. "And you please me all the time, in so many ways. But if you want to make it up to me anyway, I won't mind."

"Don't you?" As she dragged her fangs delicately across his throat, she couldn't fail to feel the fine tremors rippling through him. "You're an apex predator, and you're about to be another predator's snack."

"I'm a man," he retorted gruffly, "who's about to lie back, relax, and enjoy his woman riding him to a mind-blowing orgasm."

"Why, you chauvinist," she scolded with laughter in her voice. But her smile faded when she pulled back to look at him. His face was etched into tense lines and his eyes, those jeweled eyes that saw right through her, were aglow. The man could tease, but the beast inside him was struggling with being food for another being. She gentled him with soothing strokes of her hands through his hair. "You don't have to do this, Elijah. I can take a wrist from someone else. Quick and clean."

"No."

"A woman, if you prefer. We could go to a den. You could fuck me while I feed. It might turn you on to watch—"

"No, damn you." His voice was deep and rumbling, nearly a snarl. He caught her by the back of the neck and yanked her to his throat. "I'll be the one who gives you what you need. Do it."

Closing her eyes, she sucked in a deep, shaky breath and found her focus. His pleasure was more paramount than her need to eat, because she understood the gift he was giving her and how much it violated the very core of the predator he was. Taking pleasure from penetration took time for an Alpha male to adjust to. Some never did. She couldn't bear for Elijah to regret feeding her. And if she was honest, she would admit she hoped he'd enjoy it enough to want to do it again. To *ask* her to do it to him.

Vash licked her dry lips and parted them, her tongue stroking along the vein in a lover's caress. Twining her arms around his torso, she distracted him with the press of her breasts into his chest. Then she struck, sliding her fangs into the wildly pumping surge of rich, intoxicating blood.

He cursed and stiffened, then groaned as the rhythmic pull of her mouth was echoed by her sex around his cock. Holding his head motionless with one arm wrapped around his nape, she ran her other hand up and down his rigid back. She withdrew her fangs and licked the wound closed, sucking softly on his skin. Her mouth brushed along his throat, nibbling and kissing. When he relaxed, she struck again in a different place, sinking her fangs deep. Her cheeks hollowed on a long, drawing pull as he began to come.

He hissed, grinding her hips onto him, spilling into her.

Drunk on him, she fell into the memories carried by his blood, selfishly seeking out his thoughts of her—the possessiveness, the pleasure, the pain. In return, she flooded his mind with her own thoughts of him. Making him see how he felt inside her, the fire that burned through her when she looked at him, the deep respect and admiration he inspired in her, and the ache that only his passion could sate.

"Vashti." He jolted as she milked him into another climax, his big body shuddering as she came along with him, delicate muscles gripping him in the most intimate of embraces. Raw sounds of pleasure vibrated from his throat against her lips, rough groans of desire, a craving that was never fully appeased.

Her hunger quenched, Vash retracted her fangs and sealed the twin punctures, massaging the vein that hammered with his roaring blood. With her hands on his shoulders, she shoved him back, her mouth curving as he sprawled beneath her. He was panting, his eyes bright and hot. Leaning over him, she raked her nails down his chest and lifted her hips, then lowered again, stroking his length with the slick clasp of her body.

She didn't have the words this time around. She'd had them with Char. She'd had them as an angel. But she didn't have them now, with him. They were bottled up in her throat, burning.

But the beauty of Elijah was that he didn't need them. He *knew*. He accepted her and wanted her the way she was. He grasped that her body could say all the things she couldn't voice aloud. Her vampire body, which so perfectly connected to the primal sexuality of her lycan's.

"Take what you need," he said gruffly, understanding. "Whatever you need. And give me everything in return."

She caught her bottom lip between her teeth, riding him slow and sure, absorbing the powerful shock of pleasure every time she took him to the hilt. "I need you to come again. I need to feel it inside me."

"I'm a man," he pointed out, clearly amused. "There's only so often I can do this without recovery time."

Her mouth curved in a slow, delighted smile. "You're still hard."

"You're still naked and fucking me." He cupped her breasts, rolling and tugging her painfully tight nipples with his forefingers and thumbs. "Don't worry about me. I'm getting mine watching you get yours. Feeling you squeezing me like a fist. A hot, tight, perfect little fist. An orgasm is a just a bonus when the ride is this good."

Vash straightened and ran her splayed hands down his taut pectorals and rippling abs. Pine needles dug into her knees, but she didn't care. She had him again, right where she needed him—with her, connected to her, with nothing at all between them. No rank, no roles, no half truths or evasions. They were as bared as they would ever be. Committed. He was hers; she could make that claim now. And she was proud to be his.

"Once more," she coaxed, rolling her hips. "For me. I want to come again, Elijah, but I can't without you."

Arching up, he wrapped himself around her and rolled, taking her beneath him. His forearms buffered her shoulders and back from the prickly ground, once again displaying the awareness and consideration that she so admired.

She was pinned yet cushioned as he took over, sliding in and out, his powerful muscles flexing and contracting against her. His eyes stayed on hers, his searching gaze more intimate than even the erotic flux and flow of his body's possession of hers.

"Mine," he said. "Say it."

Her neck arched as her senses overloaded. She couldn't see, could barely hear beyond the rushing of blood in her ears.

"Say it, Vashti," he purred darkly with his lips to her throat, his breath gusting hotly over her skin. "Say it and I'll come for you."

"Mine," she gasped, wrapping her legs around him. "You're mine."

Cleansed and strengthened, Adrian slowly lowered into the backyard with a limp and satiated Lindsay in his arms. For the first time in days, he was thinking clearly, and he was grateful for that when he spotted an unknown car in the driveway. "Someone's here."

Lindsay lifted her head from his chest. "Can you do that mind-flashy-thingy and put some real clothes on me?"

He thought of the clothes she'd packed for the trip and willed a pair of black pants and an off-the-shoulder T-shirt on her. For himself, he went with slacks and an untucked white dress shirt. He was rolling up the sleeves as he moved to open the back door for his mate.

"You forgot my underwear," she whispered fiercely as they stepped into the kitchen.

His mouth curved. "No, I didn't."

Their guest was waiting in the living room, laughing over something shared with his guards. The two lycans stood at attention when he entered the room, but the lovely Asian woman who'd been entertaining them rose to her feet much more leisurely. Dressed in a pinstripe pencil skirt, silk blouse, and Louboutins, Raguel Gadara's messenger was dressed for her secular life. In her celestial one, she favored worn jeans, a 9mm, and Doc Martens.

"Evangeline." Adrian greeted her, clasping her extended hands and sifting through her thoughts via that connection, learning all he needed to know. "Good to see you."

She smiled. "You say that so smoothly, I could almost believe you."

He pivoted to bring Lindsay into the conversation. "Lindsay, meet Evangeline Hollis. Eve's presently overseeing the interior design of the Mondego casino. Eve, Lindsay was briefly the assistant manager of Raguel's Belladonna property in Anaheim. Now she's mine."

Eve shook Lindsay's hand. "Count yourself lucky to have dodged the bullet of working for Gadara."

Lindsay frowned, confused by the other woman's statement because she didn't yet know that Gadara's underlings were conscripted rather than indentured like the lycans. Adrian would catch her up later.

"What brings you by?" he asked Eve, diverting the conversation from explanations he didn't want to get into now.

She pointed at the tiny biohazard cooler at her feet. "Archangel blood. I watched Gadara draw it and place it inside. He said you'd believe me that he hadn't tampered with it or made a switch. I figured you'd mind-rape me when you touched me and prove it for yourself."

"You know me so well."

Eve laughed, but her dark gaze was hard. "There's some comfort in knowing most angels are predictable."

Lindsay looked at the cooler. "Why didn't Gadara give us the blood when we asked for it yesterday?"

"Control," Eve and Adrian responded simultaneously.

"Hell," Lindsay muttered. "This isn't a game."

"In a way it is," Eve explained. "A game Gadara doesn't want Adrian to lose, but he doesn't want Adrian to win without his help. Ambition is the Achilles' heel of every archangel. In this case, Gadara knew he had the upper hand because it was his blood to give . . . or not. He just wanted to make sure Adrian knew it, and that Adrian understands he now owes Gadara something for giving it up—it's always good to have a favor from a seraph in your pocket."

Lindsay looked at Adrian. "Well, shit."

"Lucky you, *neshama*," he teased her. "You have an entire seraph in your . . . pocket."

She shoved at his shoulder. "Why not come himself and rub it in?"

Eve's mouth twisted ruefully. "To put me in my place while insulting Adrian by sending an emissary from the bottom of the totem pole. Two birds, one stone. He's good at that."

"Wouldn't it irritate him," Adrian murmured, "if he knew how delighted I was instead?"

Eve shot a deliberate glance at the two lycans. "There are rumors. I've heard a large portion of your workforce has gone on strike. Gadara's hoping to step in and help you out with that, of course. But if you're looking to avoid his hefty commission and don't mind working with grunts under the table, I can get you some referrals. Just let me know."

Adrian deciphered the message clearly and was grateful for it. His Sentinels weren't completely hanging in the wind without his lycan "workforce." There was help available, if he decided they needed it. Whether or not he did anything with that knowledge wasn't as important as possessing it to begin with.

Eve moved toward the door. "I brought your paper in," she said, gesturing at the folded newspaper in a plastic bag dotted with morning dew. "And you should have someone pull your trash cans off the curb. I figured you're probably not used to worrying about that at Angels' Point, but some neighborhoods penalize residents who leave them out after trash day. Mortal lives are a bitch."

He stared at the newspaper as the door shut behind her. Air-conditioning . . . newspapers . . . trash . . .

"Someone's been staying here," Lindsay muttered. "We lost track of that with Vashti showing up, but she wouldn't mind the heat, would she? She wouldn't even think about messing with the AC."

"No."

"Who would dare use someone else's place like this?"

"Perhaps it's not daring," he murmured. "Perhaps it's desperation. Navajo Lake is only a few hours' drive away."

"Oh." The compassion in her eyes stirred his soul.

He could stay and wait them out, but if they feared reprisal, they'd steer clear. They would need reassurance of a different sort.

Glancing at the two lycans, he said, "Ben. Andrew. I'm going to leave you two here. You can deal with the situation. Bring whoever it is back to Angels' Point, if that's what they want. If not, let them know this property is going up for sale next week."

The two guards were quiet a moment. Then one nodded; the other smiled. "Thank you, Adrian."

"For what?"

"Trusting us," Ben said.

"And taking us back," Andrew added.

Adrian looked at Lindsay, at a loss for what to say. Her encouraging smile got him back on track. "Let's pack up and get to the airport. We need to get these samples to Siobhán."

She reached for his hand and squeezed. He wondered if she knew what that simple gesture meant to him, how much love and support it conveyed, how quickly he'd come to depend on it. On her.

He'd come to Vegas for blood and was leaving with something far more precious—a deeper connection to the woman who held his heart. In the chaos of his life, facing terrible odds and even more horrifying decisions, Lindsay was his light in the darkness. Shining even when he couldn't see her.

CHAPTER 17

"Fuckin' creepy," Raze muttered, crossing his arms as he leaned into the side of Vash's rental. "Quiet as a damn tomb."

Elijah glanced at the vampire and nodded grimly, in accord with the sentiment. His skin was crawling. They'd split up and surrounded the residential subdivision, then worked their way inward, looking for any signs of life. What they'd found was nothing. Nothing at all.

"Where are the newspapers?" Vash asked, moving restlessly. "The mail? The overgrown lawns? You can't have an entire neighborhood disappear and not leave a trail that someone can follow."

Syre opened the back of the Explorer and began pulling out weapons. "How do you suggest handling this, Vashti?"

"Two vamps on vantage point—rooftops, each end of the subdivision. Then three teams: one will take the homes in the center while the other two come around the outer circle on opposite sides. We pick this place apart home by home. The lycans can do the walk-throughs for occupants, while the vamps work on gathering physical data. There has to be a loose thread to pull somewhere."

"All right." He looked at two of the vamps he'd brought with him. "Crash and Lyric, you two are on point. Anything makes a run for it, take it down."

The two minions each selected a weapon and moved off, their bodies freshly fortified against the noonday sun by Fallen blood.

Elijah waited for further instructions, grateful for the dark sunglasses that hid how he watched Vashti. Her hair was restrained in a ponytail, her body encased in her customary black—the pants he'd shoved down her thighs earlier, paired with a leather vest that zipped from navel to cleavage. Her creamy skin and brilliant amber eyes captivated him, as everything about her did. His woman. So beautiful and infinitely deadly. A warrior whom other warriors followed into battle without question. He adored and valued her, even while she was driving him crazy.

She divided the remaining five vampires into teams of two, two, and one, then turned to him for guidance on how the four lycans should be divided. He put Luke and Trey with the teams of two vamps, and put Himeko under his watch. She could handle herself, but he'd lived—barely—through the Las Vegas attack. If they were facing something like that again, he wanted to be the one who had her back.

He and the other lycans began to undress. He pulled his shirt over his head and tossed it into the cargo space of the Explorer. Then he toed off his boots and yanked his button fly open.

"What are you doing?" Vashti snapped, having paused with her katana harness in hand.

Brows lifting, he looked at her. "Armoring up, like you."

The others continued to shed clothes and the vampires resumed the process of strapping weapons to their bodies, but he was keenly aware of their poorly disguised interest in his conversation.

Vash's gaze darted from his open fly, to Himeko, who was now in bra and panties, then back to him. "You're not getting naked here."

Himeko snorted and unclasped her bra. "Nudity is part of what we are. Get used to it, bloodsucker."

"Absolutely," Crash said, shooting a glance at her bared breasts. "Great way to kick off a hunt."

"Shut up." Vash rounded on Himeko. "And you. You've already seen what you're going to see of him in your lifetime."

Himeko smiled coldly. "There'll be others. Women with fur instead of fangs."

Vash twirled one of her katanas in a graceful arc. "Try me, bitch."

"Vashti—" Elijah sighed, knowing tempers were high. The thrill of the hunt was part of that serrated edge, but so too were Micah and Rachel's ghosts. Animosity lurked beneath the untried and tentative truce between vampires and lycans. Keeping that enmity under wraps was a priority now, considering they were about to rely on each other in a possible life-or-death situation.

"I can get naked, too," she shot at him. "Start a new trend."

"Not the same thing and you know it."

Her arched brow challenged him, as did her fingers on the pull of her zipper.

Shooting her a look that spoke volumes, he rounded the front of the Explorer and shifted, returning a moment later with his jeans between his teeth. He dropped them at her feet.

"Thank you." She picked them up and threw them into the cargo space with the rest of the clothes. Then she strapped on her blades, gave a nod to Syre—who sported a wicked-looking repeating crossbow—and they flowed outward from the vehicles to begin the hunt.

Elijah wasn't surprised when Vashti joined him and Himeko, but it was a circumstance that was far from ideal. Keeping an eye on either headstrong woman was tough enough. Having two of them at odds with each other made it dangerous.

The tension between the three of them was forgotten the moment they entered the first house. The two-story single-family dwelling was comfortably furnished and welcoming. There were no signs of disturbance. In fact, he could almost think it was a model home, everything being in its proper place . . . including the family photos on the mantel. He looked at them, noting youthful parents and three children, the smallest being an infant.

Loping up the stairs, he searched the bedrooms.

There, he found signs of life—rumpled beds, children's toys scattered on the floor, clothes spilling from hampers. There was a trash can in the baby's room that had a soiled diaper in it, and a bottle of rotting formula lay half full in the crib.

Vash entered the nursery behind him. "There are messages on the voice mail. Calls from the dad's work asking where he's been. Same with the mom and a carpool she's got going for the kids. Looks like we're on day four now."

The next several homes were more of the same. By the eighth house, Elijah decided to check the backyard as well. As with the other homes, Vash joined him after only a few moments. It struck him then that she was hovering.

He growled at her, but she played it cool. Still, he read the anxiety in her body language—she was afraid to let him do his job.

Shifting, he confronted her. "Stop smothering me."

She scowled and blocked the view from the house with her body. "Put your damn fur back on before Himeko comes out here."

"For fuck's sake. Nudity doesn't automatically equate to sex in a lycan's mind."

"She's female. In case you hadn't noticed, they drool all over you when you're clothed. When you're like this"—she gestured at his body with an impatient wave of her hand—"you're asking to be molested."

His nose twitched as he smelled the first tendrils of her arousal. "Again? On a hunt? Jesus, you're going to screw me to death."

She flushed and shifted restlessly. "If you don't want me hot and bothered, don't run around naked!"

Softened by her obvious embarrassment and understanding how helpless they both were against the pull between them, he said more gently, "I don't need a bodyguard, Vashti. Go do your thing; let me do mine."

"You say that as if it's easy. Those fuckers want you worse than the damn women do! I watched them tear you to pieces once. I won't do it again. I c-can't."

"Vash." His throat tightened at the pain he saw on her beautiful face. "Sweetheart—"

"Don't." She glared at him. So fierce and strong, yet fragile. "You got me into this mess."

"What mess?" But he knew. And if they'd been anywhere else, he would have kissed her senseless.

"*This* mess!" She waved an impatient hand between them. "You and me. Us."

"Us."

"What are you? A parrot? Yes, us."

"We're a mess?" It was very hard not to smile.

"We were last night." She ran her gaze over him from head to toe and sighed. "But we're okay now. When you're not telling me not to worry about you or trying to share your naked body with the world."

"I share my body with no one but you, my crazy vampress. God. I adore you."

"She's coming!" Vash hissed, stepping closer to shield him. "If she sees your family jewels, I'm gonna have to kill her."

"You're nuts, you know that? Certifiably insane."

And he was crazy, too. About her. He shifted back and spun away from her.

When Himeko darted out of the house at a full run, he directed her to scout one side of the yard while he handled the other. He sniffed out a dog buried in the far corner, which was confirmed by a little headstone, but he found nothing out of the ordinary. Himeko, however, whined and began scratching at the dirt.

He joined her, and they dug through fresh sod to find potting soil covering a layer of quicklime. Three feet down they discovered what was left of a child's body, identifiable as such only by the size of the bones. They both leaped back in horror.

"Oh man," Vashti breathed, her hand going to her stomach as the stench broke through the disrupted lime. "Fucking wraiths."

Mindless, my ass, Elijah thought grimly. The burial was proof of intelligence and clear, cold calculation. He looked at Vashti, frustrated that they couldn't converse while he was in his lycan form, a connection that could exist—if they were a mated pair.

Vash turned away and spoke without raising her voice. "Syre. Raze. Have the lycans check the back-yards."

He heard the quaver in her words and sensed her disquiet. She was horrified and disturbed by the discovery, shaken. He went to her, brushing gently along her hip in a gesture of comfort.

She scratched absently behind his ear. "How many wraiths would it take to wipe out a whole neighborhood? How much time would pass? Because if it was more than a few hours, they'd have to be cunning to avoid detection and I've only seen one wraith who had any working brain cells."

Raze's curse from across the neighborhood caused Elijah's ears to twitch. "We've got a body in the yard. Damn it . . . it's a child's corpse."

"Here as well," Syre said harshly. "No sign or evidence of the parent—a single mother, I gather, from the mail and photos in the house."

Elijah returned to the grave and began to dig deeper, growling at Vash when she tried to assist him. He couldn't protect her from everything, but this, at least, was a grisly task he could spare her from.

In the end, he found three bodies, all children.

"Where are the adults?" Vashti asked, following him over to the coiled-up water hose, which she turned on to spray him off.

Raze's voice crossed the distance between them. "Nothing found on the next property. No children in the household. Looks like two males lived here. Neither body is in the yard."

Elijah led the way through the house and back out to the street. He was moving on to the next property when Syre spoke. "I saw movement in a window here in my sector. Drapes are drawn, so I can't see inside."

Vash broke into a run. "Hold until we get there."

Raze met them at the house. Without a word, he led his team to the side-yard gate and they slipped into the back.

Staring at the home from the sidewalk, Elijah watched the upper windows and saw the curtains shift softly, as if with a breeze, but he heard neither the hum of an air-conditioning unit nor a fan. He also didn't hear breathing or movement, which raised his hackles. What the fuck were they dealing with?

"I don't like it," Vash muttered. "I'd rather smoke 'em out than go in. But the flames would bring fire crews, and then we'd have mortals involved."

Syre surveyed the exterior. "My team will take the upper windows. Your lycans can enter from the bottom floor. Ready?"

With a nod, Vash leaped onto the side of the house and scrambled up like a spider. Syre did the same. Elijah took one side of the house; Luke took the other. Himeko remained on point at the front, while Thomas waited in the rear.

"On three," Raze whispered, his voice drifting on the wind. "One, two . . ."

Elijah lunged through the nearest window, entering the house in a shower of glass. He'd scarcely registered that he'd landed in a small home office when he slammed into the closet door, unable to gain purchase on carpet slickened by a viscous substance. Shaking off the collision, he registered what coated the floor—the black, oily residue left behind when wraith bodies decomposed.

Himeko's frantic barking spurred him into action. He careened out into the hallway, skidding into the wall and denting it before finding traction in the unsoiled carpet. He leaped into a family room, where Himeko and Thomas were covered in wraiths. With a roar of fury, he lunged into the fray, grabbing a wraith by the neck and snapping it as he tossed the body aside like a doll's.

The repetitious report of a pistol cracked through the room as one of the vamps emptied his clip into the writhing bodies ringing the edges of the huddle. Raze waded in through the sliding-glass door, yanking wraiths up by the hair and severing heads with his blade. Elijah was tackled from the side. Fangs bit into his flank. Snarling, he kicked with his hind legs, his claws raking into the thigh of his attacker. The wraith lost its grip and fell away. Elijah turned and crouched to retaliate, aiming for the Navy anchor tattoo that decorated the pale-as-milk flesh over the wraith's heart . . .

"*Vashti!*"

Syre's shout pierced Elijah like a silver bullet. Abandoning his attacker, he bounded up the stairs. He reached the second floor and hit a wall of wraiths, the teeming mass of gray bodies clogging the narrow space. A glint of light on a flashing blade drew his attention to the ceiling, where Vash clung upside down with a one-handed grip. Her free arm slashed a katana at the upraised hands that clawed at her, trying to pull her loose.

Fear for her made him frantic, sending him scrambling over shoulders and heads to reach her.

"Not so fast, Alpha," a voice hissed. His rear leg was caught in a vicelike grip, and he was yanked into a room with the sickening crack of breaking bone.

He howled against the searing pain, his gut churning as the door was kicked shut, blocking him from helping Vash. Favoring the oddly bent limb, he faced his attacker. She tossed back silken strands of crimson hair and set her hands on black leather-clad hips. For a split second, Elijah thought he faced Vashti; then the differences came into focus through the fog of pain. The woman was too lean. Her features harsh and less refined. And her eyes were lit with a sick, mad light.

She withdrew a gun from the holster strapped to her thigh and grinned, revealing wicked fangs. "Bye-bye, lover," she crooned.

The door crashed in behind her, the paneled particleboard breaking free at the hinge and slamming into the vampress's back. The pistol went off, the shot going wide. Vash leaped through the decimated door as Elijah charged the lookalike, catching her by the arm and snapping bone in his jaws, making her drop the gun.

Vash kicked at the wraith who ran into the room behind her, then grabbed the vampress by the hair and yanked her upright. There was a heartbeat of stunned silence as the two women looked at each other.

"Who the fuck are you?" Vash barked.

Laughing, the vampress dug in her heels and leaped out the window, leaving Vash fisting a mass of hair ripped out at the root. Elijah made the jump after their quarry, yelping as his broken limb was jarred by his landing on the lawn. He chased her on three legs, nearly catching her by the ankle the moment before she vaulted over the eight-foot fence that enclosed the backyard.

Shots rang out. He heard a shout from the rooftops as one of the vamps on point joined the pursuit.

Unable to make the same jump in his condition, Elijah barreled through the wooden planks, breaking through to the backyard of the house on the other side. In the distance, he heard Vashti shouting after him, but he didn't slow or look back, driven by the memory of tiny child bones scored by fangs.

The vampress jumped over a side-yard gate to reach the front yard, and Elijah rammed through that barrier as well, so close to snaring her that he could almost taste her. His jaws were open and his lips pulled back in a snarl. So close . . .

She kicked off the ground and landed in the back of a pickup truck idling at the curb. The vehicle took off with squealing tires, choking Elijah with the acrid smoke of burning rubber. From the rooftop, Crash maintained suppressive fire, shattering the windshield with a barrage of bullets. The vampress gripped the roll bar and ducked, laughing.

Elijah continued to give chase, despite the added agony of moving from lawn to unforgiving concrete. The truck slowed to round the corner at the end of the street, and he called on reserves of strength to eke out a fraction more speed.

The vehicle exploded.

The blast was so violent it sent him hurtling backward. He tumbled across the yard, howling in frustration, his ears ringing. Vashti skidded across the grass on her knees and pulled him into her arms.

"What . . . ? What happened?"

Syre stared at the shivering minion who lay on the blood and oil-soaked family-room floor. Around him, wraiths who'd survived the melee were staked to the floor with silver-coated blades through their palms. They were far from lucid. Hissing and snapping, they writhed for freedom.

Vashti appeared at the shattered rear sliding-glass door, supporting the weight of the limping Alpha who'd shifted into human form and donned his jeans.

"What the hell just happened here?" Syre growled.

Elijah halted abruptly, causing Vash to stumble and curse. He pointed at the confused but sane minion. "That fucker bit me. As a wraith."

"Who are you people?" the minion sobbed. "Where are my clothes?"

Vashti looked at Syre before helping Elijah to a chair. "My head is going to explode if something doesn't make sense here really damn quick."

"Where are Raze and Crash?" Syre asked, having taken a quick head count.

"Putting out a car fire on the street before it attracts attention." She straightened. "Damn it. I wanted that bitch alive."

His brow arched in silent inquiry.

"The vampress who killed Lindsay's mother," Elijah explained. He looked at Vash. "There's no way her appearance wasn't deliberately styled to mimic you."

"No," she agreed. "She had roots."

"Excuse me?"

"Her hair. The roots were brown; I noticed when I ripped out a chunk of it. And I'm pretty sure her tits were silicone. They were like Princess Leia buns glued to her chest."

Restlessness forced Syre into the pacing that was normally Vashti's trait. *The blood you sent is a breakthrough*, Grace had said. *I blended it with samples of wraith-tainted blood and there was a short period of reversal.*

Adrian's blood, filtered through Lindsay and transfused into Elijah, who'd been bitten.

He pointed at the sobbing man who rocked himself on the floor like a child. "This minion was a wraith?"

"When he took a bite of me, yeah," the Alpha confirmed. "I remember that anchor tattoo. I was going to rip it off of him with my teeth."

"I remember it, too," Raze said, coming in from the front door. "I saw it in a framed photo in one of the houses we searched."

"Fuckin' A." Vash stared at the wraiths. "These are the residents? My god . . . did they eat their own children?"

The minion began to scream and rip out his hair. Syre knocked him out with a fist to the temple.

"You've gotta big fucking problem here," Elijah said. "That Vashti wannabe was one of yours and she was here, well aware of what the hell was going on with these wraiths. She was batshit crazy, but still. She's been hunting humans for sport for years now. I doubt Lindsay's mother was her first or last."

"*Syre.*"

All heads turned to Lyric, who descended from the second floor. "There are a dozen wraiths upstairs who've gone long enough without food that they're barely capable of blinking."

"She was feeding them," Vash said. "She infected them, then fed them their own children. Why?"

"There's something else," Lyric went on. "You'll want to see it for yourself."

Syre gestured for Vashti to precede him in following Lyric upstairs. They ascended quickly, picking over tarlike puddles that marked the end of wraith lives. Lyric led them to the room at the end of the hall, the master bedroom, which had been ravaged. The furniture had been tossed in the corner, opening room for the placement of a table and chairs. Writing on the wall documented the progression of the virus over a period of seventy-two hours. Handheld radios were plugged into their recharging bases. Duffel bags and a suitcase had been shoved against the closed closet doors.

"Here." Lyric pointed at the open suitcase. Amid the pile of rumpled clothes was an employee badge.

Crouching, Syre picked up the rectangular laminated badge and stared at the all-too-familiar face in the photo. His blood turned to ice as his thumb brushed over the MITCHELL AERONAUTICS winged logo.

"What is it?" Vashti asked behind him, unable to see.

He passed her the badge over his shoulder and riffled through the rest of the contents.

"Phineas," she said quietly. "But he's dead."

"Is he?"

The luggage undoubtedly belonged to Adrian's original second-in-command, as evidenced by the personal items inside, which included two molted feathers. Syre eyed the robin's-egg-blue color of the filaments, which so reminded him of the wings he'd once boasted. Each angel's wings were uniquely colored, leaving no doubt that the feathers he held had once graced Phineas's.

Elijah's voice broke the weighted silence. "They were experiments," he said, reading the writing on the wall. "See how they have them divided up by weight and gender, then again by these letters: A, B, and C."

"Here." Raze entered the room with what looked like a makeup case in one hand. He set it down on the table and released the catch, revealing a variety of vials.

"We need to get that to Grace," Vash said.

Syre pushed to his feet. "Grace needs help."

Vash walked to Elijah and handed him Phineas's ID card. "Raze knows a laboratory scientist in Chicago. I bet she could help us narrow down our choices to the best in the field."

"That's a dead end," Raze said vehemently. "I banged her and left. I doubt she'd be too charitable to my coming around again with my hand out. It'd be . . . messy."

Syre didn't point out that banging and leaving lovers was par for the course with Raze. Instead he said, "Go to her with your dick out. You know how to get what we need out of her."

"There's got to be another way," the captain insisted. "We can put out a call to the minions. There are bound to be some who have ties we can pull."

The strength of Raze's protests didn't escape his notice, but Syre chose not to delve into the reason for it now. "We don't have time to stumble around in the dark, and a recommendation from someone you know personally and intimately is a damn sight more responsible than a fucking Google search. See to it."

A muscle ticced in Raze's jaw. "Yes, Commander."

"Phineas," Elijah said softly, his attention on the ID card. He looked up and raked the room with a narrowed, searching gaze. "What the hell was that vampress into? Mortals, vampires, Sentinels . . . nothing was off-limits for her."

Syre's arms crossed. "What are the chances that Phineas isn't dead?"

Elijah barked out a humorless laugh. "No way. He and Adrian were like this." He crossed his fingers, then glanced at the suitcase on the floor. "Phineas was coming back from a trip to the Navajo Lake outpost. He stopped in Hurricane, Utah, to feed his lycans and was ambushed by a nest of wraiths. Whoever the hell that Vashti-wannabe was, she must've had a setup there, too. And after Phineas was taken out, she grabbed his shit and bailed."

"Perhaps. At this point we can't rule anything out."

"Right." The Alpha's gaze was hard. "Because it's more believable that Sentinels and vampires are working together than it is for a group of minions to fall off the deep end."

Syre conceded the point. The majority of minions succumbed to madness—mortals weren't designed to live without their souls.

A piercing, inhuman scream shattered the moment. Everyone charged downstairs, reaching the first floor as a series of gunshots reverberated through the house.

Crash stood over the sprawled body of the wraith-turned-minion. His gun was in one hand and his other was pressed over a bloody wound on his biceps. "He went nuts and lunged for me."

The minion who'd briefly recovered lay dead on the floor, his features reverted to the haunted, sunken look of a wraith. Even as they watched, the man disintegrated into an oil slick.

Rage burned through Syre, igniting a vicious bloodlust. It was quite clear now why Adrian had risked Lindsay the way he had—he couldn't afford to give up even a drop of his blood, not when all evidence pointed to it being a component of a cure for the Wraith Virus.

Syre glanced at the Alpha. Lindsay was the key to Adrian, Elijah was the key to Lindsay, and Vashti was the key to Elijah. The means he required to save his people was within his grasp, and he didn't have any qualms about using it.

CHAPTER 18

Adrian exited his private plane first, then held out a hand to assist Lindsay down the short steps.

"Wow," she said. "It's definitely cooler here in Ontario."

Soon she wouldn't notice such things. Every day the vampirism in her blood took greater and greater hold, and every day he was relieved to find her soul pure and intact. It seemed Shadoe's soul had indeed been enough of a sacrifice, leaving Lindsay's unmarred by the curse of the Fallen. Although he had doubts that the Creator paid any attention to him anymore, Adrian still offered up his gratitude for the miracle of her.

With his hand at her back, he steered her toward the Mitchell Aeronautics hangar Siobhán was using as her home base. They stepped through a slender parting between the massive hangar doors, then headed to the stairs that led down into the subterranean storage areas. The eerie quiet they descended into was very much at odds with his last visit. Then, the screams of the maddened infected minions had been damn near deafening. He'd since had the rooms soundproofed to preserve the sanity of the Sentinels who worked there.

"Captain."

He turned to face a doorway he'd just passed. "Siobhán. It's good to see you."

The petite brunette stepped out with a smile for Lindsay and a quick nod of greeting for him, but her eyes went immediately to the carrier in his hand. "What have you brought for me?"

"What you asked for." He passed it over.

"Come with me," she said, running a hand through her cropped hair, which was still damp and fresh smelling from a recent shower. As was her usual, she wore urban camouflage pants with Army-issue jungle boots and a plain black T-shirt. The hard-edged attire did little to toughen her appearance. She was tiny and appeared delicate, a ruse that had blindsided too many of her opponents to count.

He followed her and Lindsay down the hall and into a laboratory outfitted with the best equipment his considerable fortune could buy. Freezers and glass-fronted refrigeration units lined the walls, while microscopes, notepads, and laptops covered the metal tables in the center.

Siobhán cleared space on the nearest tabletop with a sweep of her hand and set the cooler down. She smiled when she opened it and read the label on the blood bag. "Wish I could've been there when Raguel gave this up. And you got a sample from Vashti, too! You'll have to tell me all about that."

"Certainly, although I expect you have information to share with me as well." Adrian pulled out a metal stool for Lindsay and stood behind her. "Where's everyone else?"

"The others are in the infirmary or out in the field." The Sentinel moved to the closest refrigerator and put the two bags inside. "I wanted us to have some privacy when I talked to you about my latest discoveries."

"Oh?"

Lindsay reached for his hand and linked her fingers with his.

Siobhán returned and leaned a hip in to the edge of the table. She was flushed and bright eyed, almost glowing. He'd never seen her look so . . . happy. "I ran tests using the various samples that were sent to me over the last few days. Lycan blood, for the most part, has no effect."

"For the most part?"

"There was one sample that was anomalous. When I tested it, it caused a violent reaction. The virus became unstable very quickly. Had I been testing with a live subject, the subject would have expired."

"What sample was this?"

"The Alpha's."

Lindsay's hand tightened on his. "Elijah's? Why?"

"I'll have to run more tests to be certain, but I believe it's because the virus was created with his blood or blood similar to it. I'm trying to ascertain whether Elijah has a unique genetic anomaly or if it's common to Alphas in particular." Siobhán crossed her arms. "Unfortunately, I can't get a hold of Reese to get more samples."

Adrian thought back to the last time he'd heard from Reese, the Sentinel in charge of the Alphas. The dominant lycans had been segregated from the others to prevent revolt, and they were used for assignments requiring the utmost stealth, ones in which a lone hunter was the best offense. "I haven't spoken to him in about three months, but he checks in regularly and reports no trouble."

"Do you scan the reports personally?"

"No, I delegate to my second."

"So it was Phineas's job, then Jason's, and now Damien handles it?"

"Correct."

She nodded. "I would suggest you speak with Reese directly, Captain. One donor wouldn't be enough for the size of the outbreak we're dealing with unless they synthesized the identified protein. They'd need a lot of Alpha blood to pull that off. I'm talking about countless pints of blood and a considerable length of research and development time."

"I don't understand," Lindsay said. "If there are genetic markers that identify Alphas, why was Elijah placed under observation first? There shouldn't have been any question as to what he was, if a simple blood test could prove it."

"This is all news to me," Adrian said quietly, while inside his thoughts were raging. How could something so vital and elementary have escaped their notice for so long? He was afraid it was impossible, which led to even darker thoughts. Lindsay had been abducted from Angels' Point by someone with wings and delivered to Syre, who'd Changed her. From that incident, he'd known it was possible that one of his Sentinels had become a saboteur, but this . . . *This* spoke of a conspiracy of breadth and far-reaching consequence. "Have you ever been to Alaska, *neshama*?"

"No."

"Well, we'll be changing that tomorrow."

"Captain?"

He looked at Siobhán. "Yes?"

"There's something else." She took a deep breath. "I've fallen in love with a vampire."

As the hotel room door shut behind them, Vash tossed her bag on the bed and shot a worried glance at Elijah's leg. "How are you healing?"

"I'm fine." He offered her an easy, heartbreaking smile. "Good as new."

She nodded, but worry knotted her stomach. Like most lycans, he hated flying, and his discomfort had rubbed her raw over the short flight to West Virginia. She'd barely paid attention to the town of Huntington as she drove through it on the way to their lodging. Her thoughts were firmly on the events of the day and how dependent her equanimity had become on Elijah's well-being. Once she'd made up her mind to keep him, everything had changed. She now had something to lose, something she couldn't bear to lose. What was building between them was too new, too rare, too precious with all its myriad possibilities. The challenges, the joys—

"Vashti." He came to her, sliding his hands into her

hair and cupping her head. "It was a broken leg. It happens."

She caught him by the belt loops and yanked him closer. "I saw you get pulled into that room and the door shut . . . I panicked. I've never felt anything like that in my life. The sheer terror. I had to fight my way to get to you and every second felt like an hour. And when I got there and saw the gun in her hand, everything froze . . . I could barely think—"

"Shh . . ." He pressed his lips to her forehead. "It's okay."

"No. No, damn it, it's not okay. I don't want to feel like this. It's too much."

"Yes, it is. Scary as hell."

"You don't sound scared," she accused. "You don't act like it."

"I fight to keep a lid on it." His voice was low and soothing. "I knew what you are . . . who you are . . . when I took you on. If I tie you down to keep you safe, I'll lose you. And since I can't lose you, I'm working on dealing with it."

That his words so closely mirrored hers was soothing, but it wasn't an answer. It didn't fix what was aching inside her chest. "I'm not as strong as you. I don't want to let you out of my sight."

He nuzzled against her and she leaned into him, her knees weakening with his tenderness. "Because you've already let someone out of your sight once and you lost him. I can imagine it's tough to take that leap again."

"This wasn't supposed to happen. I'm not supposed

to feel this way again. I had my shot. I had Char. It's not supposed to happen a second time."

Pulling back, Elijah watched her with those verdant hunter's eyes. Cool and assessing. "What's not supposed to happen?"

"You. This. Us." She squeezed her eyes shut to block out the way he was looking at her. Butterflies were having a field day in her stomach. The anxiety was killing her. "Shit. Why can't the sex be enough? Why did all this other stuff have to get in the way?"

He tilted her head back and sealed his mouth over hers. The first lick of his tongue drove her mad, goaded her to push up onto her tiptoes and capture him with soft suction. His groan rippled through her, inciting the fiercest hunger. Her desire was always smoldering, ready to combust with the slightest provocation.

Vash took his mouth with savage greed, her tongue stroking deep. Her hands shoved up beneath his shirt, seeking and finding his warm, rough satin skin. Her fingers dug into the muscles bracketing his spine, pulling him hard against her so that nothing came between them but their clothes.

His rumbling laugh vibrated against her tender breasts. "You're definitely trying to screw me to death."

"I want you," she muttered, while kissing along his jaw and throat.

"Good."

She shoved his shirt up and buried her face in the light dusting of hair on his chest, breathing in the hardworking scent of his skin. Her tongue found the flat

disk of a nipple and teased it, worrying it with fluttering strokes.

"Fuck, that feels good," he said hoarsely, lifting his
arms to pull his shirt off.

Dropping to her knees, she yanked open his fly with
frantic fingers.

"Hey." He tossed his shirt aside. "What's the rush?"

She tugged at his jeans, but he stopped her, catching
her by the chin and tilting her face up.

"Vashti." His eyes were dark with concern. "Talk to
me."

"Don't wanna talk. I want you."

He joined her on the floor, kneeling and brushing
her hair back from her face. "We're going to face a lot
of tough situations together. It's the nature of who we
are."

"Easy for you to say." She smacked his hand away.
"The chances of my dying are slim to none. You're dying right now. Every minute."

"Ah." Elijah sank back onto his heels, completely
oblivious to the stunningly sensual sight he presented—
bare-chested with his button fly parted just enough to
expose the thin, silky line of hair that led to delicious
places below. So vital and virile. A potent force of nature. And yet his days on this earth were finite. "I get
it."

"I don't think you do. How can you?"

Setting his hands on his knees, he exhaled in a rush.
"Mated lycans live longer."

"What? What did you say?"

"You heard me. And you love me. Enough that it's

driving you crazier than you already were to begin with."

She stared at him. Then she pushed to her feet, pulling herself together with as much dignity as she could muster. They weren't going to talk about this. Ever. It was bad enough without saying the words. "Go take that shower you wanted."

Catching her wrist when she moved to pass him, he stood. "I'm glad."

"Don't get excited. This place may not have hot water."

"I'm glad you love me," he qualified.

"Did I say that? I don't think I said that."

"Okay, then." His thumb brushed over the madly throbbing pulse in her wrist. "I won't say it either. Doesn't make it less true."

The sharpening pain in her chest had her stumbling to the bed. She sat gracelessly, her gaze on the blank television screen.

"Go shower," she said again.

"Join me?"

She shook her head, wondering how she would survive going through this twice. Suffering through the debilitating, devastating pain twice. And she was stunned that she could even equate the two men she loved together—one who was with her for eons alongside one she'd known only a matter of days. How could she feel this way so swiftly? Worse, there was no doubt her affection for Elijah would grow as time passed, becoming even more necessary until she wouldn't be able to breathe without him.

He lifted her hand to his lips and kissed her knuckles, then let her go. A moment later, she heard the shower come on in the bathroom. And a moment after that, she heard him singing.

The pain in her chest turned into a sweet yearning. He had a beautiful tenor, showcased by the choice of song, which she didn't recognize. But he could've sung horribly off-key, for all she cared. It wasn't his talent that seduced her, but the intimacy of sharing this downtime with him. The gift of seeing him open and unguarded.

Mated. Vash shook her head. That word didn't mean the same thing to a lycan as it did to a vampire. When Charron died, she'd gone on. Inarguably altered by the loss, yes, but capable of moving forward all the same. When Elijah mated, he would live until he died of old age or his mate died, whichever came first. He couldn't survive either circumstance.

She was still contemplating that when he emerged from the bathroom, naked and dripping wet. He shook out his hair, spraying her and the rest of the room with droplets of water.

"Hey," she protested. "Watch it, puppy."

He glanced at her as he went to the dresser and checked his cell phone. "You're doing enough watching for the both of us, cougar. You're ogling, really. My ass is burning."

"It's a very nice ass." She was startled by the throatiness of her voice. Due to his effect on her, of course. The one she'd been experiencing since she first saw him naked and bleeding in a Utah cave, his luscious body still vibrating with the threat of imminent violence.

She wasn't going to think about the end. She was going to focus on the here and now, taking everything she could from him, giving everything she had. If his life was going to pass with the swiftness of a dream, she was going to make sure they blazed as bright as the sun so that when the time came, she'd burn out with him.

She unzipped her vest and said with unmistakable possession, "Mine."

He faced her, his eyes dropping to her exposed breasts. A rumbling purr escaped him. "Mine."

She beckoned him with a crook of her finger. He came to a stop in front of her, standing between her parted knees, his glistening cock directly at eye level. When he reached for her shoulders to push her back onto the bed, she linked her hands with his and held him back, her tongue darting out to lick the length of his rigid erection.

"God . . ." His head fell back. "I dreamed about your mouth on me that first night in Bryce Canyon."

Determined to erase the memory of the last time she'd gone down on him, Vash released his hands and stroked him with her fists. His rough sound of pleasure was as beautiful to her ears as his singing. When his fingers tangled in her hair and began directing her, she gave herself over to him, allowing him to set the pace and depth, enjoying the confidence with which he took what he needed from her. It hadn't been that way with Char, who'd been reverent with her. Elijah was a much earthier creature. He was both a lycan, with a beast's base needs, and a man who understood his woman's need to cede control at times.

She tightened the ring of her lips and deepened the suction, dizzy with desire and love. The taste of him, so clean and rich and purely male, went to her head. Her sex softened and grew slick, greedy for him. Mouthing the plush head, she moaned when a hard shudder tore through him.

He gasped, his thighs trembling. "You suck me so good . . . You're so fucking hot . . ."

Lifting her head, she released him from her lips and pushed the rigid length between her cleavage. She pressed her arms tightly together, hugging his throbbing erection with the breasts he loved so much.

"Vashti." The look in his eyes was her reward, the need he revealed so stark and intimate. "You shred me."

"Yours," she said softly, licking her lips as he gripped her shoulders to keep her still. He began to thrust slowly, gently, his rhythm not quite even.

"Beautiful," he said hoarsely. "You're so damn beautiful."

Bending his knees, he quickened his pace, his breath sawing from his lungs. His eyes grew bright and feverish, his skin flushed and misted with sweat.

She felt the tension grip him, watched the tight lacing of muscle on his abdomen flex and contract with every pump of his hips. He was close; she could feel it . . .

"Enough." He withdrew and flipped her in one economical movement, bending her over the bed and shoving her pants down. With a loose fist in her hair, he pushed into her, gliding through tender, swollen tissues in a smooth, deep slide.

Her eyes closed on a whimper of delight. She lost herself in the lazy haze of pleasure, the simple beauty of Elijah's thorough, unhurried tempo. Slow and easy. Rolling his hips with a skill and control that stole her breath. Knowing just how to take her, how deep to thrust, how far to withdraw, how much pressure to exert when he ground himself into her. Her eyes stung with the purity of the connection, both raw and tender. Impossibly intimate.

He nuzzled her loosened vest off her shoulder and whispered in her ear. "One day soon, when you're ready, I'm going to mount you like this. I'm going to ride you while you arch your neck for me. I'm going to mark you with my teeth. Fuck you. *Mate* with you. Then you'll be mine, Vashti. Irrevocably. Every luscious, stubborn, dangerous inch of you. *Mine.*"

She shivered into a devastating climax with that promise in her heart. As impossible as it was, it was hers. Just as he was.

Elijah woke from a deep, healing sleep in the midst of a shift, his body jackknifing up as a man and hitting the carpeted floor as a lycan. He spun about, snarling, looking for the threat that stirred his beast. Vashti's whimper from the bed pinned him, freezing him in a block of ice.

"No!" She gasped, her body shuddering through her nightmare. "Please. Stop . . ."

Ah, God. He whined in torment, his gut churning. Focusing on his heart rate, he willed it to slow, forcing his mind to clear so he could shift back into the form that could wake her without scaring her. The form that could hold her close and give her comfort.

The few moments it took to get himself under control seemed like days. Vashti thrashed naked in their bed, her lush body jerking with remembered pain, and he had no way to fight the demons that plagued her soul. No way to avenge her. Not yet.

The moment he shifted, he lunged to the bed and caught her up, his arms banding around her as she fought against him in the midst of her dream.

"Vashti," he said gruffly, his throat tight with anger and grief. "Come back to me, sweetheart. Wake up."

She curled into his chest, her silken skin slick with a cold sweat. "Elijah."

"I'm here. I have you."

Shuddering violently, she pressed a cold nose to his skin. "Damn it."

"Shh . . ." He rocked her, his lips pressed to the crown of her head. "It's all right. It's over now."

"No." She shook her head, her nails digging into his back as she clutched at him. "I can't sleep, damn it. All I want is to lie next to you when you rest, to curl up beside you and dream with you. They fucking took that away from me."

Tipping her back to see her tear-streaked face, Elijah brushed aside the strands of damp hair that clung to her forehead and cheeks and met her haunted gaze. To see so strong a woman reduced to a terrified creature broke his heart and incited a lethal wrath that had no outlet. He could protect her from outside forces and he would, but the darkness inside her was something he couldn't reach until she let him. "Not forever. When we're mated—"

"We're not going to mate, damn it!" She struggled violently out of his arms, like a feral animal, and he released her only so she wouldn't hurt herself. "I can't breed, Elijah. I can't give you cute little fanged pups to trip over after a long day of Alpha'ing packs of lycans who want me dead."

"And I won't live forever," he shot back. "We're not perfect, but we're all we have. Damned if I'll watch you suffer when I can help you."

"There's nothing to help with! It was over a long time ago."

"Not in your mind, it's not. Not in your dreams. When we're mated—" He held up a hand before she opened her mouth. "Shut up and listen to me. When we're mated, I'll be able to share those dreams with you. I'll be able to fight off the demons that hurt you. We'll be able to talk to each other, share with each other, without a word."

Her eyes widened in horror. "I don't want you in my head."

"You had no problems digging into mine."

"That was different. We were having sex. I wanted you to feel good."

"Right back atcha, sweetheart." His jaw tightened. "You need me in your head. And *I* need to be in there. It's killing me to see you hurt like this. To smell your fear."

"I just need to stay awake." Vash began to pace, her wild hair swaying around her nude torso. "I don't need sleep like you do. I can go without it."

"Fuck that." He pushed to his feet. "Your body may not need sleep, but your mind does. Your heart does."

"You don't know what they did to me," she bit out. "I don't want you to know. You won't know. I won't let you."

Elijah crossed his arms. "Try and stop me."

"It's not necessary. We can work around it."

"No deals, sweetheart. Do you think there's something—*anything*—that could make me not want you? Don't you think I would've found that escape route before we passed the point of no return? You're right. I don't know what was done to you. But I've got the gist and a really twisted, sick, fucked-up imagination. Chances are, what I can picture in my head is worse than reality, but it doesn't matter either way. It doesn't change how I feel about you. Nothing can."

"You don't know that." She fisted the roots of her hair with both hands. "I won't risk you finding out the hard way."

He caught her when she paced by and made her look at him. "The only thing that could come between us is infidelity. In that case, you wouldn't have to worry about me walking away because you'd both be dead."

Vash stared at him a moment, her eyes bleak; then the corner of her mouth twitched. "And you call me the crazy one?"

"I'm going to make you happy." He pulled her close. The icy lump in his stomach melted when her slender arms encircled him. "Whether you like it or not. Whether you fight me or not."

"Oh, I'll fight you," she promised, her eyes clear of shadows. "That's the way I roll."

He pressed his lips to her forehead. "I wouldn't have you any other way."

CHAPTER 19

"Stick close," Elijah said as Vashti climbed out of the passenger side of their rental, her gaze trained on the massive metal gate that was the entrance to the Huntington lycan outpost. "They'll know you're mine the moment they get a whiff of you. I'd be surprised if we don't face at least one challenger here. Especially from whoever's been running this place since they revolted."

She slid sunglasses over her golden eyes and rounded the hood. "I've got your back, babe. And your fine ass, too."

He couldn't help but look twice, then stare. She was wearing one of the sleek, sleeveless black bodysuits that looked like wet paint applied directly to her skin. Black leather boots covered her from toe to knee and her long, blood red hair hung loosely down her back. For the first time since he'd met her, she wore jewelry: a stunning necklace she'd picked up that morning when she was out fetching him coffee from Starbucks. The fact that she'd thought of his desire for caffeine—a desire she didn't share—touched him. But the necklace touched him more. It was an elaborate collar of peridot around her neck, a color she said reminded her of his eyes.

The nonchalance with which she'd told him about her selection didn't fool him for a minute. The necklace shook up her usual stark mourning black in an unmistakable way. No one could miss the statement, and she'd chosen to make it with something she associated with him.

She'd gone on to tell him that her wings had been a similar color, putting a picture in his head of a ruby-haired, sapphire-eyed, peridot-winged angel with pale-as-a-pearl skin. Impossibly gorgeous, he'd thought, wishing he could have seen her that way. Then he'd pulled her close and kissed her until she went lax in his arms and her dreamy smile revealed her wickedly sharp fangs. The angel she'd been was in the past. It was the vampress who held his heart. The fallen angel with a warrior's soul. The woman who'd suffered brutality at the hands of demons and been broken only to come back stronger and fiercer than ever.

"Micah's always going to be a problem, isn't he?" she asked softly, absently adjusting the fit of her katana scabbards. "Or more accurately, what I did to him and what you did to his widow because of me."

He didn't deny it. There was no point.

"I'm sorry, El." Reaching out, she linked her fingers with his. "Not that I did it, because under the circumstances and the information I had to go on, I would do it again. But I'm sorry that it hurt you and that it's causing you trouble now."

The video screen beside the door flickered, and a stern male face appeared. "Who are you? And what do you want?"

Since the feed was closest to Vashti, she approached it first. "Your Alpha is here to check the place out. A warm welcome is expected. A little brownnosing wouldn't hurt."

Elijah sighed. "Vashti."

"What?" She strolled over to him.

The thirty-foot door slid open smoothly, revealing a party of a half-dozen armed lycans—five males and one female. Vashti looked down at the multitude of red pistol scope laser sights shimmering on her chest. A wicked smile curved her lips, and she bared her fangs.

"Behave," he admonished her before stepping forward. "Lower your weapons. She's with me."

"She's a vampire," the tall, tawny-haired lycan in the middle said with a scowl.

"Cute *and* observant," Vash purred. "I'm sorry I left the Scooby Snacks back at the hotel."

The lycan's aim lifted to center mass of her forehead.

Elijah pulled the sunglasses off his face. "Ah, but clearly his hearing is defective. I may need to put him down."

"Can I watch?" she asked sweetly.

The dark-haired lycan next to Trigger-Happy holstered his weapon and came forward. His nostrils twitched, and one brow rose as he looked back and forth between Elijah and Vashti. "Interesting."

Vash's grin widened. "You have no idea."

The lycan extended his hand to Elijah. "I'm Paul. We weren't aware there was an Alpha in charge."

Vash stepped closer, clearly protective. "Why send a messenger when he can take care of it himself? Your Alpha takes the hands-on approach."

"We have a hierarchy here," Trigger-Happy said tightly. "You'll respect it, or you can find another outpost to shelter you."

She shook her head. "Definitely no treats for you."

Trigger-Happy took aim.

In the time it took for Vash to pivot out of the way, Elijah shifted and lunged. He knocked the blond down and ripped his throat out in one fluid movement.

Gunshots fired around them. Elijah spun in a snarling crouch, prepared to attack again . . . only to find three of the lycans nursing bleeding trigger hands and one of the males standing with both arms up in the air and his gaze rigidly trained on the ground. Vash held Paul's pistol in one hand and the back of his neck in the other, her arm straightened so that he was forced to his knees on the ground.

Elijah shifted forms and walked toward his discarded clothes, admiration and respect for his woman filling him in a heated rush.

Vash glared at the female lycan. "Close your eyes, bitch. No peeking. You see any part of your Alpha but his face and you won't live to regret it."

He pulled on his jeans first, for Vash's sake, then

used his shirt to wipe the blood from his mouth and chest. "I'm lenient about many things," he said to the group at large. "But I won't tolerate disobedience or threats of any kind against Vashti. Are we clear?"

Two of the males shifted forms at the mention of who she was, unable to restrain their agitation. The snarl he shot them had them sitting, if shifting restlessly. "Let Paul get up."

Vash released the man, but kept her gaze trained on the others.

Paul straightened, raking Elijah with a sweeping glance. "I've never seen a lycan shift so fast."

"Betcha never seen a lycan who's nailing a vampress either," Vash said. "Syre's second, no less. It's a whole new world."

Elijah arched a brow at her. "Didn't I tell you to behave?"

"I don't take orders from you when I'm not naked."

He decided not to give her any more ammunition. "I need access to your data center, Paul."

"Yes, Alpha." Paul gestured through the gate. "I'll show you where it is."

Elijah was deep into working on the data when Vash's cell phone rang. Excusing herself, she stepped out to the hallway and answered, managing a smile when Syre's face appeared on her iPhone screen.

"Vashti," he greeted her. "How are things faring in Huntington?"

"I don't know yet. They're digging for the goods now."

"What is that on your neck?" He frowned. "Is that . . . jewelry?"

She flushed. "Yeah. What's up?"

"Have things smoothed out between you and your lycan?"

"I'm keeping him." She figured it was best to get that out of the way.

Syre's smile revealed his fangs. "Excellent."

Her fist clenched at her side, her mind's eye seeing the fork in the road ahead and the decision she'd soon be forced to make between the two most important men in her life.

"Can you speak privately?" His smooth, soothing voice had the opposite effect, making her hackles rise.

"Not yet." Vash glanced up at one of the lycans on guard duty in the hallway. "Nearest soundproofed room?"

He jerked his thumb down the hall, his gaze cold and hard. "Two doors down on the right, bloodsucker."

"Thanks, Fido."

Once she was inside alone, she cocked her ears and listened for anything other than her own breathing. She kicked the walls one by one, listening for the telltale sound of a pocket where a bug could be hidden. When those checks come up clear, she nodded. "Okay. I'm good. What's up?"

"I'm heading with Raze to Chicago now to follow up with his contact there. Torque is covering for us while we're in the field." Syre leaned back in his chair. "As for your lycan . . . there's something you need to know."

Her heartbeat skipped at his tone. "Oh?"

"His blood caused a remission in that wraith yesterday for a reason—he'd just drunk filtered Sentinel blood through Lindsay. When Grace tested Lindsay's blood via the needles and other paraphernalia that you had the presence of mind to retain, she found the effect to be even more pronounced. It's highly likely that pure, undiluted Sentinel blood—or perhaps all angelic blood—is the key to a cure for the Wraith Virus."

She heaved out her breath and nodded grimly.

"You suspected that," he noted.

"I knew it had to be something major in order for Adrian to let Lindsay come with me." She ran a hand through her hair and paced, her heels clicking across the tiled floor. "Fuckin' A. This could explain why he took my blood. He probably figures we might still have similar blood properties."

"I've sent Grace blood samples from me, Raze, and Salem. We'll see what she turns up. With any luck, this trip to Chicago will prove fruitful and we'll be able to get her the help she needs to speed things up." He paused a moment. "Also, there was an incendiary device found in the wreckage of the pickup truck. It's possible it was set off by remote."

"How would the person with the remote know to activate it?" Her mind scrambled ahead. "Unless they were watching."

"We found pockets of C4 all over the wraith house. It was a trap."

"Why didn't the house go up? If they saw the truck pull out, they definitely saw us in the house."

"We don't know. Perhaps your double had the remote for the house in the truck. Or the receiver was defective. Salem is leading a team through the property now. Torque is working on tracking the purchase of the C4. Hopefully we'll have some answers soon."

Vash rubbed at the icy lump in her chest. "Until we've got a better handle on this, watch your back in Chicago. And keep an eye on Raze. There's something between him and that lab tech you're visiting."

"I caught that. Keep me posted."

Syre's austerely beautiful face faded to black and she blew out her breath in a rush. She turned when the door opened behind her.

Elijah filled the doorway and the fear that had been sliding through her eased its grip.

He held his hand out to her. "We've found what you're looking for."

Vash squeezed Elijah's shoulder as she read the data on the massive van-sized monitor on the wall. "Three lycans," she said. "Three against Char and Ice. They shouldn't have been able to win."

He looked at her, studying her face, wishing he knew who she'd been on the phone with and what they'd told her. Her usual vivacity was subdued, concerning him. "Do you believe the accusation that Charron's fledgling incited an attack?"

"It's possible." Her troubled gaze met his. "Ice was problematic. He was struggling with bloodthirst and he lacked self-control. I was leaning toward putting him down, but Char thought he could turn the kid around. I was so busy with my duties as second that it was hard for me to deny him something that gave him pleasure and kept him occupied."

Elijah read between the lines. They hadn't been equals, not as he and Vash were. "But Ice survived the attack—"

"Only by hours. He'd been burned too badly by the sun."

"—while Charron was brutalized."

She nodded. "The attack was especially vicious. So much so that I thought maybe the demons had gotten to him before I arrived. But the body reeked of lycans, and the disemboweling had been done with lycan teeth."

The demons. A chill moved through him. Pulling her close, he placed his lips to her ear and asked, "How soon after Char's death were you attacked?"

She yanked back. "Who said I was—" Then she scowled. "An hour. Thereabouts."

"An hour . . ." He crushed her to him, squeezing her so tightly she gasped and struggled. "I'm going to find a way to raise them from hell and kill them all over again."

"Elijah." She softened and let him love her, pressing her lips to his jaw. "Always avenging somebody . . . except when I get in the way."

He turned back to the monitor, keeping an arm around her waist. He spoke to the lycan named Samuel who manned the keyboard. "Can you pull up their histories and display them side-by-side?"

Samuel typed in the necessary commands and Elijah studied the results. "Same month and year of birth for all three," he noted.

"And they all died the same year," Vashti murmured. "Within a few months of each other."

"Same litter, Samuel?"

The lycan frowned at the monitor. "We don't have many triplet births, but let me pull up their breeding charts . . . Huh. There aren't any. That's weird."

"We can check their blood," Elijah said. "Send someone to cryostorage to pull their samples."

Samuel picked up the phone embedded in the workstation and passed along the order.

Vash's fingertips kneaded restlessly into his hip. "Would that be unusual for brothers to hunt together?"

"Depends." His gaze remained on the monitor. "At a younger age, no. But these were breeding-age males. They should have been spread around among the outposts."

"Widening the gene pool," she filled in drily. "How romantic."

"Explains why their information is so similar. Doesn't explain why they died. Samuel, why isn't there a notation as to cause of death?"

Shrugging, Samuel said, "Depends on the situation at the time and the thoroughness of the tech. Remember, this room was Sentinels-only before the revolt, and most of them don't give a shit how we die."

Elijah pulled his ringing phone from his pocket to silence it, then noted Stephan's name and took the call. "What've you got?"

"A few hundred lycans," his Beta said drily. "I'm back at the warehouse. As the teams move across the country, they're running across expat lycans and sending them here. Someone needs to be here full time to process them."

"Thank god you've got initiative."

Stephan laughed. "If I bothered you with every administrative decision, you'd bite my head off. Perhaps literally."

"You're too valuable. I'd find something else to torture you with."

"Listen, there's something else."

The sudden gravity in his Beta's voice set Elijah on alert. "What?"

"Himeko's telling everyone you've mated with Syre's second."

"Hmm . . ." He watched as Vash stepped in front of him with a frown, her vampiric hearing ensuring that she heard every word. He smoothed the line between her brows with soft strokes of his thumb. "Not yet. She's still getting used to the idea."

There was a long pause. "Alpha, I hate to point out the obvious—"

"Then don't."

"Vampires can't breed."

"Thank you for the recap."

Stephan was not amused. "It's my job as your Beta to inform you of concerns in the ranks. Don't mock me for doing it."

"I would never mock you—I respect you too much. In return, I ask that you don't talk to me like I'm an idiot. I'm doing everything I can to the best of my ability. That's all anyone has a right to know. My personal life is my own. If there's a problem with that, tell the

others to direct their energies to finding the Alpha outpost. Then we can have a democratic election and
everyone can have a say."

Vashti's gaze darkened. *Not funny,* she mouthed.

No, it wasn't. The only way another Alpha could
gain control of the packs was by taking Elijah out. They
wouldn't get the respect they needed to lead without
that victory.

"I'll keep you posted," Stephan said.

Elijah killed the call and returned his attention to the
monitor. "Now, where were we?"

The ringing of the phone in the workstation interrupted as if on cue. Samuel answered. "Did you double-
check? Well, check again."

Vashti's gaze narrowed. "Wanna bet the blood's
missing?"

"Don't like the odds," Elijah replied, not surprised
when Samuel proved Vash's hunch correct. "Okay,
then, pull up their photos."

"No problem. Let me see . . . Ah, here's one. Peter
Neil."

A familiar image popped up on screen and Elijah
scowled. "I know him. Worked with him a time or two.
His name isn't Peter."

"A sibling, maybe?" Vash queried.

"No. See the scar on his lip? Same guy."

"Is he here?" she asked Samuel.

"I've never seen him before."

"He's dead," Elijah said curtly. "Killed in a nest raid
about twenty years ago. I was there when it happened.
Do you have head shots of the others?"

Whistling, Samuel tapped out another string of keystrokes and another picture popped up. "Here's Kevin Hayes."

Vashti sucked in a deep breath.

Elijah's remaining patience thinned dangerously. "Wrong photo."

"That's the one that was shot on intake," Samuel insisted.

"It's a mistake. That's Micah McKenna."

"McKenna, huh? Hang on. Okay, there's a Micah McKenna in the system. Yeah . . . you're right. He came in the same day as Kevin. Maybe the photos got switched around and misfiled. Here's the one from Micah's file." The same photo popped up. "Someone fucked up."

But Elijah's attention was riveted to the history data that had opened along with the photo. His gaze skimmed through it, finding all the expected information—registered mate, archives of transfers and kills, breeding chart.

"He lied," Vash said. "I asked him his age and he said—"

"—fifty." Micah's official record put him at eighty years old, which made it possible for him to have killed Charron. He'd been too young at fifty—the perfect alibi. "Where's the third lycan's photo?"

"Here." Samuel pulled it up. "Anthony Williams."

His fists clenched with recognition. "Look up Trent Parry."

"All right . . . Yep, he's here, too."

"Well, look at that," Vash muttered. "The same photo as Anthony."

Elijah's entire world tilted to the side, skewed by the realization that the men he'd trusted had betrayed him and every other lycan.

She began to pace. "It's a fucking cover-up. They created a paper trail for three imaginary lycans and absolved them of guilt in Char's death. Why, damn it? Why did the Sentinels protect three rabid dogs?"

He shot her a look that warned her to say no more. "Samuel, get me copies of all these files, on both a flash drive and disks. Look up a Charles Tate, too, and throw him in the mix. He's the one using the alias Peter Neil."

Vash stopped directly in front of him. "Is Trent dead like Micah and Charles? Have I been hunting ghosts?"

"Trent was with me in Phoenix during the trip when Nikki attacked Adrian and we found Lindsay." He pressed his lips to her brow and murmured, "You may have to fight her for him. She wants him, too."

"Why?"

"I'll explain later. For now, let's get out of here."

CHAPTER 20

Vash didn't realize how furious Elijah was until they returned to the hotel and he began shoving things into his bag.

"Elijah." She reached out to him as he stormed past her.

"Get your shit. I want you out of here. I don't trust this place. Don't trust what's left of that pack."

"Elijah."

"I'll throw it together if you won't," he growled, grabbing toiletries out of the bathroom. "But you'd better not bitch at me if something gets left behind."

When he emerged, she stepped right into his path. "Will you talk to me, damn it!"

"What?"

"You're pissed."

"Goddamn right I'm pissed." He tossed the things in his hand on the bed and growled. "You know what Rachel said to me before she incited the rebellion at

Navajo Lake? She said, 'It's all on you.' Now I have to wonder if I've been manipulated in ways I haven't figured out yet. It's certain they wanted you and me to kill each other. If we hadn't fallen into rut the minute we scented each other, one or both of us would be dead. We'd never have spent the time together that led to where we are now, and Syre would be out for someone's blood."

"You think Micah's the one who planted your blood for me to find?"

He crossed his arms, straining the armholes of the T-shirt he'd borrowed after getting blood on his own. "You killed Micah's partner but kept Micah alive to interrogate. Why not the other way around?"

"He had a big mouth. Taunting me and being an all-around asshat. It was easy to pick him."

"He *made* it easy. And I think it's possible you recognized his scent from Charron's attack without realizing it. Maybe you even recognized it from Nikki's abduction. That knowledge might've been there in the back of your mind."

"I have Char's killers' scents ingrained in my memory. I wouldn't miss that."

"I once had to argue my right to claim a kill because a badly wounded lycan had bled all over the body. It smelled like her, more so than me, because of the blood. If Micah had access to my blood to frame me, certainly he had access to others'. Considering the trouble involved in creating that paper trail, dumping a couple bags of blood around Charron's body would be the easy part. And we both know how a disemboweling smells.

That could explain why the attack was so vicious—they wanted the stench to cover up their identities."

She sank heavily onto the bed. "Why?"

Elijah crouched in front of her. "To break you. I think they've been trying to do that for years. First through Charron's death, then through me. Micah's the thread there. You can't tell me that's coincidence. I won't buy it."

"No." She exhaled harshly. "I'm not buying it either."

"And we can't forget about your double attacking Lindsay's mother. Lindsay grew up planning on killing you her whole life."

"They would've had to know who she was. That she had Shadoe's soul inside her."

"Yes. Just as they'd know Adrian or Syre would find her, and through them, she'd find you. It explains why she wasn't killed along with her mother. In my experience, the minions who go batshit have a liking for children's blood."

"I've heard it's sweeter," she murmured absently, rubbing at the ache in her chest. To think of Char dying because of her . . . "I'm not important enough to go to this much trouble for."

"You're important to Syre. Very much so. And so was Phineas to Adrian." He caught up her cold hands in his. "This is psychological warfare—cripple the primaries by taking out their seconds. Micah likely deliberately sacrificed himself for the cause—just as I now suspect Rachel did. They wanted me in a specific headspace to achieve their aims."

"To put you and the lycans on the high ground? Is that what this is all about? To make you the dominant faction?"

"I don't know." He scrubbed a hand over his face. "That wouldn't explain the doctored files and missing blood; only Sentinels had access to cryostorage and data centers. And your double brings vamps into the mix, too. Why would they want lycans at the top of the food chain?"

"Vamps delivered Lindsay to Syre . . . after she was taken from the Point by a Sentinel."

"Right. We've got the wrong vamps, lycans, and Sentinels involved here. The question isn't just who's dirty, but are they dirty together?"

Pulling a hand free, Vash cupped his face with it, then told him about the conversation she'd had with Syre.

He cursed and pushed to his feet. "I have to go back. I have to go back to Adrian."

She gained her feet, too. Her heart pounded. *"What?"*

"The Sentinels are wide open. Once it gets out that their blood is the cure, they'll be sitting ducks. They need help. I have to at least attempt an alliance."

"They can take out a hundred vamps a minute, if they wanted to. They never really needed you."

The look he shot her was dark . . . and decided. *"We* need *them.* For all their faults, they keep the minions in check."

"Minions are dying, El!" But she knew with a sinking heart that she wouldn't be able to sway him.

"I need to go back if only because Micah worked so

damned hard to force me to leave. There's a reason for that, and I'm not going to just play along."

"What about me? I need you. My people need you."

Elijah tugged her close and pressed his lips to her brow. He held them there for a long moment, the beat of his heart slightly faster than it should be. "They've got you, sweetheart. You're a one-woman army."

She caught his belt loops, holding on tightly. Her chest and throat burned. "You can't ask me to make this choice. It's not fair."

His hands pushed into her hair, brushing it back from her face. He looked down at her with such tenderness, she could hardly breathe through the pain of it. "I'm not asking you to do anything, Vashti. I'm telling you what I have to do."

She stood frozen as he extricated himself and walked away. She watched him collect the items from the bed and take his stuff to his bag and her stuff to her bag. Separating them. Dividing them up.

"Fuck you, lycan." Her fists clenched at her sides. A surge of malicious satisfaction moved through her when he paused in surprise. "You can't make me love you, then just fucking walk away. We're in this. You and me."

"I'm not walking away." He faced her and crossed his arms. "You're mine, Vashti. Nothing can change that. If you haven't figured that out yet, we've got bigger problems than the war breathing down our necks."

The fist around her heart loosened. "Then what the hell are you doing?"

"Letting you be who you need to be. Letting you be

the woman I love, even if that means you're on the other side of the world, on the other side of the line. If I make you go my way, I'll lose you. I know that, because if you try to force me to go yours, you'll lose me."

"I can't live that way, El." Anxiety slithered through her, making her sick and cold. She began to pace. "We can't be apart, working against each other. We have to find a compromise we can live with."

"Tell me what that is," he said softly. "I have to call Lindsay and tell her the vampire most likely responsible for her mother's murder is dead, which will be both a relief and not, because she wanted to do the killing herself. Then I'll follow that up with the news that I probably got her father killed, since I handpicked the team of lycans sent to guard him and one of those team members was Trent. After that, I get to tell Adrian that Syre knows Sentinel blood is the cure and pretty soon more vampires will know, so now the clock is ticking. In the meantime, Syre's got rogues infecting his ranks and I've got lycans who are deliberately sabotaging my relations with both sides. Where's the middle ground?"

"Switzerland."

His brow arched. "You want to run off to Switzerland? That's your plan?"

"No, we'll *be* Switzerland. You and Lindsay will form a loop, Syre and I will form a loop, and you and I will remain one unit. We'll bridge the gap between the two. Right now, the biggest priority for everyone is the Wraith Virus. If we're all fighting the same enemy, it makes sense to combine forces."

"Since when did common sense prevent war?"

"I don't think Syre would go to war without me. He would certainly think twice about it if I objected. If you can convince Adrian that the risk to the Sentinels is too great without your support, we might be able to hold them both back. Especially if they know we're all being set up. They're not going to want to play into that any more than you do. It's worth a shot."

"Okay."

Vash came to an abrupt halt, shocked that he'd capitulated so easily. "Just like that?"

"It's messy, complicated, and will probably come back to bite us in the ass. And the Wraith Virus isn't really a lycan problem—"

"Aside from the fact that you seem to be especially tasty to them," she interjected.

"There's that, I suppose." He resumed packing. "But we'll do our best."

Relief hit her like a Mack truck. That might've been why she blurted, "And I want to mate with you."

Elijah froze, his hand suspended in the process of zipping his duffel closed. "*Vashti.*"

She spoke in a rush, her heart racing and her palms damp. "I know it's selfish. If someone's really out for my blood and they manage to get to me, I'll take you down with me. I know lycans don't live long after losing a mate, but—"

He faced her and the look in his eyes nearly leveled her. "I'll go down whether we're mated or not. I thought you knew. I'm already there, Vashti. I think I've been there since you gave me that pep talk in the cave."

Vash stumbled straight into his arms. "You're the

worst thing that's ever happened to me. You've fucked up everything."

He laughed, and the sound unknotted the stress and fear inside her. "And we're just getting started."

"We'll be able to communicate without words, right? We'll have that advantage."

"Among others." He brushed her hair back from her face. "We'll be stronger as a connected unit . . . and more vulnerable. They'll know how to hurt us."

"So we won't tell anyone. I'll be your fanged piece on the side and you'll be my boy toy. We'll let those who want to believe that we're using each other believe it, but we'll know better."

"You don't have to do this," he said softly. "I can wait until you're ready."

"I'm more than ready. Just try and stop me, baby."

She called Syre and told him about what she'd learned of Charron's attack. While she did so, Elijah called Lindsay and told her he needed to meet with both her and Adrian. Then Vash and El finished packing and headed to the Huntington Jet Center to wait for one of Adrian's private planes.

They were finalizing the paperwork for the return of their rental car when an agency employee rushed in with a manila envelope in her hand.

"Mr. Reynolds," the pretty strawberry-blonde called out, wearing a winsome smile that made Vash take a possessive step closer to her man. "You left this in the backseat."

"That's not mine." He frowned and soothed Vash by failing to even register the clerk's attraction to him.

"It has your name on it."

He accepted the envelope and opened it, withdrawing the contents. Photographs. Shots taken through a paned window, like something a private investigator would snap of subjects unaware they were being surveilled. Vash recognized the Sentinel in the photos instantly.

"Helena," she murmured. "Wow. She's being naughty. With a hunky guy."

"Mark," he identified grimly. "A lycan from the Navajo Lake pack."

The import of a Sentinel shagging a lycan slowly sank in. Hell, a Sentinel shagging anything was earth-shaking news. "Fuckin' A."

He flipped faster, turning the frame-by-frame shots into a mini-motion picture. The couple came together in a passionate embrace, their mouths melding . . . clothes shedding . . .

Then a masked figure was in the room with them, standing over the bed, his posture so menacing it caused the fine hairs on her arms to rise. The next shot was of the window with the curtains drawn, followed by several photos from inside the room, scenes of a carnage so horrifying her stomach knotted—Helena with sightless eyes, her beautiful wings clawed from her back, her lover lying pale and bloodless on the floor with twin punctures in his neck. The time stamp in the lower-right-hand corner of the pictures told her the shots had been taken nearly a month ago.

"What is this?" she whispered, devastated. "Where did it come from? What the fuck are we supposed to do with it?"

Elijah shoved the envelope into his duffel. "Someone's sending us a message we'll have to decipher."

They swiftly wrapped up their business at the rental counter and headed over to meet their plane. The silence stretched out, comfortable between them even when thick with a clusterfuck of lies and questions.

Vash linked her fingers with his while they waited in the concourse. "Are you sure about going to Alaska? It's a long flight, El. Maybe a video conference would be better. Or we can wait until Lindsay and Adrian get back."

He glanced at her. "Didn't I mention that Adrian's jets have a sleeping cabin?"

"Oh?" Heat swept through her, melting her trepidation over the days to come. "No, I think you forgot that part."

He bent toward her and pressed a kiss to her temple. "You'll be a mated woman when we land."

"Well, then." She rested her head on his shoulder, allowing herself to savor the precious gift of having someone to lean on. "You may just learn to like flying after all."

Dr. Karin Allardice was running late, as usual. Grabbing her briefcase off the passenger seat of her sleek black Mercedes AMG, she unfolded from behind the wheel and set one stiletto-heeled foot on the ground.

The morning was cool, the sun still hovering low in the sky. In front of her stretched the wide lawn that filled the space between her designated parking spot and the entrance to her laboratory. The lush blades of grass still glistened with dew, and the parking lot around her remained silent and empty. In a few hours she'd be brownnosing one of the most prominent philanthropists in Chicago. A donation of several million would give her a good start, but she knew that was wishful thinking. The best she could hope for was a fund-raising gala, another endless evening of overpriced food and drinks during which she'd grovel en masse with her hand held out.

As she straightened from the driver's seat, she was startled to find a man standing by her car. She was briefly confused as to how he'd appeared out of nowhere, then the question fled her mind. Everything she'd been mulling vanished from thought as she faced the most gorgeous man she'd ever seen.

He extended his hand. "Dr. Allardice?"

Dear god, his voice was as delicious as the rest of him. Throaty and warm, like fine, aged whiskey.

"Yes? I'm Karin Allardice." The moment her fingers touched his, a spark of awareness shot up her arm. Shaken by the strength of her physical response, she shut the door and took a quick, deep breath to regain her composure. "Can I help you?"

"I certainly hope so. I've been told you're a preeminent virologist. Is that correct?"

"That's very flattering." She pushed her hair back from her face. "My primary focus is virology, yes."

The soft light of the early-morning gilded him, enhancing the natural sheen of his thick black hair and the beauty of his caramel-hued skin. His eyes were the most unusual shade of amber, quite breathtaking when framed by such thick, dark lashes. His mouth was a voluptuary's wet dream. Firm and sculpted, the lower lip was just full enough to make her think of sex while the upper was etched with the sharpest edge of sin. He wore a three-piece suit like nobody's business, and when his mouth curved she lost her breath.

"I've recently been made aware of a new viral strain, Dr. Allardice. I'd really like your opinion on it."

"Oh?" She forced her brain to resume functioning. "Well, I'd be happy to take a look, Mr.—"

"Syre," he provided. "Excellent. I was hoping you'd be cooperative."

The flash of unnaturally long canine teeth was the last thing she registered before the world went dark.

For a brief moment after Dr. Karin Allardice woke,
she was struck with confusion. Her surroundings
were unfamiliar. She couldn't remember how she'd
gotten where she was. She tried to recall what she'd
been doing before she lost consciousness. . . .

"How are you feeling, Doctor?"

She bolted upright at the sound of a low, purring,
masculine voice. Her gaze darted around the room,
settling on the dark figure lounging in a wingback
chair in the corner. It was *him*. The man with the in-
sanely gorgeous face. She hadn't forgotten him. In fact,
his face had been foremost in her mind, both asleep
and awake.

Blinking into full awareness, Karin focused on him.
He sat with unnatural stillness, as if he were actually a
photograph or painting. Although that was unnerving,

it afforded her the opportunity to study him and to prove to herself that her recollections of the man's beauty hadn't been exaggerated. They weren't. If anything, they hadn't done him justice.

"Karin," he prodded. "Are you feeling all right?"

A shiver moved through her at the sound of her given name spoken in that decadent voice.

"Where am I?" she asked hoarsely.

"Virginia."

"*What?* What are you talking about?" She lived in Illinois. She'd met this man in Chicago, in the parking lot of her laboratory. He'd approached her, asked for her opinion . . .

Then *kidnapped* her? Or had she come voluntarily? Why couldn't she remember?

He stood then, in a rivetingly graceful rise. His body was as much a work of art as his face. He was tall and leanly built, with powerful shoulders and forearms. He wore black slacks and a neatly pressed blue dress shirt rolled up at the sleeves, the picture of easy, casual elegance.

But the urbanity of his clothing didn't diminish the air of danger that clung to him.

There was a hardness in his luminous amber eyes and an edge to the determined set of his sensual mouth. As he crossed the room to her, his stride was both inherently sensual and predatory.

His outer masculine beauty was a facade, she thought. It beguiled, luring her to forget pesky things like the mystery of how she'd ended up in a different state in a strange bed without her knowledge or recollection.

"What do you want?" she asked, swallowing past a painfully dry throat. Her heart was racing in her chest, her breathing too quick and shallow. A quick glance down assured her that she was still dressed. She lay atop a sumptuous turquoise-hued silk coverlet in an equally luxurious room. She was unrestrained, but that didn't make her feel any less trapped.

"I told you," he said easily, pouring a glass of water from the pitcher on the bedside table. He handed it to her. "I need your help identifying the cause of a disease."

"You abducted me!" she accused, staring suspiciously at the water until he took a sip of it himself. "Which branch do you work for? The Feds? CDC? Homeland Security?"

His mouth curved in a slow, devastating smile.

"Don't," she snapped. "What did you use? A pressure syringe? What was the drug? I'm highly sensitive to drugs. I have a condition—"

"Lupus. Yes, I know your kidneys are delicate, Doctor. I didn't use any medication on you."

She exhaled her relief. Unless this business had something to do with Plasma X, she had no interest in taking on another top secret government project. And this degree of aggression was completely unacceptable to her. Nothing could justify rendering her unconscious and taking her without her consent.

"Answer my questions," she demanded.

"I'm Syre, and I don't work for anyone." He sat on the edge of the bed as if they were familiar enough with each other to warrant such intimacy.

I'm Syre, as if that explained everything.

Looking at him over the lip of her tumbler as she drank deeply, Karin noted Syre's caramel-hued skin and the slightly exotic slant of his eyes. His unusual name and cultured voice hinted at a foreign heritage. He was the most flagrantly handsome man she'd ever seen, as decadent as dark chocolate rolled in solid gold leaf.

And he'd taken her across state lines.

The first tendrils of real fear slithered in her stomach, but when she spoke, her words came clear and strong. "Am I free to leave?"

He stood and held out his hand. "Come with me."

Aware that knowledge of her surroundings would be vital to figuring out how to escape if she had to, Karin set her glass on the table and slid her legs off the bed. She accepted his assistance to stand, then moved to the window first, pushing the sheer curtain aside to look out.

A Rockwell-esque town lay before her—with the addition of dozens of motorcycles lining the curbs. It gave her a slight feeling of security to see numerous people milling on the street below and the lack of bars caging her in. She could scream and dozens of people—many of whom were intimidating-looking bikers—would hear her.

Turning away from the view of freedom, Karin faced Syre and found him standing very close by, watching her intently. She held her breath as he reached out and ran his fingertips along her hair.

His stunning good looks and smoldering sensuality mesmerized her. As near to her as he was, she could smell the spicy scent of his skin and take in the amazing perfection of his face. He was gorgeous in a way she'd never seen before. Eerily perfect and breathtakingly beautiful. The darkness that surrounded him seemed less sinister in proximity. More melancholy. Almost . . . haunting.

She exhaled in a rush, wondering if it was reckless desperation that had driven him to the insane act of abducting her from her job, her hometown, her life. Maybe someone close to him was ill. It wouldn't excuse him, and it certainly didn't mean she'd stay to help him, but it made his actions far less scary.

"My shoes?" she asked.

Stepping back, Syre pointed to where her heels had been neatly arranged against the wall. Karin slid them on, and he ushered her out to the hallway.

With his hand at her elbow, he led her down a flight of stairs to the ground floor, then through a heavy metal door that had been concealed behind a bookcase that swung out and away from the wall. The dichotomy between the warm, comfortable home she'd woken in and the sterile area they entered was striking. Instead of warmly polished hardwood stairs, a utilitarian metal staircase took them down into what resembled a hospital wing.

With just the opening of a door, they'd gone from wainscoted rooms and claw-footed furniture to austere concrete floors and a palette of unrelieved gray and white. The sense of surreality that fogged her mind was exacerbated by the abrupt change in her surroundings.

"This medical facility was completed very recently,"

he said, leading her down the halogen-lit hallway. "My chief researcher was using a converted warehouse previously, but I needed her closer, and she needed better facilities and equipment. As do you."

Two technicians in lab coats passed them—a large, ruggedly handsome male with golden eyes and a tall blonde who couldn't seem to look away from Syre as he passed. Both techs paid deference to him with slight bows of their heads, which he returned with a far more regal and arrogant dip of his chin.

He was clearly someone very important, a man used to giving commands and having them obeyed. Who was he? And how much trouble was he going to give her when she didn't toe his line?

"Are the infected individuals here?"

"Some of them are." He opened an unmarked door and she found herself in an observation room.

Karin moved to the viewing window and saw the rows of infirmary beds, in which freakishly gray patients lay comatose. Gray hair, gray skin. As if all of the color had been sucked out of them. They appeared almost like black-and-white figures in a colorized film.

"How are they presenting?" she asked.

"You'll have to talk with Grace about that. I don't know how to speak medical jargon, Doctor, but I can tell you my people are dying by the hundreds and the Wraith Virus is spreading quickly."

Wraith Virus? She faced him and immediately regretted it when some of her synapses fried at the sight of him. "Why haven't I heard about this?"

"Because it's need-to-know, Doctor. Until now, you didn't need to know."

The possibility of a government cover-up seemed more likely by the minute. Still, as bizarre as her present circumstances were, she nevertheless was fascinated and tantalized by the unknown. She couldn't fight the greedy curiosity to know more. To know everything.

"I'd like to look at their charts," she said, turning her attention back to the viewing window, "but I can't commit to becoming involved. I have other things on my plate at the moment, and the way you brought me into this has made me very uncomfortable. I'm a private citizen whose rights you've trampled. I have work that needs my attention and—"

"Doctor." There was steel in Syre's voice and it effectively cut her off. "*This* has become your one and only priority. You will work on the Wraith Virus until you find a cure."

Her mouth fell open and she met his reflected gaze. "The hell I will! I—"

"I'm a desperate man, Karin." He moved to the rear wall and leaned his shoulder into it, crossing his arms. The casual pose did nothing to mitigate the restless energy he gave off in waves. He was a coiled threat, waiting to spring. "And you're nearly as desperate as I am."

"I'm not—"

"I can give you the healthy body you've never had. I can give you all the time in the world to conduct your research and tests. I have limitless wealth at your disposal. I can give you everything you've ever wanted and more."

Karin wondered if she was still unconscious and dreaming. She shoved her hands through her hair, feeling awash in confusion and frustration. In the glare of the fluorescent light above her, she saw her face in the glass and her wide, dilated blue eyes. First and foremost, she needed to understand one very important point. "Am I a prisoner?"

"You'd rather be playing with petri dishes in a lab than saving actual lives?"

"Don't take that fucking tone with me!" she snapped, fury overriding every other emotion. "You've taken me from my home and work, and you've given me very little information to justify why. You evade my questions, and you've yet to give me a satisfactory explanation for who you are and what authority gives you the right to disrupt my life. You——"

"What life?"

"Excuse me?"

"You work and you sleep. You have no kin. Your colleagues are your only friends." His gaze was a nearly tangible weight on her back as he watched her with hawklike focus and spoke so coolly about her personal affairs. "I'm offering you a life of good health and purpose——"

"It's not up to you to decide that my life, such as it is, isn't worth living!"

Syre straightened. "I'm giving you the opportunity to find a cure for something—*anything*—in your lifetime. It's highly doubtful you will without me. Your lab suffers from underfunding, and you yourself are suffering from a debilitating disease that's severely shortened your lifespan. I can erase both of those problems."

"You're doing me *a favor* by conscripting me?" she shot back, telling herself to focus on the patients and not his stunning face. As ridiculous as it was to argue with him with her back turned, it was far safer than looking at him directly. "Is that the way you see it?"

"Yes, actually," he drawled. "A little gratitude would be nice."

Karin snorted. "You need far more help than I could ever give you, since I'm not a shrink and you could seriously use one. I made peace with my life and my disease—which is incurable, by the way—long ago."

"Ah." He nodded. "I see what the problem is now."

"Took that long, did it?"

"You don't believe me."

He thought *that* was the problem? "Let's say I did believe you. You pretty much blew whatever chance there was for us to work together by taking me against my will. And by crossing state lines, my abduction is a federal offense."

"You say that as if the laws of your government apply to me."

The rhythm of her heartbeat faltered. *Your* government? Jesus. If he was a foreign dignitary, it was possible he had political immunity and—

Where was her tablet? She'd had it with her when they'd met. Sensitive information was on it, including memos regarding Plasma X. If that were to fall into foreign hands . . .

"Karin."

Her name struck her like the crack of a whip. She jolted.

"Look at me," he coaxed.

She'd been trying to avoid doing that, so she could keep her wits about her. There was something deeply compelling about Syre, from the underlying cadence of his speech to the way he watched her in a very nonobjective way.

"Look at me, Karin," he repeated.

Turning her gaze away from the rows of patients, she did as he ordered. And gasped.

His eyes were aglow, shining as if illuminated from within. Then he smiled and revealed . . .

Fangs?

She stumbled backward, tripping over her own feet, but he was there to catch her. He'd moved so quickly, he had been no more than a blur, crossing the distance between them in the blink of an eye.

"What are you?" she gasped, her mind scrambling.

"I am capable of making all of your problems go away." He slid one arm around her waist, while the fingers of his other hand pushed through her dark hair and brushed it back from her flushed face. His touch shimmered through her, making her thoughts scatter.

"There are several reasons why I chose you, Karin. The research you're so desperate to get back to is one of them. You've spent years analyzing that blood sample the Feds sent you, haven't you? It's degraded, but still amazing. You know it's radically different from anything you've ever come across, but you haven't been able to isolate how because you don't have enough to work with and your grants are insufficient to provide you with the resources you need."

She swallowed hard. "Is it . . . yours?"

"Doubtful. I'm rarely hurt. In fact, it's been a century at least since the last time. But I do have a limitless supply of more like it."

His gaze swept over her face and it almost felt as real as the brush of his fingers. His voice was low and smooth. Intoxicating. She felt herself relaxing, the tightness in her muscles loosening. The low buzz of pain in her joints faded from her perception.

The smell of his skin was delicious. Karin found herself breathing just to inhale more of it. The feel of his body against hers was surprisingly—but not unpleasantly—cool, and it was stirring a heat in her blood. The fear she'd been nursing since learning her location was a distant concern.

"I have what you need, Karin," he murmured, his gaze on her mouth. "I have what you want."

Dear god . . . Syre was a greater threat than she'd given him credit for. He was as seductive as the devil himself, a creature not quite human and yet imminently desirable. And he knew it. He knew the spells he could weave with the promises he made, both spoken and unspoken. He understood the power he wielded with his looks and sinfully sexy body. He didn't need bars on the windows or guards at the doors.

He intended to make her his captive. And he was going to do his best to make her want to stay that way.